MW01120625

HIGH HEELS

Patricia Anne Healey

Chère Suzette,
Ja suis
très heureuse
que tu aimes bien
l'histoire!
Merci.
Patricia Anne
February 1, 2013

Copyright © 2012, Patricia Anne Healey

All rights reserved. No part of this book may be reproduced, stored, or transmitted by any means—whether auditory, graphic, mechanical, or electronic—without written permission of both publisher and author, except in the case of brief excerpts used in critical articles and reviews. Unauthorized reproduction of any part of this work is illegal and is punishable by law.

ISBN 978-1-105-44172-1

Publisher
Pat Healey Inc.
Arlington, Virginia 22206

First Edition, May 2012

PUBLISHER'S NOTE
This is a work of fiction. All modern characters either are products of the author's imagination or are used fictitiously, and any resemblance to actual persons, living or dead, events, or locales is entirely coincidental.

A LULU BOOK
To purchase this book contact
www.lulu.com

Acknowledgements

I owe thanks to many people—to my friend, Suzi Borgo, for her unwavering belief from the very beginning; my granddaughter, Micayla Anne Bowman for her encouragement and critique; and my writing workshop groups for their fellowship, caring and red ink. I will always owe the teachers and clergy, from elementary school through college, for helping me live life even when they didn't know I needed help.

Finally, a debt of gratitude to The Johns Hopkins University Master Of Arts instructors, David Everett, Mark Farrington, John Gregory Brown, and Richard Peabody, who taught me the technique of writing while leaving the story telling to me. I especially owe Richard, who pumped me full of self-esteem as I took my darkest chapters out of the closet for all to read.

Dedicated Lovingly To

Moonbeams

the loyal heartbeat at my feet during the ten years it
took to write this novel.

1

"You can muffle the drum, and you can loosen the strings of the lyre, but who shall command the skylark not to sing?" Kahlil Gibran, *The Prophet*

By the time I reached twelve years old, I knew that I was going to leave. I sat on the bed and looked out the window most of the day. Every afternoon, my mother slept in her bedroom with her face towards the hall steps so she could see me if I tried to go downstairs. She was the only person I knew who slept with her eyes open. Sometimes if I were quiet, I could sneak by her bedroom, though usually I heard the standard question.

"Dolly, where are you going?"

I gave the usual answer, "Downstairs."

"Why?"

Sometimes I had a reason, but it was never good enough.

"No, you stay up here. There's no reason for you to go downstairs."

The sinking feeling in the pit of my stomach was there as I went back to my bed. The house was quiet. My brother, George, thirteen, and my sister, Brenda, eight, both managed to disappear every time my mother called for assistance. My brother was exempt from doing anything anyway. He did what he wanted to do. His only chore was to take out the garbage, and even for that, I had to make sure that I properly wrapped it. If any garbage spilled when George carried it out, I would, of course, receive any blame. There was something about being a boy that gave him special privileges that didn't seem fair.

Brenda was not asked to do much because she was completely incompetent at everything. She had enormous fears and would, upon the slightest provocation, jump wildly about. She had a constant need for my attention, and I really got along better when she hid from us. If she wasn't around, she couldn't cause trouble. During the better times, when my life was relatively peaceful and I was allowed to be on my own without some tiresome chore to be done, Brenda couldn't resist butting in to anything that might be going okay. She delighted in deliberately ruining anything I might be lucky enough to have under control. When she upset things, my mother blamed me. Any commotion was my fault and made me more vulnerable when either my brother or my sister was around. They made the commotion, and I was to blame. It was simply easier to do everything that needed to be done myself.

There were no radios that we were allowed to listen to and no TVs that we were allowed to watch. There were no pictures on the wall, no plants to water, and no magazines to read. Comics, of course, were not allowed, except the ones hidden in George's room. The one television, in the living room, was my dad's. We were not allowed to use it except if we were invited to watch with him. He watched only news or boxing. Boxing was an important sport in our house. My dad was Irish and had lived a leisurely life in Boston, complete with sports, parties, and "the good life" as he called it, before my grandfather lost all their money in the stock market crash of 1929. It was only then that Dad had to quit Columbia College and help support his mom. Leftover from those days was one of my dad's favorite pastimes—boxing. The television was relegated to Dad for watching the fights, and when he wasn't home, it wasn't on. I never saw any sense to "the good life" of boxing matches, those ugly men with bloody faces and sweaty bodies.

I was not allowed to use the phone without permission, and when my mother napped, I was not allowed to disturb her to ask. Asking didn't make any difference anyway because she needed to keep the line open for calls from her teaching clientele or my dad's work. If someone phoned me, she simply said that I could not come to the phone. I hated that. She always answered the phone. It was hers. She would ask who it was. I received few calls, and it made me feel lonely when even the few I did receive, I was not allowed to answer. She was intent on making sure that no one was finding out anything through me that she didn't want people to know. She carefully questioned everyone who called. If she liked what she heard, she would say that I could call back later. If I did what she wanted the rest of the day, I could sometimes call back, usually not. If she didn't like what she heard, she would hang up, come and find me wherever I was, crush my cheeks between the fingers of her right hand, push them in so they met on the inside, and say, "Keep your big mouth SHUT."

Once, I made the mistake of telling a teacher that my father slept most of the time when he was home. When my mother found out, my mouth hurt for two days and there were cuts along the inside where she had rubbed my mouth against my teeth. Another time, I told a friend that my mother didn't iron sheets. Again, my cheeks were smashed against each other while my eyes sent tears to ease the pain.

"Some day maybe you'll learn to keep your big mouth SHUT," she'd say, as her fingers painfully indented my cheeks.

Gradually, I learned to tell people only what I knew would be acceptable to my mother. Sometimes I would say stuff I knew she would like so they would pass her questioning. She didn't like most of the people who called anyway, especially if they were either very rich or very poor. She liked Suzanne and Geraldine, not Lynne or Janie. Lynne was nice. I liked her. My mother hated Janie. Janie's dad took us ice skating and my mother didn't want me to get involved with them because she didn't like to reciprocate rides.

Janie taught me how to ice skate, and I caught on immediately. My Aunt Theresa made me an ice skating skirt. I didn't like the skirt much. It was maroon and full and made me look too fat. I knew from past experience that I'd better like it. My mother beat me if I didn't appreciate the things my aunts did for me. I learned to like a whole bunch of awful junk; dusty crocheted doilies, over-ripened fruit, burnt toast, and hand-me-down dresses. I never said anything about what I liked or didn't like. When I wanted ice skating lessons, she said I could take sewing lessons. I cried and cried when she wasn't looking.

I labored in sewing class, made a green dress and won second place. The girl who won made a purple suit. It was really ugly. My green dress was also pretty ugly, too small with large gruesome shoulder pads. The material was gabardine, and gabardine really looks awful on a twelve-year-old girl. My mother called all the neighbor ladies and bragged about how I had made this gabardine dress. She made me wear it all the time. The other kids made fun of it. All the teachers liked it. Well, they pretended to like it. I was sure they thought it was hideous. The material was the big thing. Gabardine was expensive.

The only mirror in the house was in my sister's and my bedroom. My mother would come into the room and ask me how she looked. I would always have to say she looked nice, so sometimes I'd say "nice" without looking. When she figured that trick out she would just stare at me until I'd look at her. And those big breasts would be stuck out so far. Her clothes were spotted, especially on the top of her breasts. I guessed it was easy for her clothes to be spotted because her breasts stuck out so far. Many times at the dinner table, I saw drops go onto her breasts, which she would flick daintily with her two fingers. The spots caught my eye and made me even more uncomfortable because I didn't want to appear to be noticing any flaws in her dress.

She looked at me a lot. When she folded the laundry, she sat with the laundry in her lap and I changed in front of her, handed her my dirty underwear, and waited to get the clean underwear back. I was cold and self-conscious. It took a long time for her to give out the underwear. I was getting breasts then too. Sometimes my aunt was there with her, and they'd laugh at how shy I was.

"Grace, did you know that those two dinky little freckles have to be dressed in the closet?"

Aunt Grace didn't answer at first.

My mother didn't take the hint. "She's overly modest, Grace. You'd think she'd realize that I am her mother after all. What's wrong with a child who won't let her mother look at her, I'd like to know."

Finally, Aunt Grace said kindly, "Just let her be, Anne. She'll outgrow it."

That is when I would have to take off my undershirt and wait for her to hand me the clean set of underwear.

I stood in front of both of them, arms crossed over my breasts. There was less than a foot between the undershirt that was being offered and my naked body. More than once, I saw a shirt come out of the laundry basket. I dropped one of my arms to take it, but my mother put it back on her lap, folded it slowly, and smoothed it out.

Finally, I got the message. The correct behavior was to stand there, arms at my sides, so she could get a good look. When she looked at me, I saw a combination of a look that I did not understand and another look of jealousy.

There was something wrong with my mother. The idea came to me out of the blue. *There was something wrong with my mother—something beyond my understanding—something that could not be explained.*

I stood for what seemed like forever, hands at my sides, as she paused and gave the last shirt in the laundry basket to me.

I learned to obey every order, follow every command, because if I did not, things went badly for me.

Every two or three months, she called me into the bathroom. She had a habit of calling me in there to talk over the day. Lucky for me, she didn't bathe often. It made the bathroom scenes less frequent, and that was a certain advantage. The dark side was that she smelled awful most of the time. There was not much toilet paper, and she didn't wipe herself after she went to the bathroom. She had diarrhea a lot. The brown liquid ran down her leg. Because she kept the toilet paper out in the hall, she would be seen because she hiked up her skirt or nightgown when she came out in the hall. I was always embarrassed when I saw her. I couldn't help looking because I did my homework on the bed, which faced the hall, and I'd always glance up at the wrong moment.

Today, she called me into the bathroom to help her with the bath. I sat on the toilet with the lid down facing her. She had the biggest boobs imaginable. They hung down way past her fat belly and kind of rested on her stomach. Both breasts had huge, dark brown nipples with a dark, huge circumference around them. I had never seen any breasts that big. My own breasts were a light brownish pink, which suggested that they could become dark brown at any moment. There didn't seem to be any sign of the large circumferences that my mother had, and I could not differentiate my nipple from the outer circle, so I felt somewhat safe, but never totally. My breasts were small, and that was reassuring. In the right light, the pink seemed pinker, not really brown, so perhaps I had escaped the fate of huge brown ugly breasts. My younger sister, Brenda, seemed to have fuller breasts already, and the nipples were more dark brown. I hoped that I was spared.

My mother leaned forward. Her huge breasts fell heavy, into the water. She looked like an ugly version of Cleopatra, as she demanded to be worshipped and administered to in the bathtub. She started talking to me about things she wanted me to do the next day. I made a list. I liked to make lists because it was an excuse not to look, even though it was hard because my glasses steamed up a lot in there. If she caught me looking at her breasts, she'd give me a dirty look, so I was always trying to find other things to look at. That was no easy task in a bathroom with no windows, no towels, and no pictures on the wall. Even if I did manage to find something on those barren walls to distract me, she would chastise me for not paying attention, and I'd be right back in the same dilemma again. There was no place to look where I would not see breasts. They were everywhere—big and fat and everywhere.

She started in with the list.

"Junior will deliver the chicken at about four o'clock."

Junior was the delivery *boy*. It was a strange name for someone who was tall, fat, balding, and at least fifty years old. I didn't question it though. Everyone seemed to accept Junior as a *boy*. He wore glasses hanging off his nose that were spotted. He came in by the kitchen door wearing a butcher's apron all splattered with blood and was always in a hurry.

Mother continued as she washed under her arms. There was a lot of hair under her arms.

"After Junior delivers, you need to take out the chicken, wash it, salt and pepper it, and place each piece in the baking pan with the skin to the bottom."

Washing the meat was a pretty disgusting job. It was all bloody.

She went on, "The fattier part of the meat is on the bottom, and the bony side of each piece of chicken should be face up. After you check and see that each piece has the skin to the bottom of the pan, get some margarine from the refrigerator and place a drop or two on each piece. At five o'clock, put the baking pan in the oven at 350 degrees. After twenty minutes, turn all the pieces on the other side and cook for thirty minutes. While the chicken is baking, take the two pounds of carrots out of the refrigerator. Grate the carrots and add the raisins and peanuts. And don't do the carrots like you did last time. You didn't grate them to the end. You put too many big pieces in the garbage. Each carrot must be grated to the end."

I protested, "The grater scrapes my knuckles. Sometimes, they bleed."

"What millionaires do you think we are that you can throw away perfectly good carrots to save your precious little fingers? Don't leave so much waste. Grate them to the bottom. And I will check when I get home so don't try to get away with anything. Then mix them with a little mayonnaise and put them in the refrigerator. Your father will be home at five. If there is not enough milk for his coffee, go to Corbello's store and buy some. Buy the smallest container they have. And don't buy anything else. That store is too expensive, and your father can't stand Mr. Corbello. We can't let him make those huge profits on us.

"There's money on the mantel. Set the table for six. Marian Hamill will be coming home from school with me. Don't forget to sweep the dining room before you set the table. Wrap the garbage for George to take out. Make sure you tie it securely. Last time, you didn't, and your father got angry because George spilled some of it on the way out. You really must be more careful when you wrap it."

"I'll be home about six with Mrs. Hamill. Be sure and say hello to her and make sure that you are sitting quietly in the living room before we arrive. I don't want her to think I run a noisy household."

I wrote some of this down, but mostly I just pretended to. I didn't really need to write anything down, since it was usually the same or about the same every day. My friends at school knew about the lists. Sometimes Suzanne would ask me to go over to her house to visit after school.

At almost the same moment, we both remembered the list. "Oh, the list, Dolly, there is always your list. You can't come, I know." Suzanne looked as sad as I felt.

My mother interrupted my thoughts. "Dolly, look at your mother when she talks to you. Why are you still looking down? Look at me."

I looked at her.

"Look your mother in the eye when she talks to you, Dolly."

I did. Her breasts were everywhere. It was impossible to look her in the eye. I saw only breasts.

"Now, please wash my back."

This was awful, but good at the same time because I knew it was the last thing I had to do and it would soon be over. There was only an inch of water, so I could see her whole body. Her stomach rolled over on top of her fuzz. Dad made the rule that baths could only have an inch of water. My sister and I were bathed together in about an inch of water to save money. We stood in the tub like two stiff totem poles while she washed us. It was cold that way. Hot water was at a premium, and my dad was cheap. He was obsessive about the hot water bill. Even a penny over and things became troublesome for my mother. He saved half of his salary every week because he wanted to be rich again, like his dad was before the depression. He believed that if he didn't spend any money and saved it all, he would eventually become rich.

I had this way of washing her back so that I actually never touched her and she couldn't tell. I would let the washcloth hang down slightly so it seemed larger on her back. I don't know if she knew that I cheated. She never said anything.

If I slipped and touched her skin I would feel like throwing up, and that scared me. I threw up a lot, and my mother got angry.

She'd tell people, "Dolly upchucked again in the car on the way home."

I finished her back. She was usually pretty dirty, and by then, the bath water had become pretty scummy. When she said "lower," I knew I had to do her crack. She would lean over, and I washed the crack. I used my trick with the washcloth so it seemed as though I went lower than I did. Not much fun. I thought of several ways to drown her. I never tried any of them. An inch of water probably wouldn't have done the job. Once, out of desperation for a way out of this, I suggested she start taking showers instead. She said she couldn't because the water on her head made her dizzy.

When I finished, I could go. So I left her in the scummy inch of water and went back into the hall. *One of these days, I'm going to leave this place. I'm just going to get in the car and go.*

The cool air felt good even though it steamed my glasses again. In the comfort of the cool, clean air, I went back to my room and cried. It was over, until next time and the time after that and the time after that; endless days of waiting.

2

"Now, Voyager, sail out forth to seek and find." Walt
Whitman

Hazy sunlight awakened me as I heard my father taking
a shower. Morning was my favorite time of the day,
reminding me that I would soon be at school. My
homework was always ready. I was always ready.

My mother was in my closet searching for
something. She kept her clothes there because she liked
to use my full-length mirror. She called this bedroom
that should have belonged to Brenda and me, "the
dormitory." To her, it was a free-for-all room. Everyone
could come in and get whatever they wanted at any
time, and everyone did. She didn't spend much time in
her room with Dad. It was her way of saying, "This
whole house is mine, Dolly; nothing is yours to keep.
Your room is a dorm, public property, and so is
everything in it, including you."

"If you don't like it, lump it," she said one day as I
protested her taking over yet another of my dresser
drawers, which left only one for me.

The hangers in the closet started moving fast.
Brenda woke up with a start and looked around. She
was scared, as usual. My mother pushed the hangers,
one by one, back and forth over the rod, harder each
time. The motion got faster and the hangers crackled as

they banged into each other. As I moved to get out of bed, the clothes picked up speed and started flying over the rod, faster and faster. A blouse fell on the closet floor. It wasn't the one she was looking for so she kept on. Some skirts fell, a coat, shoes got kicked into the corner as she looked for her blouse.

I checked under my bed to see that my homework was out of her reach. Brenda or George seemed to take delight in destroying my homework from time to time. They consistently made fun of my hard work. They hated that I was smart. Actually, I really wasn't that smart. It was just that I had nothing else to do except read or study. When Brenda or George destroyed my homework before I went to bed, it didn't matter because there was always my time spent in the closet and plenty of time to do it again. I worked and prayed in the closet a lot. Sometimes, I was so frightened that I asked God, "Dear God. If you just keep me from going crazy, I promise I'll never ask you for anything else."

I would hide in there from George in the afternoons when he was home, but, more often, I would redo homework in there after everyone was asleep. I would pretend that I was Abraham Lincoln. Here I was, doing my homework in my own log cabin by the dim light of the closet, waiting to grow up to be President. I put the homework under the bed, got up the next morning, and retrieved it before the others were even ready for school. I could leave before anyone scribbled on it or wrinkled it up. From time to time I forgot to put it safely under my bed. When I left it out, I'd make myself as small and invisible as possible and quietly move it somewhere safe before the full bloom of her rage took hold.

"Don't you dare leave for your precious school, until you clean this up. Don't just stand there like a bump on a log. Clean it up. What are you standing around for? Get to work. It's embarrassing, the stuff you tell those teachers at your dear school. Sometimes I think I should send you away to school so no one will know about your crazy ideas." She made a gesture with her finger indicating I was "crazy in the head" as she put it.

I couldn't see, and I couldn't find my glasses. "I'm trying to find my glasses," I answered, full of fear.

"What, poor thing, you can't see? Well, will this help?" She grabbed my head from the back and pushed my face into the dresser top. "Now can you see this filth, Miss Queen Bee? Now can you see? Are you close enough? Clean it up. And don't go to school until you do."

Her hold on my head relaxed, signaling that it was over. Carefully, still with my head down, I glanced sideways at her. Even without my glasses, the familiar look of satisfaction as she stuck her nose up in the air and left without her blouse was all too clear.

The room became deadly silent. Brenda was in a state of shock, staring at me, and I trembled, trying to figure out what to do next. At first, no thoughts helped me, but then I began to see what to do. The room needed cleaning up, and I had to do it fast because I was already probably going to be late for school. My glasses finally appeared on the floor near my dresser, and with my sight restored, I sorted everything out that needed sorting and placed everything back in its rightful place in my drawer. My sister's drawer looked good for the first time in a while, and I separated my clothes from hers and folded everything. I was not dressed and cold, but I managed to get everything back together again in a reasonable way. Fortunately, nothing was broken this time. I picked up my miniature statue of the Holy Family from the floor, kissed it, and put it under my pillow for safekeeping. Brenda was still staring, not saying a word. She was not much use after one of Mother's episodes and usually couldn't do anything except sit and stare into space. Today was no exception. Brenda had the same look in her eyes that she had when she would pick up cats by the tail and watch them scream; hate mixed with awful fear.

I dressed, picked up my books, checked to see that my homework was still intact, and left the room, leaving poor Brenda to get dressed by herself.

Downstairs, my mother was already fixing breakfast for Dad. He didn't look up from the newspaper as he asked, "Don't you want any breakfast, Dolly?" Sometimes I thought he was as scared of my mother as I was.

I said that I already ate. I was used to lying to him. Telling him wouldn't do any good because he would discuss it with my mother and I'd only be punished later for telling Dad. Lying seemed the only way to get to school without more trouble.

A voice from the kitchen reminded me that she heard everything. "Don't let her go to school without breakfast, Spence. What will I look like to those teachers? Of course, they'll ask her if she'd had breakfast, and of course, she'll say no. She tells everything. Nothing shuts her up. You get in here and have some breakfast, Miss."

She threw a piece of toast on the table. "See, it's burnt. You made me burn it because you got me so upset. Now eat it and get out of here. And don't go telling anyone that your mother doesn't make you breakfast in the morning." My father's newspaper, in front of his face, safely covered his view of the world.

I walked up Linden Street and entered the corner side of Oak Avenue School, an old school. The dark, wooden boards of its staircase were sunk in the middle from all the people who had walked there before me. I wondered about them. What did they find to do after this beautiful school? Did they grow up, wear high heels, and go to work? Did they earn their own money? I hoped it was so because it was going to be true for me. In my high heels, I would earn my own money. I would have thousands and thousands and thousands of friends everywhere in the world and a little brown dog named Buster Brown who would wait for me to come home at night. It would happen for me. *Just wait, Mother, just wait.*

The steps shined back at me because Ray Smith, the colored janitor, oiled them all the time. The sun was reflecting, as usual, off the dark, wooden banister that Ray polished and polished each day. I watched his dark hand on the white rag rub one spot at a time. He rubbed and then looked, rubbed again and looked again, until he was satisfied that there were no spots. Then he took one more quick brushstroke with the rag and moved to the next part of the banister. His hands were gentle as he worked, like my dad's.

The beams of sunlight mixing with the soft dust of the air created a cloud in the stairwell, almost like a mist that could actually carry me to the heaven that was sixth grade. They shined through the large windows and calmed my spirit as I turned the corner of the first landing. I could see Miss Roberts at the door of the classroom. *Sixth Grade.* I was a sixth grader, and this was Miss Roberts, the best teacher that any child could ever know.

Margaret, my mother called her. Her name sounded like bells when my mother said it. Miss Roberts had gone to normal school with my mother. In the normal schools, it took only three years to get a teaching degree. They were all colleges now, and it took four years to get a teaching degree. My mother was proud to have been head cheerleader and the first Italian to be allowed to stay in the girls' dorm. My mother bragged because she was the first Italian hired in the Edgemont school system. My mother boasted about just about everything she ever did.

This morning, Miss Roberts was standing at the open classroom door as she always did, to greet everyone with the same good morning.

"Good morning, Dolly," she said.

"Good morning, Miss Roberts."

The classroom smelled of varnish, chalk, and freshly bathed teachers. I looked up at the large squares running across the top of the blackboard. Inside each square were Palmer method writing examples. Each letter of the alphabet had its own square, and inside, the sample letters were perfectly written, one in upper case and one in lower case. I still couldn't make a proper capital D. I took a look and wondered why mine never came out quite right.

Miss Roberts smiled once more as I took my seat. It was not an ordinary smile. It was a smile just for me. It said, "Hello Dolly, my favorite little student. I'm so glad to see you." She never said all that out loud to me, but her face said it.

She hadn't hugged me this morning. Sometimes if I passed her in just the right way she gave me a little hug against her girdle. She had a hard girdle, but it felt good. She smelled like roses and her elbows were always clean.

I often wondered how she kept her elbows white. I looked at my own. They were gray.

I was the second-to-shortest person in the class. When we lined up for gym class, we lined up by height, shortest to tallest, so I was always second. Today, Nancy Whetherspoon wasn't there, and I had the first place in line, my favorite spot. As Miss Roberts spoke to the class, she turned me around facing the rest of the line, so that she could rest her hands on my shoulders while she talked. As she touched me, I went straight to heaven. It was the softest touch in the whole world. She smelled like an angel. Her girdle was strong against me, and I felt good. If I had my way, I would have spent the rest of my life exactly in that position.

Today my body was confused after the beating, as I joined gym class. At the climbing rope, where I usually scrambled right to the top, my legs refused my commands, and after several inept tries, dejected, I returned to homeroom class only to find that the lace of my shoe had been torn in two with my efforts. Tears came to my eyes. I didn't want anyone to see. I kept looking down at my shoes.

Miss Roberts asked me what was wrong, and I started to cry. She looked worried. "Did you have any breakfast?"

"Yes, Miss Roberts," I answered softly because I hated to lie to Miss Roberts. She leaned down, and the smell of roses spoke softly, only to me. "Let me take you to see Miss Hartwick. Maybe she can help."

I was really scared. Usually, people didn't go to the principal's office except to be punished. I racked my brain for what I might have done wrong. Miss Hartwick was the principal and had a reputation for being mean. The boys, who were always in trouble, called her "Strict

Hartwick." If she saw me crying, perhaps she would punish me. I held back my tears and went to the office. Miss Hartwick had already heard I was coming and was sitting at her desk waiting for me. She was twirling the pencil that she normally held in the bun of her gray hair.

"Sit down, Dolly. I want to talk with you."

I shook. "Am I in some sort of trouble?" I asked. "Did I do something wrong?" I started to cry again.

"You did nothing wrong, Dolly. You are much too hard on yourself." She went out and brought back a glass of water. The glass was painted with tulips and stems and green leaves all over.

When she saw me admire it, she asked, "Do you like the glass? A student of mine a long time ago did that for me. She was just your age when she painted it, and now she's an artist. She sends me beautiful paintings from all over the world. So you see, people who leave this school do wonderful things. That's going to happen to you some day, Dolly. Some day you will leave this school and build your own life."

She asked me if I had had any breakfast.

The champion liar in me spoke again. "Yes, Miss Hartwick."

"I'm not punishing you. Even if you had done something that deserved punishment, I wouldn't punish you. In my opinion, you're a beautiful, quiet, intelligent little girl, and you've already punished yourself too much. You won't be punished by me. I think perhaps you should rest here a while and go back to class later."

Oh no, I thought, I would miss science.

She must have read my face because she asked, "What is it, Dolly? Would you rather go back to class?"

"My project. I did a science project." The knot broke again. I couldn't stand it anymore. My heart was broken. No class, no science, all my work for nothing. I sobbed.

Miss Hartwick waited until I had stopped crying. She had moved closer to me. She smelled good. "Really? What did you do?"

I started to explain, and she suggested, "Why don't I just come along and watch you show Miss Roberts and the class your project?"

She said the right words: Miss Roberts. My eyes must have told her so because she smiled. "Wait for me, and we'll go back. I'll only be a minute." I waited while she wrote a note to herself and placed it where she could see it. She took my hand, and we went back to class. She didn't seem like "Strict Hartwick" to me.

Miss Roberts looked worried as we approached. "Is everything all right?"

"Yes," Miss Hartwick answered, "we just had some big feelings that had to get out."

I showed my science project to the class while Miss Hartwick and Miss Roberts stood in the back and smiled. They liked it. I showed the class how I made the soundboard, how I hammered nails on the board different distances apart. I demonstrated how the rubber bands made different sounds depending on how tight they were stretched across the nails. I showed them that if the nails were wider apart, the rubber band made a different sound than when the nails were closer together. I explained about sound waves through the air, about vibrations, and all the while, Miss Hartwick and Miss Roberts were well within sight, smiling and smiling and smiling their unwavering approval. I smiled back. I couldn't help myself. I was pretty proud.

Next, we all went to Nurse Carlin's office to discuss blood typing. Those who had chosen the blood typing project showed their charts, and we figured out what their blood type might be. Even though, I had no chart, I explained that I knew mine would be type OO because both my parents were type OO. I explained what my dad had explained to me about the recessive gene. I was type OO positive.

I stayed after school that day. It was my day to rinse the blackboards before Ray came in to clean up the room. Miss Roberts sat at her desk correcting papers. The classroom was quiet and peaceful, as she and I worked together, no other children to interrupt—no Brenda, no George, just peace. Sometimes she would look up and smile that beautiful smile of hers, the one that shined right out of her eyes, not just her mouth.

I washed the blackboards for as long as Miss Roberts wrote on each paper, in perfect penmanship posture, at her desk. I dipped the fat sponge into the water over and over again and slowly made long streaks straight top-to-bottom on the blackboard. As usual, I started at the top and went down to the bottom of the board, careful not to get water on the sill where the chalk was kept. The sill was made of wood and it was important to keep it dry. I started again at the top and went down in a vertical row until the whole board was finished in the same pattern of top to bottom rows. It was important to make the sponge strokes straight rows from the top down so the blackboard would dry with the least streaks on it.

All too soon, Miss Roberts put the papers away, walked to the closet for her coat, and smiled at me.

"Let's call it a day, Dolly." She took an admiring look at the blackboard. "You can really do a job on those blackboards. I've never seen better," she said as she helped me with my coat.

"Good night, Mr. Smith," she called over her shoulder, as we headed for the stairs together. Her flowing coat brushed my shoulder, and my whole body tingled with love.

"Good night, Miss Roberts, ma'am," returned Ray.

We walked down the shiny oiled steps together. I didn't touch the beautiful banister because I didn't want to make extra work for Ray.

3

"When you hear the cannons, go towards them."
Anatole France

It was Friday evening. Things were pretty scary on Friday nights because my dad stayed out late every Friday and sometimes Saturday because he worked the night shift. It was really strange because when the phone rang, Mother told me not to answer it. When I asked her why, she said because she was afraid it was dad's office calling. But why would dad's office call him if he was there working? I didn't ask her that. I just wondered. I had a feeling asking would not get an answer and would probably get me a swat across my face for questioning my mother. She hated me questioning her about anything, and I was afraid anyway when Dad was not at home until late.

When he was home, my father sat at the head of the table, otherwise it was empty. I always sat at the foot of the table. My mother sat to the right of my dad, George to his left and Brenda sat next to George's left. I used to sit next to George, but I moved because he was always punching me in the stomach or poking me in the ribs. My mother didn't eat with us except when Dad was there or when we had company. Dad wasn't home for dinner except on Sundays, so most of the time, like tonight—it was George, Brenda, and me in the dining room. George was pretty much in charge.

I set the table for supper. I knew what the supper would be. Every Friday we had fish sticks with macaroni and cheese. I didn't like the A&P fish sticks because there were small annoying bones in them. Some of the other brand fish sticks were better, but A&P brand was the cheapest so we always got those. I did like the macaroni and cheese. My mother made that herself.

"Dolly, come and help me serve the supper, please."

I left Brenda and George waiting at the dining room table and went into the kitchen to serve the food. My mother put the dishes on top of the stove.

"Bring those dishes in to everyone, Dolly," she commanded as she cleaned off the sink. I took the two dirty potholders from the drawer and carried the macaroni casserole dish into the dining room. I returned and carried the fish sticks to the table. There were six fish sticks. *Two each*, I said to myself as I left them in the middle of the table and went back to get the drinks.

I went to the refrigerator to find the milk. My mother helped me make the drink for George. He wanted chocolate milk. George got angry if he didn't get exactly what he ordered. To spare us all the wrath that only George could deliver, my mother helped me. I took some cocoa from the cupboard and mixed it into the milk. I carried the two glasses, one for Brenda and one for George, to them and went back into the kitchen to get my own. I returned and sat down at the foot of the table. There were two fish sticks on my plate and no macaroni. I looked up. The casserole dish was empty. They had eaten all of it.

George looked at me and grinned. There was nothing left for me except two fish sticks. I was too hungry for the fish sticks to be enough.

George laughed a horrible laugh. My sister was looking at me with the "ha, ha" look she always got when George bested me, which was often. She was giggling, her eyes shining with sheer glee.

"Hey, Dolly, hungry, ain't cha?" George said and laughed and laughed. He poked Brenda in the ribs. "What are you laughing at, stupid? You'll be next." Brenda quieted immediately. George never kept allies for long. He didn't need any.

"You got an appetite like a truck driver, for someone so skinny, now don't you?" He grinned a malicious grin again.

I yelled into the kitchen. "Mom, George and Brenda ate everything. There's nothing left for me." She didn't hear me.

I repeated myself. "Mom, there's no food left. George ate it all before I got there. And now he's hitting Brenda."

"Just ignore him, Dolly. I can't do anything with him. And Brenda needs to learn to stay away from him." That brought a quiet sneer from George as he turned his hateful gaze on me.

"Well, what can I eat?" I asked.

"That's all there is. I don't do any shopping until tomorrow morning. Just go into the dining room and sit down. You'll have to make do."

He had won again. I looked at my empty plate and cried. I cleared the table, washed and dried the dishes, and went to bed, but I couldn't sleep and was awake with a stomachache when I heard the front door open. I glanced at the clock. It was three a.m.

"Is that you, Spence?" I heard my mother call downstairs from the bedroom.

No answer.

"Spence, is that you?" Her bare feet hit the floor with a thud as she got out of bed to call again. She was at the head of the stairs.

"Is that you Spence?"

There was still no answer. I was getting scared. What if it wasn't Dad? Why doesn't he answer? I grabbed the miniature statue of the Virgin Mary that stood next to my bed and put it under the pillow. It had to be him. Who else would get in with a key? I prayed quietly out loud. "Please, St. Jude, let it be him. Some of what I do you may not like, but please help me now. Make sure Dad is home. I can't live alone with my mother. You know that."

I heard my dad's voice finally answer. "What is it?" My mother responded with something I couldn't hear, and her lonely footsteps went back to her bed.

I awoke to daylight coming into my window. I took the statue from under my pillow and put it back on my night table. It was Saturday, so I didn't get up. I was really hungry though, so I was going have to get up soon. I picked up my latest Thomas Wolfe book, *Of Time and the River*. The house was quiet because Dad slept late on Saturday and Sunday, and it was a great time to read. In the book, my favorite hero, Monk, was finally on his way to becoming a successful writer.

A few hours later, I was still reading when Dad, looking clean and neat as always, came into my room and sat next to me on my bed. He smelled great after a shower. He didn't like after-shave lotion so he smelled exactly like himself, clean and washed and just like a father should smell. He had on a clean yellow sport shirt, my favorite color.

"Hey, Dolly, how're ya' doin'? Your old man got home a bit late last night so I didn't tuck you in. I thought you'd be asleep." I drank in the beautiful whiff of cleanliness next to me.

"I wasn't asleep, Dad. I heard you come in. Were you at work?"

"Hmm, yeah—I guess you could call it work. I was at a very serious prayer meeting. What were you doing up so late anyway?"

Dad didn't know that I knew what he meant, so I didn't say anything. A "prayer meeting" is a group of men throwing dice to win money. It's called that because they get down on one knee when they throw the dice.

"I had a stomachache. What do you do, Dad? What is your job? I need to know for a form at school. I have to write down my father's occupation."

"Tell them I'm a technological technician. Here, take this pillow and put it on your stomach. It will make you feel better." He handed me a pillow from Brenda's empty bed.

"What is a technology technician?" I said it wrong. I couldn't pronounce it.

"Nobody's quite sure. That's why I keep my job. Nobody can figure out what I do."

I laughed. I heard from my aunts that my dad was a real intelligent man, so I knew he was only joking. Whatever he did do for a living, my dad was good at it; that much I knew.

"The pillow made my stomach feel better. Why is that?"

"Because it's warm and the warmth of the pillow will help. Do you feel like something to eat, Dolly? Your mother just got back from the grocery store. I'm going to make breakfast."

"Yeah." My dad made the best omelets.

"What would you like? Omelets or French toast with bacon?" It sounded like we were going to have a feast. Mom might even have brought onion rolls from the bakery. My dad liked onion rolls.

"Omelets."

"Omelets, it is."

My dad went downstairs. I heard him talking to my mother. "Anne, she had a stomachache again last night. What's wrong?"

"She didn't seem ill to me, Spence."

"Well, that's what she said."

Now I was in for it. I read about the Marquis de Sade one of the days when I sneaked into the adult section of the library. My mother was like him.

I knew I was getting it again. I just lay there waiting for the sound of her heavy weight on the steps.

I heard her coming up from the kitchen, lurking in the halls of the night again carrying the tools of her trade, an enema bag and hot water. An enema bag is a frightening thing that is supposed to be used if you are constipated. With my mother, this enema bag was her constant companion. She carried the water from downstairs to heat it exactly right, so you could hear her coming up the stairs huffing and puffing with the weight of the contraption.

Her limp on the stairs made an eerie sound as she ascended from below. She told me once that she was born with one leg shorter than the other. I knew what she was thinking as she labored up those stairs, how she had to do everything herself without help. Dad didn't help her much. He was always watching the boxing matches. He didn't seem to care what went on, as long as he didn't have to get involved. If I asked him anything, he'd get quiet, and just say, "Ask your mother."

"Did you have a bowel movement this morning?" she asked, as she rolled me over on my side.

"No."

She put down a small cotton sheet and pushed it under my bottom.

"Lift up, Dolly, I have to put the sheet down."

I peered back at her over my side as I lay there waiting. She was incredibly ugly, her face twisted itself into this familiar martyred expression as she ordered, "Turn over, Dolly." I was ashamed because I knew that my bottom disgusted her, so I avoided looking at her face as she grabbed me and opened the hole to see better. She loved her big chance to jab it in. She seemed to be almost having fun.

"Bend your knees all the way up Dolly." I obeyed as I was taught. The room became still as the only thing left to do was wait. The hardest part was waiting in the bed because I was afraid the hose was leaking. I think that's why she put down the extra sheet. Sometimes, it was only a towel or a cloth. A lot of times she missed and jabbed it anywhere near the hole, which hurt more. She pushed and I could feel it, feel it inside, as the water came up and hurt. I could tell when the water was coming because I could feel her uncork the thing. There was some kind of small metal plate that kept it all together. I know because it was hanging in the bathroom once, and I figured the whole thing out. The way one metal piece clamped on another and that prevented the flow of water and when she unlatched it, the water could flow. They never taught us that in science class. I figured it out by myself. Sometimes the water was too hot, but I didn't dare say anything because she would have to go downstairs again and it was bad to make extra work for her.

She always had a helper. Today, Brenda helped by holding the enema bag. It was my own fault. I should have never told anyone about the stomachache. She cured stomachaches with enemas. Whoever was my mother's helper would be told what to do.

She commanded Brenda, "Lower it a little, Brenda. Make it higher than that, Brenda."

How she loved that. Giving orders to my sister as she did her bidding, that was her favorite fun. I hated her. I would like one chance to get her back. But I could never even touch my mother's bottom, no less stick something in it. I would rather have just beaten her up until she bled everywhere and watched as her blood dripped on the carpet. I prayed for a chance to run away some day. My day would come. *Hate, sweet hate, walk with me, and be my friend. Think up whatever you want to do because some day we'll get her back, we'll get them all back—George, Brenda, the whole lot of them.*

Hate answered me with her own fury. She was hot in my belly. I could feel her heat all through me as I confessed silently to her that I hated my mother—that I hated her so much that I was willing to destroy myself just to get her back. She was in the air I breathed, the food I ate, and she had no idea how much I hated her. Neither did anyone else. No one is allowed to hate mothers. It was a sin, but there were so many mothers—there were more mothers than insects, crawling everywhere, always ready to slam the door on somebody else's happiness.

I heard the witch command, "Stay in bed until I tell you that you can go."

Lying on my side, with my backside exposed, I kept pleading with her. "Can I go to the bathroom now? I'm cold."

"No, you're not ready. If it's too soon you won't go." She looked over at me. I must have looked a pitiful mess, completely panicked with my bottom jutting out into the cold air of the bedroom.

"Don't move. I don't want you to leak anything on the bed."

"Please, I can't hold it any more. I know I have to go. I'll go. I promise." I felt as though I was going to go right in the bed.

No answer. *Some day I'll get her back, some day I'll...*

Finally, she said yes, and I ran as fast as I could to the bathroom. My sister, who was also on the sadistic side, took delight in watching me run for the bathroom in the panic of not knowing if I could hold it long enough to make it. Brenda loved to watch. Her face was a mixture of fear and glee: glee to watch me suffer, and fear of her own turn next time anyone found out that she was sick. She even dared to make fun of George when it was his turn to get it. He didn't get it as much as I did. He was smart enough not to tell when he had a stomachache.

I ran into the bathroom, but as soon as I got there, I couldn't go. The only thing that came out was water from the enema. I waited. I strained. Nothing. I spit into the toilet to see if I could make it look like I went. Not enough. Wait, it looked a little brown. I tried spitting again. No luck. I was supposed to call her when

I was done. If I didn't go, she would give me another one. I sat down and tried again. I was straining and straining, but I just couldn't go. I was going to be there all day.

Why did I always screw up? I hated her. I hated them all. I opened my big mouth again and got into trouble. Why did I never learn? I was desperate with pain and fury.

"Dolly, where are you? I got your omelet cooking." It was my dad from the kitchen. He was right. I could smell the omelet. I hoped for cheese in it, too.

"Come on down, I made western omelets with ham, peppers, onions, and cheese."

I didn't need a second invitation. I hopped off the toilet, flushing it real fast. I hadn't gone, but with my dad in the picture, I might be able to get away with it. I started down the stairs.

"Dolly, don't flush the toilet. I want to look," came the words from my all-seeing mother.

"Dad called me. I already flushed it."

"I thought I told you to never flush the toilet. Did you go?"

"Yes." I lied, again.

"Well, go ahead and have your breakfast. Your dad is waiting. And don't eat too much. You might get an upset stomach again. Your stomach is always queasy."

I went into the kitchen. Dad was there with a chef's apron on and was cooking up a great pile of omelets on a special wrought iron skillet. It was a long and narrow skillet that was made in such a way to cover two burners at once. I could see that he had several omelets underway on either side of the skillet. They were formed like pancakes, and he flipped them over and over like an expert. I could see pieces of onion, ham, peppers, and cheese protruding out as they turned in the air.

"You know what makes these omelets good, Dolly? It's the Worcestershire Sauce in them. Not many people know that. The Worcestershire Sauce adds just the right flavor."

I couldn't disagree. They were great omelets. The cooking smells made me have to go to the bathroom. I pretended to be getting ready to wash my hands and set the table and went into the downstairs bathroom and went. I was glad because that funny feeling in my bowels was gone.

I set the table for everybody. Although George wasn't home, I set a place for him because if he came home in the middle of the meal, I would have to get up. I set one all the time, just in case.

Brenda joined us, as was her habit every time Dad fixed me anything. Nothing was mine, even my dad's company. Even with her there, we had a great breakfast feast. Dad joked with me about my huge appetite.

"You don't seem sick to me, Dolly. I guess your mother's right. You've got a hollow leg," my father teased.

"She *was* sick," my blabber-mouthed sister volunteered. "She had a stomachache and had to have an enema. I helped." She was pleased with herself again, as any idiot would be.

My father buttered an onion roll and handed half to me. He never seemed to notice what was going on with my mother's constant enema punishments. What a perfect team they seemed to be. He never questioned her infinite medical wisdom. He thought she was perfect. I understood, in a way because whenever there was anyone around, my mother was a complete angel.

She was always talking about helping all the little children who were her students. The people listening to her didn't know that little of her concern applied to me.

I just kept waiting to grow up. It would be better. Hate was my friend now, and together we would make it to age eighteen together.

4

"Love the little trade which thou hast learned and be content therewith." Marcus Aurelius

I usually went to the nine o'clock children's Mass on Sunday. I liked the children's Mass because I could sometimes sing the hymns with the Catholic school children. The Blessed Sacrament Church congregation was divided into groups. The Catholic school children had reserved seats. They would march in near the beginning of the mass and take their seats. They sat on either side of the middle aisle. The rest of the congregation sat in the back or in the side aisle pews. Sister Josephine or Sister Marie, depending on which Sunday, came next, passing hymnbooks to only the Catholic school children. If I wanted to use a hymnbook, I had to walk to church early and make sure that when I sat on the side aisle I was the first person in that pew. Sometimes, the Catholic school children would then push the hymnbook over the divider to me so we could read it together. Not all of the children did this, so I had to be lucky to get a seat near the center pew and be next to a girl who would share. Certain girls would always be willing to share. One of those girls, was a pretty red head who smiled and blushed almost all the time, Mary Alice O'Connell. When she came into the pew, she would smile right away letting me know that she was glad to see me and would share her book with me.

Pentecost Sunday was my favorite hymn day. I was glad when Mary Alice managed to sit next to me especially on that day. Sitting next to me was not an easy feat since she had to jostle all her friends around so as to get the seat near me. But faithfully, when she could, Mary Alice opened her hymnal and pushed it over the railing so that I could see it. We sang all the hymns together.

> *"Come, Holy Ghost, Creator Blest,*
> *And in our hearts, take up thy rest,*
> *Come with thy grace and heav'nly aid*
> *To fill our hearts which thou hast made,*
> *To fill our hearts which thou hast made."*

The final hymn every Sunday was another one of my favorites, "Holy God We Praise Thy Name." First, the Catholic school marched out the central aisle singing together. I was left without a hymnal, but it didn't matter because I knew this one by heart. Each Sunday, I sang as Mary Alice waved goodbye and signaled me that she would wait for me outside the church so we could walk home together. Soon, we began to pick a start time in the morning and meet on the corner so that we could also walk to mass together. She always tried to sit next to me so that I could share her hymnal. I hated to say goodbye each day because I was happy to be with Mary Alice and away from my mother for that precious hour and a half each Sunday.

§§§§§

Mary Alice and I began to go to daily mass together. Today was the *First Friday of the Month*. In the Catholic Church, if I went to mass and received communion on the first Friday of each month for nine consecutive months, I would have the "grace of a happy death." This meant that I was guaranteed a spot in heaven. It was a pretty important series of days. I had already collected more than the nine First Fridays, but I continued going anyway because I had become friends with Mary Alice and we liked to go to church together. Every First Friday, rain, sleet, snow, or shine, Mary Alice and I met on the corner to walk to church and giggle over stories about school.

Since Mary Alice went to Catholic school, I envied her. My mother didn't give me a reason why I couldn't go to Catholic school, but I was pretty sure it was because we couldn't afford the uniforms. I wore only hand-me-down clothes, and buying uniforms seemed like a big expense. I really wanted to go to Catholic school, but I accepted learning about it through Mary Alice.

I had lots to tell her, too. She depended on me for stories about the public school. Her school was for girls only, and she listened with rapt attention as I told stories about the boys in my class. I made up a few stories along the way. One of my biggest sins was the number of lies I could tell in a week, a rather large amount.

Today, Mary Alice was at the corner to meet me as usual, but she was late so we had to run the three miles to the church to get there on time. She was talking excitedly as we ran, about the new priest at Catholic school, still unknown to me. She was flushed from running, but she kept talking, breathless and happy.

"His name is Father McAvoy. He's taking Monsignor Tobin's place. Monsignor is too old to continue. Father McAvoy is young and cute. All the girls at school are in love with him." It looked to me like Mary Alice was also in love with him, as her face changed color with excitement every minute.

When we arrived at church, I realized that the small hat I was wearing had blown off. "Mary Alice, my hat is gone. I have no hat to wear into church. If I go back to find it, I'll miss mass. What do you think I should do?"

Mary Alice was confident. "Why don't you come in anyway? You don't want to miss mass, and there are not many people at the seven o'clock mass. No one will notice. Your hat is small anyway. I don't think it's noticeable even when you have it on."

"Is it a sin not to wear a hat in church?"

"No, it's not a sin. Girls have to wear hats to show respect for Our Lord, but I don't think it's a sin if we forget. So come on in. No one will even notice."

She strode down the aisle in front of me, past the rows of nuns in black garb in the back on the right. They were there every First Friday, and we knew some of them. There was one in particular we didn't like at all. Her name was Sister Lucy, and she was known to be mean. Mary Alice said she had hit Chris Minion with a ruler. The idea was to stay away from her as much as possible. The second nun in the row was Sister Marie, the nice one, who was kind and helped everyone as best she could. She taught the religion class on Mondays. Monday was the day I got off early from public school to go to religion class. I liked going to the class and saying, "Good afternoon, Sister Marie," as she smiled at me.

Mary Alice chose the first row on the right as she always did. I genuflected and entered behind her. I no sooner had I knelt down than I felt a hard tap on my shoulder and someone pinched my arm. I was startled and turned towards the disturbance. It was Sister Lucy, her face grim, thin, and hard.

She whispered in her raspy voice that everyone could hear, "Come with me, young lady." She grabbed my arm in a way that hurt and dragged me out past the rows of nuns. They stared at me, as horrified as I was. The embarrassment was more than I could stand, but she wasn't through with me.

At the back of the church, in full earshot of all the others, she faced me, still pinching my arm hard and pulling me towards her face. "What are you doing in church without a hat?"

"But, I—"

"Don't give me any 'buts,' young lady. It's imperative that you wear a hat in church to show respect for Our Lord. You have been disrespectful to God, and I don't care about any 'buts.' Now, go on home and don't come back until you have a hat to wear." She gave me a shove towards the door, turned, and went back to mass.

I was dejected. It wasn't fair. I had a hat, but it had blown off. She wouldn't even listen. I didn't want to walk all the way home without Mary Alice.

The tears flowed almost on their own as I looked around for a place to wait for Mary Alice. Between the church and the rectory there was a small garden with a statue of the Virgin Mary set up as a water fountain. It was a warm day and the water was flowing. I decided to wait in the garden. I exited the side door of the church, crossed over the garden, and sat in the corner behind the wall on a nice warm stone.

Only then, did I look up. A short distance in front of me was a priest in black garb with a black prayer book under his arm walking peacefully on the other side of the garden. He didn't see me. I didn't dare move. He was clearly occupied with his own thoughts as he knelt by the statue. I couldn't leave because to get back into the church lobby I would have to go past him.

I sat and waited, hoping that he wouldn't see me. After he said his prayers he would probably go back inside the rectory, and I could go and meet Mary Alice.

The priest stood up. As his knee steadied him, he bent over slightly, and I saw inside his cassock. It was the first time I had ever seen what a priest wore inside his robe. It was less interesting than I expected: a long white chemise with lace trim on the bottom. It seemed funny that a man would wear a skirt with lace around it.

As I was staring, I heard, "Hello, Miss, may I help you?"

"Hello, Father."

"Have you been crying? What's your name?"

"Dolly Morgan, Father."

"What's the matter? Why aren't you inside at mass?"

I knew I had to tell the truth. You don't lie to a priest. I was afraid I would be punished again but I told him. "Sister Lucy made me leave because I lost my hat on the way to church and I have no hat. I'm missing my seventeenth First Friday. I'll have to start over." I started to cry again.

"Have you gone to seventeen First Fridays in a row? All by yourself? Well, God bless you, Dolly."

"No, Father, I'm not allowed to come by myself. I come with my friend Mary Alice. We walked here together. I'm waiting for her to walk home with me."

He smiled. "Oh, Mary Alice O'Connell. I know her. But, wait a minute, Dolly, you haven't missed mass yet." He looked at his watch. "Do you have anything you could wear instead? Perhaps a handkerchief?"

"No, Father." I shrugged indicating that there were no pockets in my skirt. I had nothing.

"Wait one minute. I've got an idea. I'll be right back."

He walked quickly into the rectory and returned with a clean, white, ironed man's handkerchief.

He attached the handkerchief to my head with one of the bobby pins in my braids. He hurt my head when the pin went in.

"Ouch."

"Oh, sorry, Dolly, I'm not doing this right. There, wait a minute, there you are."

It still hurt but I didn't want to tell him.

He took my hand. "Come with me, we still have time. God needs little girls like you in his church. Don't worry about a hat. Go and take communion, and if you are ever crying again, be sure and come and tell me. God is your friend. He doesn't want you to cry in His house."

He kept my hand as we walked into the church, and he walked me past the sisters and up to the row where Mary Alice sat. I entered the pew as Mary Alice turned towards us.

She got beet red and said in a whisper that was much too loud for church, "Hello Father McAvoy."

Father smiled softly but didn't answer. You're not supposed to talk in church. Mary Alice just kept staring. Her face got redder as she stared.

He walked back down the aisle and out of church as Mary Alice stared after him, her mouth open. "That's him. That's Father McAvoy. Did he talk to you? What did he say? Was he angry about the hat?"

I became aware of the nuns watching us. "Shh, I'll tell you later." I concentrated on communion and my final prayers.

Mary Alice almost skipped down the aisle as we left. She was bursting. "You are soooo lucky. He is soooo nice. Tell me what he said. Exactly. Don't leave anything out."

I explained about the meeting in the garden and the handkerchief.

"Do you think that I could I go with you to return his handkerchief?" Mary Alice asked.

I hadn't thought about having to bring the handkerchief back, but I saw her point. "Okay."

We walked back to the rectory together and left the handkerchief with Mrs. O'Rourke the rectory housekeeper.

"Father is in church getting ready for the next mass, but I'll return his handkerchief," she told us in a thick Irish accent as she shut the large dark rectory door.

After that, Mary Alice and I got into the habit of deliberately walking in the church garden so we could wave to Father McAvoy before we went into church. Many times he stopped his prayers and spoke with us. We got so we would save questions for him, which he always answered. One day I got up all my nerve to ask him a question that had been bothering me a lot. My mother had hit me when I had asked her, and she sent me to my room that day. It was a big risk to ask it again, but I wanted to know.

"Father, if Adam and Eve only had two sons, Cain and Abel, then where did they get their wives?" I asked.

"That's a good question Dolly," answered Father. I was relieved.

The answer was difficult to understand. He said that the Bible was not always to be taken literally. Sometimes the stories were symbolic. He also explained that the Bible was handed down by word of mouth and some information was missing. It could be that the wives simply had not been mentioned.

I had my answer. I wondered what had bothered my mother so much that she had hit me, but I didn't ask about that.

Mary Alice and I told another friend, Connie Green, about Father, and she started coming to mass with us. Our little band formed, and we followed him about everywhere we were allowed. There were some moments when Mrs. O'Rourke shut that dark rectory door quickly, but we were undaunted.

I was now going to church every day instead of just on First Fridays. Sometimes Father would wait for me outside of church, and after mass he took me into his office at the rectory and talked with me.

One day, I could tell he had something important on his mind. I waved from a distance, not wanting to disturb him. He walked over to me. "Hello, Dolly, I've been expecting you. I thought that you and Mary Alice and Connie might like to have communion breakfast with me one day. Would you like to? You pick the day and let me know."

When I told Mary Alice she got totally red and spent hours figuring the best day to do it. Connie was ecstatic. "How did you get him to invite us? Did you ask him?"

"No, he asked me."

"Wow."

We chose one Sunday, and after mass we went with him to the rectory where there was a table set for four, with a white linen tablecloth, white cloth napkins, silver forks, knives and spoons, and even a silver butter knife. We never had cloth tablecloths and napkins at home except at Christmas and Easter. The fare was wonderful. Mrs. O'Rourke served juice, eggs, bacon, and the best biscuits. She was fat and had huge breasts, but she didn't scare me like my mother did. In fact, she seemed quiet and nice. She laughed a rosy laugh whenever Father made a joke. Sometimes, she was clearly eavesdropping as she served us.

"Father, lord and beggorrah, they ask a lot of questions," she exclaimed as she served.

Father answered her. "That's how they learn, Margaret. And, actually, it's interesting conversation. Pull up a chair if you would like to join us."

"No, Father, I have my chores to do before I go home today. Perhaps another time." She smiled at each of us and left the room.

It was Mary Alice's turn. "Father, Avery Steerforth says there is no God. He says that I can't prove there is a God. No one can."

"And, who, pray tell, is Avery Steerforth?"

"He's a boy at school. He's a Protestant. He makes fun of us because we think there is a God, and he wants us to prove it."

Father McAvoy thought for a long moment.

"Mary Alice, sometimes people aren't blessed with the gift of faith. Be glad that God gave you the gift of faith. That is how we believe in God. He gave you and me the gift of faith. I wouldn't bother about Avery if I were you. He may not believe himself, but for us, God is true and that is all that counts. Don't you remember how many times Jesus Christ was tested by people with little faith?"

We remembered. We shared all the different stories we knew about how many times God and His Saints were tested.

I told my favorite story. "I like the one about the Jesuit priest, Father—the story about the little boy who tried to put the whole sea into a pail and couldn't do it. Remember?"

"Yes, I remember. Do you remember what happened, Dolly?"

"Yes, I do. A Jesuit priest by the name of Father Thomas was walking along the beach trying to understand the mystery of the Holy Trinity. As he walked, he came upon a small blond boy filling a small pail with water from the ocean. 'What are you doing?' he asked the boy. 'I am putting the ocean into my pail,' answered the boy. Father Thomas exclaimed. 'Well, you can never do that, little boy. You will be here forever.' The little boy answered, 'I can put the ocean into this pail sooner than you can explain all of God's mysteries.' And then the boy disappeared."

"That's right, Dolly. We don't have to explain everything to Avery either. We have the gift of faith."

There were lots of other questions. Every time I was troubled, I went to the church and asked for help.

One day I missed Sunday Mass. I knew it was a mortal sin. I went in to tell Father.

"Father, I overslept and missed mass. It's a mortal sin."

Father looked down at me with the kindest expression on his face. He thought for a long moment and answered me in a soft voice as though he knew something important about me. "Oh, no, it isn't a mortal sin, Dolly, not for you. With you, God lives in your heart. You don't need to come to church to be with Him. He is right inside of you." He pointed to my heart. He was right. My heart felt much bigger now that I hadn't committed a mortal sin. And I didn't have to worry if I missed again. God was in me.

I started going to church after school. Every chance I got I would go and Father would be there after in the rectory to talk with me. We talked about boys and kissing and if there really was a God. All the questions I never had the nerve to ask anyone else, I asked my friend, Father McAvoy.

My friendship with Father McAvoy became known at home. My sister, interfering as usual with anything I tried to do, started telling her friends about Dolly's friend, the priest. Actually, she also told just about everyone else who would listen. My mother knew about it, but she seemed glad. She started putting money into little specially printed church envelopes with our name on them each Sunday. On Christmas and Easter, the envelope was pretty thick. She had never done that before. Until Father McAvoy, she had felt her Sunday contribution should be anonymous.

One day at one of the communion breakfasts with Connie, Mary Alice, and me, Father McAvoy started talking about an idea he had. He wanted to start a girls' group called *The Sodality of Our Lady*. We would start with Mary Alice, Connie, and me, and we would get other members as we went along. We would meet once a month on Tuesday evening.

"Do you think you could come?" he asked all of us.

I started to cry.

"What is it, Dolly?"

Mary Alice answered for me. "Her mother never lets her go anywhere. She won't be able to come."

"Well, let's all ask our mothers and see what happens." Father answered confidently.

I nodded, but I had no intention of asking. I knew the answer.

The other girls said they would ask. I didn't want Father to have the club without me, but it looked like he was going to.

Mary Alice and I walked home dejected.

"Do you think you could ask your father?" she asked me.

"No," I answered easily, "he never does anything she doesn't want. And she'll never let me go." I realized I was saying "she" again. My mother said it made her sound like the cat's mother and I was to say Mother when I spoke of my mother. I didn't care what I called her right then.

The subject was closed. Mary Alice, Connie, and Father were going to have the sodality without me. I went home and set the table for supper.

Shortly after dinner, as I was washing the dishes in the kitchen, the telephone rang. I was not allowed to answer the phone, so I waited for my mother to come in and take it. She picked up the telephone on the wall next to the sink.

"Hellooo." She had this funny way of saying hello, kind of uppity, like she was a queen or something.

She acted a bit surprised as she started to speak. "Yes, Father McAvoy, I know you. I have seen you at eight o'clock Mass. Is anything wrong?"

There was another pause as she listened to a long talk from the other end of the line. Then, she answered,

"Well, thank you, she is my oldest girl. She has spoken to us about you. Thank you for being so kind to her."

My heart stopped. It was Father McAvoy, and he was calling about me. I kept doing the dishes, pretending that I was not listening. I ran the hot water. My mother signaled me to shut off the water with a real dirty look. She reached over and hit me.

"Yes, she's an outstanding student. Do you know that I'm a teacher myself? I'm a substitute at Oak Avenue School." She bragged every chance she got.

My sister came in from the living room and unashamedly sat down to listen in. She listened in to everything that concerned me. She thought she was in charge, too.

Brenda went back to tell my father. I heard her talking to him in the living room. She loved to impart news, especially about me. She was the biggest tattletale imaginable.

"It's Dolly's friend, the priest. He's calling Mother. I think it's about Dolly."

My father absentmindedly answered as he usually did when he was reading the paper or watching TV. "Oh, Father McAvoy. I've heard about him. Sounds like a really nice guy."

"Dolly is friends with him. She talks to him *all* the time." More unsolicited information from Brenda—no answer from Dad.

Not being able to rustle up any trouble with Dad, Brenda came back in and started whispering to me. "It's your friend Father McAvoy. Mother is talking to him about you. Something about a sorority. You're going to be in a sorority."

"Not a sorority, Brenda, a sodality." I corrected her while trying not to appear too excited. One thing was certain. If I acted like I wanted anything, I didn't get it. The best stand to take was nonchalance about everything.

Brenda started helping me by drying the dishes. She only helped in order to be next to the phone so she could hear the conversation.

"A sodality for girls, that does sound like a nice idea, but I have no way of getting Dolly to the church." After a long pause, my mother continued, "My husband might be able to drive her, but I'll have to ask him."

She was as nice as pie to Father McAvoy. I knew my father would drive me if she asked him. It was always her decision about me. He did whatever she wanted. Asking him was just a stall tactic. This meant that she was at least thinking about it, but I wouldn't know until she hung up. Sometimes she could be as nice as an angel to the grown up on the other end of the phone and then, the minute she finished, she could easily beat me up for telling them something she didn't want anyone to know.

She hung up and didn't say anything. I wasn't showing a speck of interest. That way if she said no, I could pretend I didn't want it. What I hated the most was her saying no after she found out I wanted something. She loved to do that.

I finished the dishes and went upstairs while Brenda followed me around.

"Leave me alone. I have to do my homework," I said to Brenda, who was whispering loudly about the whole situation.

She was too excited to leave me alone. "You might get to go out at night. You might get to go. Dad will drive you. I heard them talking."

I sat on my bed and picked up my book, *Pathfinder*. It was a great book. In *Pathfinder*, the Indian was always in the beautiful woods by himself enjoying life on his own. He could take complete care of himself in the woods. He knew how to hunt and fish, pitch camp and make a fire for his supper. He had his own canoe, and he roamed the Hudson River with the fish.

There was some talk downstairs between my mother and my father, and I heard my name from time to time.

"Sure, I'll take her. Only once a month? I'll take her at 7:30 and pick her up at 9:00. I can give Mary Alice a ride too. That Father McAvoy is supposed to be a real nice guy. I'd like to meet him myself."

I might be going. Could it really be true? It was getting more and more difficult to concentrate on my book.

My mother finally came upstairs, dumped herself on my bed, and pontificated for about twenty minutes on how nice she was to let me go. I had to promise to clean up the dishes before seven and mop the kitchen floor before I left. I had to promise a whole bunch of other stuff. She knew she had me cornered. Finally, she got off my bed and went downstairs. I was free to be happy. I danced around the room very softly to the Al Jolson music in my head, *Swanee*. I was as happy as Al Jolson must have been when he sang that song.

"The folks up north will see me no more when I get to that Swanee Shore." *I'm really good at Al Jolson*, I thought as I knelt down in the same way that he did to take a bow. The bow was to my appreciative audience of one, the full-length mirror on my door.

Sodality meetings were organized, and my father drove me each month. He picked up Mary Alice and Connie on the way. I felt proud because they thought my dad was extra nice. Between my dad and Father McAvoy, Mary Alice, Connie, and I got to ask a lot of questions.

"Father, I don't understand the point of learning the ten commandments." I brashly told Father one day.

He didn't get angry. He looked at me, a little bewildered. "Why, Dolly?"

"Because isn't the second commandment enough? 'Do unto others as you would have them do unto you.' If I do that, then I don't need to know anything else."

He looked at me again, now with a look of delight. "That's true, Dolly. You're absolutely right. For someone like you, we don't need any more commandments except the first two: 'Thou shalt love thy God with all thy heart and Do unto others as you would have them do unto you.' Those are God's two greatest commandments. But some people need it better explained so we have the Ten Commandments and the Commandments of the Church. But for you, you are right, you don't really need to bother to learn the commandments."

"Actually, I already know them Father. I was only wondering about it."

Father smiled and answered, "You're like St. Thomas Aquinas, Dolly, and he did a lot of thinking, too. Keep up the good work and ask me anything you want to know."

At another meeting, I asked, "Father, why is kissing boys a sin?"

"Well, because sometimes when a girl kisses a boy, it can be a cause of excitement for the boy."

"The boy, Father? But, *I'm* the one who gets excited."

Father McAvoy laughed a huge laugh. I never saw quite that big of a laugh before, and I never saw one quite that huge after. I didn't get the answer.

One day Father walked with me to the public library. He knew that I loved to read.

"Dolly, can you help me find some books for the younger children? I need to start a remedial reading class for some of my students. I'll go with you to the library, and we'll take a look."

Father McAvoy talked with the librarian about some books for the younger children, and I was left to wander among my own book friends. I loved having Father along but the library was my kind of place, and I didn't really need him there. I could get lost in the library all by myself. Father McAvoy knew about my friends in the library. Fictional characters were my favorite people. I told Father about all of them.

I especially loved *The Web and the Rock*. The story was so beautiful that I felt as though I had walked right into the book and was sitting next to Monk Webber, the main character. I knew Monk, and I agonized with him as he wrote his manuscript. I walked with him to look in the mailbox every day, and I suffered with him when he despaired over his rejection letter. I could not believe it; I took hope. The book was only half read—surely there was some mistake. I continued to read. It took two whole books, but Monk turned his despair into fame. And through him, I saw that if Monk could succeed, then so could I. We were aliens in an alien land, Monk Webber and me, but we had each other.

I went with *David Copperfield* when he received his beatings, and he came with me when I received mine. Together, we learned endurance. From the *Count of Monte Cristo*, I learned the power that comes with being on time, and from each of my fictional friends, I took solace, felt less alone and less afraid. I took from each author self-esteem, knowing somewhere, that if I could read these books, I could read other books. I dreamed of growing up, wearing high heels, going to work, and earning my own money. They made me feel less alone, my friends from all over the world: *David Copperfield*, *The Pathfinder*, *The Great Gatsby*, *The Count of Monte Cristo*, and my littlest friend, Huw, as he worked in the coal mines with his dad in *How Green Was My Valley*. They each had their parts in bringing up Dolly, and they would be my friends forever.

Father McAvoy took out some books for the younger children, and we walked back to the church together. I helped him arrange the books in his classroom and then went home. My mother didn't get angry with me much when I was involved with Father McAvoy. His influence on my mother was astonishing. One day I was even allowed to go to a dance with the boys' club of another church. My mother initially said no, but Father called her, and it ended up that my father became one of the car pool drivers. Mary Alice, Connie, and I went to the dance together. Mary Alice giggled at all the boys all evening long. She knew more of them than I did because she knew some of the Catholic school boys from other functions. She introduced me to Patrick Sheldon, getting all red when she did it. After, she said he was the cutest boy at St. Paul's school. She was right. I talked to him a bit. He was studying to be a priest—too bad.

My long talks with Father in the rectory garden continued for a long time. He had a lot of good ideas for our sodality. Our group grew to over twenty members, and we had social functions. We had communion breakfasts, dances with other schools, field trips, group discussions with Father, and trips to the library. There were dozens of small jobs that Father seemed to love having helpers for. Sometimes, certain ones of us were chosen to do community service.

I was good at keeping track of money. Every Fourth of July I helped my dad count the dimes at the Firemen's Carnival booths. I became the Treasurer of the sodality. There were no dues but I kept track of refreshment money.

Father seemed to have found my mother's Achilles' heel. Every time she said no, he'd speak with her. I asked him once how he got her to change her mind.

"She isn't really against you're going, Dolly. She just worries about your getting hurt. She also knows that children are the handmaidens of the Lord and God watches over you. I just have to remind her of that from time to time."

So that was it. God was in charge. God was actually the only person my mother was afraid of. She was constantly saying her prayers to one or the other of the saints, trying to get them to help her out.

My father made fun of her. "She's upstairs banging her rosary beads again," he'd say to my brother.

Yes, Father McAvoy had God power in our house. My mother's contributions to the church became more and more generous. As a reward for my mother's numerous contributions to the church since his arrival, Father McAvoy let us have the original *Lady of Fatima* statue from Lourdes in our living room for a week. It had been sent from France, and it was a big honor to have it in our house. My mother set up kneelers and chairs, and all the neighbors came to pray for miracles. I had to kneel right next to it all day, every day for a week. I didn't mind.

When I went to confession, Father McAvoy told me what a wonderful child of God I was. He never actually said so but he made it clear in any number of ways that my sins were really not important to him or to God.

I had the same sins and got the same penance every week.

"Bless me Father for I have sinned. It is one week since my last confession. I lied thirty-two times; I disobeyed my mother thirty-two times. " These two sins went hand in hand because when I disobeyed her, I lied to cover it up.

"For your penance, say the *Hail Mary* three times, and now—make a good Act of Contrition."

I spoke next. "Oh my God, I am heartily sorry for having offended Thee. And I detest all my sins because of Thy just punishment, but most of all because they offend Thee oh Lord, Who art all good and deserving of all my love. I firmly resolve, with the help of they grace, to sin no more, and to avoid the near occasion of sin."

The "firmly resolve" part was hard because I knew every week it would be the same. To resolve not to do something again when I knew perfectly well I was going to didn't seem right. It felt like I was lying to God. I told Father McAvoy about my worry, and he said it was okay because the spirit could be willing even though we know the flesh is weak and God understood that. I didn't really believe him, but I took his word for it. Sometimes, I just had to believe Father to get by.

"Goodbye, Dolly, see you at Mass. God bless you, now. " I heard the confessional door close softly behind me as I knelt in the back pew to say my penance. There was peace in that church with the new priest, a quiet, gentle, kind peace—a peace that entered my heart and stayed with me for years and years.

5

"Fortune favors the Brave." Virgil Aeneid

One of my mother's sisters, Rosa, had a daughter, Rosamarie. They lived in a stone Tudor style house with a screened in porch, next door to a doctor and opposite a lawyer. Their section of town was called Edgemont Acres.

Rosamarie's dad was a vaudeville dancer and a lively guy. Max liked to make grasshoppers, a drink that's green and sweet. I liked Uncle Max a lot. He and I both liked to dance in his living room—the waltz, the Charleston, the polka—and we sang Broadway songs. He liked to sing Al Jolson as I danced along with him.

He said, "You have a good sense of rhythm, Dolly. You ought to be a dancer."

My mother didn't like Max. She said Max was a drunk and Rosamarie was a spoiled princess because she was an only child and Aunt Rosa gave her anything she wanted. My mother made fun of her a lot.

She said, "You mean that princess, the Queen of Sheba, Rosamarie? What did her mother hand her today?"

Today was a bad day. Rosamarie had decided to marry. My mother was upset and had arranged for her to go and talk with my Aunt Jean who lived at Lake Mahopac. Aunt Jean, as Rosamarie's godmother, was naturally expected to talk her out of marrying Renaldo, a foreigner from Venezuela. Naldo, as we called him, was very handsome with dark tan skin, thick wavy black hair, and black eyes. He talked to Rosamarie in English with an accent. I loved his accent. It made me dream of *Arabian Nights* and far away places where I might some day learn new languages and talk with anyone I pleased without my mother interfering.

Naldo, in a white jacket and navy blue trousers, walked like a movie star, with a confident air, and smiled at me from time to time. When he and Rosamarie talked, they talked in Spanish. I tried but never could understand exactly what they were talking about. I liked listening, though, because the sound of the language was beautiful. All in all, I loved having them around, especially with the Spanish. They paid no attention to me as I quietly listened to the melody of the language. I was pretty good at being invisible, and it was even easier when people didn't expect me to understand.

Every once in a while I heard the name "Aunt Anne" through the Spanish, sharply spoken, interfering with the softness of the language. My cousin said my mother's name in a way that made it clear she hated her. There were other hateful words, too. I could surmise the most amazing stuff without knowing the language.

My mother and my Aunt Rosa wanted Rosamarie to marry Will Dugan. Will was Irish like my dad. But it was clear; Rosamarie did not want to marry Will. She wanted to marry Naldo.

Naldo went home, and Rosamarie stayed over at our house in order to go to Aunt Jean's lakefront home upstate the next day.

In the morning, Rosamarie and I were quietly sitting in the living room until my mother's heavy steps invaded us. She stood in front of Rosamarie, giving orders. "Rosamarie, George is on his way down for breakfast. I don't want him going out without breakfast. Make him some English Muffins, some bacon, and juice. He likes bacon."

Rosamarie looked at my mother and then at me. I could tell she was wondering why she should make George breakfast. She didn't say anything.

I looked back at Rosamarie but didn't say anything either because I had never once seen George make his own anything. My mother or I usually fixed all of his meals. Rosamarie didn't move.

My mother spoke again, "Hurry up Rosamarie, he's waiting," like he was some kind of king.

George bounded down the steps, two at a time, and headed for the dining room, clearly in a rush, impatient to get going. I couldn't see him since I was sitting in the living room with Rosamarie, but I knew exactly where and how he sat. He always perched at the head of the table, where my dad usually sat, and held his knife and fork upright in each hand waiting to pounce on whatever I served him.

Rosamarie nonchalantly got up and went into the kitchen. I followed. She cut an English muffin in half, buttered it and put it on the table.

George took a big bite, "Yuk," he gagged, "you didn't cook it."

I stifled a laugh with all my might.

"Rosamarie, you must broil the muffin," my mother yelled from the front door as she put her hat on and left.

Rosamarie waited until my mother was out of the house and went casually back into the living room, with me, not as casually, following her.

She sat, picked up a magazine, got this huge smile on her face, and winked at me. She called to George, "That's how I make English Muffins, George. You have to eat it like that." She was smiling that big smile of hers. She looked at me again and cracked up laughing. I didn't dare laugh for fear he would hear me, but I was having the time of my life.

We heard George's chair go crashing to the dining room floor as he stormed out of the house, furious. I peeked into the dining room. He had left the English muffin with the big bite in it on the table.

I looked at Rosamarie. She smiled back at me—that huge wonderful smile. She had successfully antagonized George, which was great fun. Here was a real princess, or even a queen. Only a queen could successfully make George mad without getting beat up. Only then did I realize we were alone, and I began to laugh. Rosamarie eagerly joined me, and we laughed our heads off for a good ten minutes.

My mother returned in a bad mood but not because of me for once. The trip to Aunt Jean's was off to a rocky start. Rosamarie was refusing to go.

"Rosamarie is stubborn," my mother spoke to me as I set the table for lunch. "She is a real disappointment to her mother. She thinks she can have her way about everything."

"Is she going to get married?" I asked.

"She better not," my mother quipped back. My mother and Rosamarie did not speak much. The silence in the house was gloomy, but Rosamarie would look over at me and smile that big, confident, devilish smile.

I checked again. The project was there. I picked it up and held it. This had not been my first choice for a project. My first choice was the health project. We were to chart the blood types of our parents and try to guess our own. The school nurse, Miss Carlin, was going to help us understand the purposes of blood typing. I really wanted to know my blood type. I was hoping that I was O positive because that was my dad's. My dad gave me his: type OO+. I made the chart in different colors with all the boxes to fill in. I filled in my dad's. My dad said my mother's was also type OO+, and I filled that in. I told him that we were to have our blood typed in school to check if our charts were correct.

"Yours will be easy," he said, "because type OO+ is recessive to everything. Two type OO parents always have type OO children."

I asked my mother for hers, just to be sure.

She said, "What? It's none of the school's business what my blood type is. Do another project."

"But," I argued, "I've already started this one."

"That's too bad, Miss Lazy Bones. Do another one."

I put the first project under my bed and chose the second choice on the class suggestion list, an experiment with sound, which needed no help from anyone to complete except the librarian. Things were always easier without family.

I went to the library and found science magazines on the subject. My dad did end up helping, which I didn't mind. He gave me a piece of wood, some nails, and permission to use his workbench after school. Since this one had been my second start, I definitely wanted to protect it from damage. I held on tight.

"Where is my blue blouse?" She turned her special hateful gaze towards me as the hangers sped by in front of me, like movable weapons, with their own energy. "Find it." Tempo was picking up. I could feel the rage taking hold of her—soon rage would be in charge of all of us. Brenda crouched in the corner, her eyes wide with fright.

My mother threw the clothes on the floor and at me. "It's not here. Where is it?" she yelled, now more to herself than to me as she attacked the heap of clothes. I saw the blouse I had just ironed come flying back at me. She went from the closet to the dresser, all the while yelling, "Find my blouse. Did you find it yet? Look how nice and ironed your stuff is, selfish little girl who never does anything for her mother."

That wasn't true. I ironed for the whole family. It was impossible to keep up with it all the time. She rummaged through all the clothes in my sister's drawer and put those in the same heap. I sadly realized it was going to be difficult to sort everything out. Brenda was quiet. We were both just staring, waiting for the final explosion. Everything came crashing to the floor now— the lamps, the radio, all the knickknacks on the dresser, my aunt's picture, my miniature statue of the Virgin Mary—it all went to the floor.

"Your room's a filthy mess," she yelled as she threw everything down. After the lamp, it was my books. I desperately clung to my homework, knowing that if she messed this up, I wouldn't have time to do it over. I hung on. She swung at me, I ducked, and she missed. That made her even angrier.

"This dresser is filthy dirty. When are you going to clean it up? Come over here and look at this mess." She grabbed me by the cheek to show me the caked-on dirt of the dresser. I was still holding on to my homework project. She hit me, this time she didn't miss, and said,

My mother was right. Rosamarie was determined to get her way, and she was going to do whatever she wanted. I would have loved to have the nerve to defy my mother like that.

Aunt Rosa arrived to pick up Rosamarie to take her home. Things were pretty quiet. Aunt Rosa looked at me and smiled as she called to my mother, "Anne, how about letting Dolly come with us to our house. She can spend the night." Those words couldn't have been better received by me. I could sleep over with Rosamarie. I was thrilled and also glad to get away from my mother's ranting about Rosamarie for a whole day.

My mother strutted into the living room and stood by me, "Well, I don't know Rosa, she hasn't even made her bed, yet," displaying as always that sick infinite power she had over me.

Aunt Rosa responded firmly, "She doesn't stay with Rosamarie much, and you can see how happy she is to be invited. You need not say no all the time, Anne."

"Alright, but she's to be home first thing in the morning."

"That's no problem at all. I'll drop her off myself." Both she and Rosamarie turned to me with big smiles. I was afraid to smile back. I wasn't out of the house, yet, and my mother would reverse the invitation if she thought I was too happy. Instead, I put my head down and smiled to myself.

Aunt Rosa, Rosamarie, and I arrived at their house just as Uncle Max returned from work. Uncle Max was tall and wiry, and when he walked, he almost danced, his feet hardly touching the ground. He wore rimless spectacles, which he was always pushing back on his nose. His hair was totally gray. He looked distinguished with a small moustache. Noticing me right away, his

eyes lit up, "Hello, Dolly—you look beautiful, as always.
How about having a nice cool drink before dinner?" He
said to all of us at once.

"Good idea, Max." Aunt Rosa brightened. "Let's
have a drink in the sunroom."

We followed her, listening to the inviting clink of ice
cubes from Uncle Max at the bar. It was a peaceful
evening, no George, no Brenda, no Mother—just nice
people being nice to each other. Aunt Rosa hurried
upstairs to change and returned in a long blue dress.
Her hair was pushed down to cover her ears. Aunt Rosa
had the biggest ears you could ever imagine. She didn't
like them and was always covering them with her hair.

"Here you are, ladies," and with a little bow to each
of us, he handed a grasshopper to my aunt, another
drink I didn't recognize to Rosamarie, and a Shirley
Temple, which is ginger ale with cherry juice that turns
the drink to a pretty color pink, to me.

The grownups chatted as I, trying ever so hard to be
as ladylike as Rosamarie, sipped my own drink. It was
difficult just to sip—the ginger ale was cool with ice,
and I was thirsty. No one talked about Naldo. I'm not
even sure Uncle Max knew him. They talked instead of
George M. Cohan, who was trying to get a group of
people together to work in movies instead of Broadway.
He had invited Uncle Max to join them. Uncle Max was
not happy with the thought of Hollywood.

"No," he said emphatically to Aunt Rosa. "I could
never be in movies. It's too low class."

"But, if he offered you a steady job, it might be
worth a try." Aunt Rosa crossed her legs and smiled at
me. She leaned over and put my hair over my ears, and
then she patted her own ears as if to make sure they too
were covered.

Uncle Max repeated, "No. It's Broadway or nothing for me."

The subject changed, not too easily, to flowers. Aunt Rosa liked African violets. They were lined up on the windowsill of the porch. She was fussy about watering them.

"Be careful not to get the leaves wet, Dolly," she said, as I offered to water them, "because if you get the leaves wet, the flowers won't bloom."

I chose the pretty green watering can with a long, narrow spout to water each plant for her.

That night, I slept with the princess named Rosamarie. She had her own room. It was a small room with twin beds. The furniture was dark brown mahogany with a dark brown dressing table and white linen curtains, bedspread, and dresser scarves. There was whole closet full of magnificent clothes, all for Rosamarie. The only people I knew with a closet all to themselves were my aunts, and they were grownups. I didn't have my own closet, but I didn't have many clothes anyway. I certainly didn't have a whole closetful of them.

There were pictures on the wall of the bedroom, all of Rosamarie. She explained each of them to me. "This is my mother and me when I was twelve. We were at Hunter Beach where we go every year. And this is my father dressed as Al Jolson. He was doing a Jolson imitation and someone snapped his picture. She picked up a large framed picture on the dresser. "This is a picture of me playing the piano at a recital that I was in last year." She smiled as she told me. She seemed to enjoy all of her pictures. I could tell she liked telling me about them. I could see why my mother called her a princess. She was treated like one. I could only wish for such wonderful treatment for myself.

She let me try on some of her clothes. I tried on her bra, but it didn't fit so we stuffed socks into it. I tried on her red, off the shoulder blouse. *Wow.*

She asked, "Would you like that blouse? I have many others, and you seem to like it so. Why don't you keep it for yourself?" She found a peasant skirt in the closet and I tried that on.

Rosamarie looked, "I think there is a brown skirt in there that would go better because it's smaller. This one is too big. Look in the back of the closet. There should be a brown one there that I outgrew. If it fits, you may have it."

I was aghast. "Don't you think we should ask your mother if you can give it to me?" I asked. I didn't want to get Rosamarie into trouble because of me.

"Why? They're *my* clothes," Rosamarie answered with a clear sense of ownership. She seemed to think the idea of telling her mother was silly, so I didn't say anything more about it. I was instantly jealous of her clear sense that certain things belonged strictly to her.

I was looking at the clothes to choose the other skirt when she came close to me and smiled her huge smile. Still smiling and looking at me, she juggled a huge, white box down from the top of the closet. How small she looked as she almost lost her balance under its weight.

"Dolly, I have something to show you. But first you must promise never to tell anyone—ever."

I promised.

The box opened. Out tumbled a beautiful satin white gown with rows of little buttons up and down the sleeves. I looked at Rosamarie. Her confident smile flashed back as she said, "I had it made for me. It cost two-hundred dollars. I'm eloping tomorrow with Renaldo." She pronounced the name Renaldo in Spanish. She usually called him Naldo, but tonight she seemed to be thinking in Spanish. "I am leaving to be married in Venezuela."

Naldo. I almost died. Rosamarie was eloping with the most handsome man in the world. I thought about the two-hundred dollars for one dress. The entire lot my father built our house on cost three-hundred dollars. How would they get that huge dress down the ladder? And the window, it was so high up and small. What would happen when Mother and Aunt Rosa found out? The sky would surely fall.

I woke up the next day to find Rosamarie's bed unmade and a sense of silence in the house. She had disappeared. I tried to figure out how she got out of the house. I looked out the window of the bedroom for a ladder, but there was none. The cousin with the beautiful smile was gone, and Aunt Rosa was crying as she spoke on the telephone with my mother. I was to go home immediately.

Aunt Grace came to get me in her big maroon Pontiac. Aunt Grace was one of my favorite aunts. She was a third grade schoolteacher and had her own money to spend. Aunt Grace liked high-heeled shoes and Pall Mall cigarettes. They were written Pall Mall on the pack, but they were pronounced "Pell Mell." She had piles of shoeboxes in her closet. Brenda and I played in the closet for hours trying on the beautiful shoes.

Aunt Grace's car was sparkling clean and shiny except for a pile of cigarette butts in the ashtray under the dashboard, which hung open because it was stuffed full. There was the usual pack of cigarettes, Pall Mall, on the dashboard. The car smelled of cigarette smoke.

I settled into the gray plush seat on the passenger side. It was nice to be in the front to watch out the window from a higher vantage point. I tended to get motion sickness and was car sick a lot in the back, but George always got the front seat. I never understood why George always got the front seat even if I was sick in the back. If I felt sick, my mother would stop the car and let me out for a while, but no one ever offered me the front. As we drove, Aunt Grace pushed the cigarette lighter into the dashboard, and it closed with a click. A few seconds later, it popped out, and she lit a Pall Mall with the bright red glow inside of the lighter.

"See, Dolly, you're a witness. I do *not* light one cigarette from another. That's the definition of a chain smoker. I'm not a chain smoker."

I didn't really see a big difference, but I didn't say anything.

"You know not to touch the lighter, don't you Dolly?" Aunt Grace reminded me. "That red color means it's very hot."

She returned the lighter to the dashboard. This time she did not push it in all the way. A few minutes later, she pushed in again, waited until the lighter popped out, put one cigarette into the ashtray, and lit another from the hot center. As we drove, each time she finished one cigarette, she lit another, but always with the lighter.

My mother was at the door waiting for us.

Aunt Grace didn't even say hello. She went straight to the problem as she lit another cigarette. "Well, she's marrying a jerk; I'll tell you that, Anne."

"I think he's handsome," was my unsolicited opinion.

"Handsome is as handsome does," my mother snapped at me. She looked at me sternly. "Did you know about this?"

"No." I remembered the promise. The lie was easy.

My mother poured Aunt Grace a cup of coffee and they sat down at the table. My mother shot me another menacing look, which usually meant "You'll pay for this later."

She knows. She always knows everything.

Aunt Grace was frantically lighting cigarettes, one from the other.

My mother turned to me. "Go upstairs to your room." I was worried that she might have guessed, but I wasn't going to tell. I didn't care if I got a million beatings; I was as certain of that as Rosamarie seemed to be when she said she was going to marry Naldo.

Aunt Grace came to my rescue. "I doubt she knows, Anne. Rosamarie would be too ashamed of herself to tell anyone."

I didn't go to my room. Instead, I perched at my usual spot at the top of the staircase to listen, the image of the beautiful wedding gown alive in my head as Aunt Grace's smoke traveled up the stairs with me.

My mother, nervous, was talking fast. "Grace, you really are smoking too much. You're a chain smoker."

"No, I'm not a chain smoker. I seldom light one cigarette from another, and that is the sign of a chain smoker."

"Well, you do that when you're nervous. I've seen you." My mother was determined.

"Only, when I'm upset." Aunt Grace was equally determined.

My mother, still agitated, went back to the problem of Naldo. "What is this going to do to poor Rosa? What could that selfish child have been thinking of?"

My mother answered her own question as she launched into one of her usual lectures. "Rosa spoilt her, Grace. That's obvious. She handed her everything and now Rosamarie thinks she's a princess and acts like one. She does whatever she wants and doesn't give a thought in the world for her poor mother."

That was the beginning of the end for me. No one found out from me about the secret, of course; the secret was locked in my heart just as I had promised. Grownups don't get secrets out of little girls. Yes, Rosamarie eloped and I never told, but the sky did fall, and right on top of me. My mother refused to let me see Rosamarie again or ever mention her name. The spoiled princess was considered a black mark on the family. She had married a foreigner and was a bad influence on the younger children. No one mentioned her name again. When they had to refer to her, which wasn't often, they called her, "Persona non grata".

I didn't see Rosamarie after that. I heard she had moved to Venezuela. *Well, one day I would just get on a plane and go and visit her.*

Every day, I walked past her house on my way home from school, hoping to see the beautiful princess and her handsome groom, but the house was dark. The stones seemed to reflect how cold their home was without Uncle Max. There was no piano music, no Al Jolson imitation, just the cold stone of the house and the lonely lace curtains still in the window. It was clear that there was no one behind them.

One day, as I passed, there was a for sale sign on the lawn of Rosamarie's house.

FOR SALE
BATTISTA REALTY
TELEPHONE: EXEL 8-3000

I missed Rosamarie so much that I wrote a diary about her and me, but my mother found it, threw it out, and beat me up. The beating didn't hurt as much as when she threw the diary out. In the diary, I had changed my name to Rosamarie and my mother was furious. I didn't understand. It was only pretend. I could never be Rosamarie.

6

"To strive, to seek, to find, and not to yield." Tennyson

One afternoon, I received an invitation to visit a friend who was important to me because she was the most lonesome looking girl in the school and I thought I had a chance with her. The other girls didn't talk to either one of us much. The second reason that I liked Judy was because she had tan skin and beautiful dark eyes. I longed for the thick eyelashes that seemed to frame her jet black eyes exactly right.

I didn't know why the other girls didn't talk with Judy, but in a way, I was glad. If the other girls took her over, she would not want to be with me. I learned that when I brought Joan, a new girl on my block, to school her first day. We had been friends most of the summer the year she moved in almost next door. After the other girls took her over, she didn't bother much with me.

Judy seemed to want a friend, and I was more than willing. We'd meet on the playground and eye each other most of the time. One day, another girl, Linda, broke her arm falling from the monkey bars in the playground right next to where Judy and I were standing. She let out an awful yell and ran into the school with her wrist hanging down completely without any support. I was pretty scared.

"What happened to her?" I asked Judy.

She looked at me and spoke. Her black eyes were even prettier up close. "She broke her wrist. That's why it's hanging down like that."

I was glad to have someone who knew more than I about such things, and I started to ask her a lot of questions each day on the playground. She told me a lot, too. She knew all about what each child had. When one of the boys, Michael, mysteriously disappeared from school one day, Judy seemed to know all about it. She said he lived near her. Miss Carlin, the school nurse, had to take him home because he had lice. He wouldn't be back until it was cleared up.

One conversation led to another, and I started helping Judy with her homework. Sometimes I even did it for her. I had a lot of time after school and had no problem adding a little extra work to my time in the closet at night. I liked being in the closet with the dim light and the peace and quiet. It was no trouble to help Judy.

One day I went to school without my homework and hers. I explained, "Sometimes my sister messes it up. She's younger and doesn't know any better. Don't worry, I'll finish at recess."

"Did you tell your mother?"

"No."

Judy didn't say anything, but she didn't seem to mind the missing homework.

Judy's mom found out about me doing Judy's homework. She asked Judy to bring me home for a visit. She wanted to talk with us together.

When Judy invited me, I wanted to go so badly that I didn't tell my mother. I had begun to see that I couldn't tell my mother ordinary everyday events because she would prevent them or interfere in a way that made doing them impossible. When I received an invitation, not only did she say I couldn't go, but she made sure that I never received another one. Usually, she'd call the girl's mother and insult her.

I sensed that there was something wrong with my mother, that's all. I learned to stay out of her way as much as possible, get whatever work she wanted done, and then disappear. It didn't always work; although, many times I remained safe in the closet during one of her raging episodes. I stayed there all night and knew that there was something very wrong, but that is all I knew.

I avoided telling my mother about the invitation from Judy. If the timing was right, I could work in the visit and get back home before my mother got home from teaching school. There was no sense to tell her and face the same old never ending phrase, "No, you may not go."

Judy was glad to have me come.

"What should I wear?" I asked her.

"Oh, anything you want to play in. We can go to the lot behind my house. I have a cap pistol, and you can use it."

Judy had a cap pistol. I was not allowed one because as usual, girls in our house were left out of anything fun. My brother had one. I had a play gun and could pretend to be the Lone Ranger, but it had no caps with it.

Judy was going to lend me hers. That was the next best thing. And best of all, Judy wanted me for a friend.

She told me how to walk to her house from my house. I went home, did my chores, and changed. I wore my gun belt and holster, but I left my toy gun home. I was kind of ashamed of that gun. It had no caps, and my brother's friends had told me that it was not worth much as a gun. When the boys' guns cracked and smelled of smoke, my gun would quietly click an impotent click, click.

I had no trouble walking up Halstead Avenue to the railroad tracks that divided us. I passed the liquor store, Sal's drugstore, and Arturo's beauty parlor. His name was written on a large frosted glass window: **ARTURO'S BEAUTY SALON**. I knew the way well from the days of walking to the train station to meet my dad.

I was not prepared for what I saw at Judy's. It was not a house as I understood one to be. The neat manicured lawn that my father kept and that I had come to accept as the definition of a proper house was conspicuously absent at Judy's house. There were boards placed to serve as a sidewalk to the front door, and underneath, there was grass trying to grow but not anything like the beauty of my father's lawn and the large pretty slates that were the sidewalk to my door. I walked over the boards with Judy, and we entered the house. Judy's mother was hanging laundry in the living room. I had never seen this before. There was dirt packed down from walking, instead of a floor. There was a small faded pink rug, but it was not anywhere big enough to cover the dirt.

The bigger shock came next. Judy's mother turned to say hello and smiled a big toothy smile full of large white teeth, the whitest teeth that I had ever seen. And then I understood. The teeth weren't that white—they seemed bright white because they stood out against the dark black skin of Judy's mother.

Judy's mother is colored, I thought with sudden fear. *What should I do? Did Judy tell her mother that I am white? Will she send me home?*

But Judy's mother didn't seem to notice. She was warm and happy and welcoming.

Judy had not seemed colored to me. Her skin was slightly tanned and her lips were small and her nose was like my mother's, not like a colored person would have. That day I matched Judy with a word, a word I had heard in school. I heard my mother say it once, too, when she was on the phone. The word was "mulatto." Judy was mulatto.

Judy's mom took us into the kitchen. I saw the cookies and a bottle of cold milk set out on the table. Judy's mom smiled. "Judy told me that you love chocolate covered graham crackers. I bought them especially for you and Judy today."

That was a good start. It didn't look like she was going to punish us for the homework stuff.

Mrs. Davis put out some cups for the milk and continued. "Judy tells me that you help her with her homework. I think that is nice of you. I have seen some of what you do, and you are a smart little girl. Judy is lucky to have you for a friend."

I didn't say anything. I got the feeling she wasn't finished.

She offered me the plate of cookies, and I took one and put it on the napkin in front of me, not wanting to eat before Judy was served. Mrs. Davis again offered the plate. "Go ahead, Dolly, take another, enjoy, they're all for you and Judy." I took another one from the plate and settled it, too, on the napkin.

I looked at Mrs. Davis, who put the plate in the center of the table and continued talking. "There is something I want to tell you and Judy. I don't mind you helping Judy. I think she is lucky. But I would like it better if you would only assist her. I don't want you to take her homework to do yourself. Do you understand the difference? Do you understand why?"

I didn't answer, as she seemed to be ready to say more. She looked at me, took a breath, and wiped her hands on her apron. "There is an old saying, 'neither a borrower nor a lender be.' That is true of money, but it is also true of knowledge. Judy mustn't borrow knowledge, and you mustn't lend that knowledge. You can help her; yes, even teach her about all those books you love to read, but her papers must be her own. They shouldn't be borrowed. Do you understand what I mean, the difference between helping her and doing it for her?" Mrs. Davis placed her hands on the back of Judy's chair and waited.

I didn't really understand, but I said that I did and that I was sorry.

She softened her stance. She seemed almost afraid that she had hurt me. "No, you don't need to be sorry. You're a nice little girl who was helping her friend. You have nothing to apologize for. But you must tell your mom, and after the weekend, on Monday morning, first thing, as soon as you and Judy get to school, the two of you go and tell the teacher. Miss Roberts needs to know that the work is not Judy's."

I was scared. I didn't want to do either one of those things.

Judy looked at me. "I'll say it was my fault, not yours, Dolly. You didn't do anything."

"It's nobody's fault," said Judy's mom. "You didn't know. If you do it again, then it's somebody's fault, but not yet. Now go and play and Monday everything will be better. Never worry about tomorrow until it's yesterday."

She smiled down on us, that big toothy smile, until we finished our cookies and milk. We went outside, and I played all day with Judy's cap pistol. I had been invited somewhere and this was an event not to be forgotten. Most of all, I had a friend. Her name was Judy Davis. What a pretty name!

My father talked often about the other side of the tracks and how dangerous it was. It didn't seem dangerous to me. It seemed wonderful. I was visiting the other side of the tracks, and everything was fine. I would have liked to tell my dad about the day, but something did stir in me, a vague feeling of danger. Judy and I formed a club. We called it The Red Circle Club. We used a Red Circle coffee can and promised to put our money in it to save for the cigarettes Judy seemed to want us to have.

"I'll teach you to smoke, Dolly, and you can teach me all about those big books you read in the library." Judy smirked; I think making fun of me a little. I didn't mind a bit. It was just like Heaven up there in our house with all the trees around us, trees that seemed to reach straight up to God all day long.

I was astonished. "Judy, does your mother know you smoke?"

"Of course not, silly, and don't you tell her. Swear!"

We put our hands on the coffee can and swore secrecy about everything we told each other forever.

The colored men, dressed in muddy overalls, were coming towards our tree as they returned home from work with their lunch pails. Some of them waved to us, and we waved back. It was time to go home. I would have to hurry to get there before my mother or I'd be stuck with another lie to confess on Saturday. Judy walked me to the railroad tracks. She and I both knew that she should leave me there. We didn't say anything—we just knew.

"Can you come over tomorrow?" Judy asked.

"I can't. It's Saturday. I have to stay home on Saturday and watch my little sister."

"Can you come over on Sunday? We can go up to the tree house again."

Boy, I would have loved to but there was old, fat Uncle Vincent, the dentist. "No, my uncle comes on Sunday. I have to stay with him." I hated Sundays. The men and the living room smelled awful from smoking cigars all afternoon. I wasn't allowed to leave the house because I needed to show respect to them and stay home during their visit.

"When can we meet?" Judy was insistent.

"We can meet at the children's Mass at church. I usually help Father McAvoy after Mass, but I don't have to. We can go to your tree house after that." That would work for me because my mother was used to my staying after church to help Father McAvoy.

"Great." Judy was smiling. I was smiling so much that I was embarrassed. I hoped she didn't think me a fool for being so excited.

She didn't seem to mind what surely must have been a silly grin. She just smiled all the more.

"I can go to any Mass I want." She spoke like someone who ran her own life. "The children's Mass is at nine o'clock. Is that the one?"

I answered, "Yes," as I secretly envied her freedom to do what she wanted.

"I can get to that Mass. See you then."

Judy and I turned away from each other as we went our separate ways. I was enveloped by a cloud. I had a friend. My steps were fast and light, my heart on fire.

As I rushed home, I should have known—a bell should have rung, or some instinct or warning should have entered my head. I saw nothing, heard nothing except joy as I smiled and smiled and almost cried out loud with happiness.

As I crossed the street, I looked up. From Arturo's Beauty Salon came a big fat woman, raging, and her little permanent curler rollers protruding under wisps of hair everywhere. That dark silhouette was too familiar to be ignored. I froze. The figure caught up with me, still raging, the eyes bulging, the arms flailing, and I heard that all too frightening and familiar voice.

"Where have you been? I just saw you cross the tracks." The figure punched and pinched and shoved. "You are not allowed to play with colored people. Are you crazy?"

My hands shot up to protect my face as my mother's relentless blows stung my cheeks.

"How dare you! Put your hands down! You are not to resist your mother's punishment! Keep your hands down."

Hard as I tried I could not keep my hands down. Each time I saw the fists flying, my body betrayed me; my arms tried to protect me.

"Put your hands down or I'll give you a beating you will never forget!"

The hands punched, the feet kicked. I did the best I could, tucking my hands between my knees. The blows fell again. *Please God, help me keep my hands down. Help me be a good girl and keep my hands down.*

God answered. I put my hands between my knees, hard. God gripped my knees himself and pushed. I felt His strength and together we held my hands away from my face as my mother's blows met their mark. My glasses fell to the ground as my face burned with pain and embarrassment. I hoped no one could see us under the darkness of the bridge overhang. I didn't dare hit back. A child should never hit back at her mother; it's a sin.

The storm abated as quickly as it came. Suddenly, my mother turned and, without speaking, crossed the street into the beauty parlor, her back signaling the end of yet another beating. I was on my hands and knees moving my hands around until I picked up my glasses, relieved to find them unbroken. As I put them on, they felt funny, a little bit crooked on my face, but I couldn't stop then, I had to find Father McAvoy.

I ran all the way to the rectory. My mother beat me to it. I saw her car pull away as I turned the corner. I was crying, my face smarting from the salt of the tears, as I saw my friend, Father McAvoy, behind his desk, looking down at the floor. On his desk was one of my mother's church contribution envelopes.

"What is it, Dolly?" He didn't look up and smile at me as he usually did.

"Father McAvoy, please, Father, my mother said I can't be friends with Judy any more because she's colored."

My heart was breaking. I was praying Father McAvoy would intervene as he sometimes did to help persuade my mother.

I sobbed, "Why Father, when all of God's children are equal must I give up Judy? Doesn't God love her, too? If she's equal, she can be my friend, and everyone is equal in God's eyes. That's what I learned, Father. That's what Sister Marie told us. Please Father, tell my mother to let me keep Judy."

"Do you mean Judy Davis? I know her."

"Yes."

Father McAvoy looked sad. Hope was lost as his answer came back. "No Dolly, if God wanted you to be friends with Judy, He would have made her skin the same color as yours. God wants to keep the races separate, He does not want them to marry and change the color of His children."

"But, Father, Judy is a girl. I'm not going to marry her."

"Yes, but she may have a brother, or someone you might meet through her."

I gave up then. The decision was made by God. No one dare argue with Him.

Father McAvoy took a closer look at my face. "Dolly, I think your glasses are crooked. And there is a red mark on your cheek."

I remembered Phyllis's fall on the playground and the champion liar in me spoke, "Yes, Father, I banged them on the monkey bars at school." I never thought I would ever lie to Father, but if I told him, anything could happen to me, and him. I could never, never tell him. I couldn't even tell him in Confession because he always recognized my voice. The burden of silence weighed on my shoulders as I said, "Thank you, Father, Goodbye."

Father looked lonesome as he stood near his desk to bid me goodbye. "Goodbye, Dolly, God bless you." He knew more than he was telling me, too.

7

"What gets us into trouble is not what we don't know, but what we know for sure that just ain't so." Mark Twain

There was not much left to do except head for the library, where I would find the only sure friends I had. I sat down in my usual place, next to the row of books on the bottom shelf. I took the book about my friend, Monk, *You Can't Go Home Again,* down off the shelf and held it. *I can't go home again either, Monk.*

I leaned on the shelf with my left arm touching all the books and cried. My stomach didn't feel like a stomach. It felt like a big hole in the middle of my body. My mother had won again. She had taken Father McAvoy from me. He didn't want to be with me. He wanted to be with her. I had no money to contribute to the church. I had nothing to give anyone.

The next time I looked up, the windows of the library were dark with the night sky. I had never been out alone at night. I went to the librarian, took the card from the back of the book, and handed it to her. The library was deserted, and I saw, for the first time, the dim, yellow library reading lights. The quiet, the peace, and the books all around comforted me, invited me to stay a little longer, but I knew I couldn't.

Mrs. York took my book and stamped it. "Dolly, you are out much too late. I didn't see you back there or I would have sent you home. Now, hurry and go home. Do you know the way?"

"Yes, Mrs. York, I walk to church every day, and I can take the same way home."

She handed me my book. "You have two weeks from today. Will that be enough? It's a big book."

"I already read it twice," I answered. I didn't tell her that I just wanted to hold it and feel Monk near me.

Mrs. York responded with approval. "Yes, Thomas Wolfe—it's a good book. Now, hurry home, Dolly."

As I walked down the hill towards home on Maple Avenue, I looked up. The stars were everywhere. They looked very bright. I saw The Big Dipper and asked her to swoop down and pick me up, but she didn't.

I'm going to have a hard life, I said to myself. I was all alone, and to God, what happened to me was small. He had other little children who need his help more. I would have to make it on my own.

The stars came down and wrapped themselves around me. They were my friends, too. My glasses felt a little funny. They were bent, but I could still see fine in the bright starlight. I looked up at the moon. I had to wonder what the man in the moon was thinking. He looked sad, and I didn't see why. It must be great to be him—hanging in the sky with nothing to do all day but watch the world go by.

As I turned the corner of my street, my dad's car pulled up alongside me. He jumped out of the car.

I looked at him expecting punishment. He was standing straight and tall but when I caught his eye, there was softness in them, a look of relief, that I had never seen before. Then as quickly as it came, the look disappeared, his body relaxed and he said, "Well, you're a sight for sore eyes. I've been all over town looking for you. I went to Father McAvoy. He's terribly worried about you. He said that you had been there this afternoon, but he hadn't seen you since."

"I fell asleep in the library."

"I see. What have you got there?" He looked at the book that was cradled in my arms.

"*You Can't Go Home Again*, by Thomas Wolfe."

"You sure do like that Thomas Wolfe guy. Well, he can't go home again but you can. Come on home with me. You must be hungry. I'll make you a sandwich."

Oh, boy, one of Dad's sandwiches. Great. He was right. I was hungry.

He opened the door for me on the passenger side, and I got in. I tried to straighten the frame of my eyeglasses, but it wouldn't budge. My dad smelled good, his arm around the back of the passenger seat, checking me out.

He leaned forward. "What happened to your glasses? They look crooked."

Uh, oh. Here comes another lie. "I banged them on the monkey bars at school."

"Hey, that's a humdinger of a bruise on your cheek, too. Your mother better not find out that you were on those monkey bars. She doesn't like them." That meant he wasn't going to tell her. *Good.*

There was a light, gentle odor of cigarettes as he leaned forward. "Let's take a look-see at those rims." He gently took the glasses off my face and held them up to the car light. He blew on them a couple of times and then held them in his hand. After a few times of this, he adjusted one side, looked at them again against the light and handed them back to me. "There, you go, Princess.

They were a little bent. I think they're okay now." He took a white handkerchief out of his pocket and patted my bruise a little. Even though my cheek stung when he touched me, he made me feel better. He was like that. He could always make me feel better. My heart felt warm as I put the glasses on and a little surprised because I knew I had tried to straighten them myself with no success. "How did you do that, Dad?"

He answered me as he shifted the car into gear and drove off. The whirr of the motor reminded me that one day I was going to have a car and drive myself right to the ends of the earth, away from here forever. "Oh, I just warmed the plastic of the frame with my hands and warm breath, which made the plastic softer so I could bend it back to its original form. If that doesn't fix them let me know and we'll go to Walt and he can help us." Walt was Mr. Berry, the optician, who made me my glasses each year.

We drove quietly down the street and turned into our driveway.

Dad opened his door. "Wait, here, Dolly, I'm just going to open the garage door, and we'll go in the garage way."

He walked down the driveway, opened the garage door with one arm, and walked back towards me. He seemed to swing along with the garage door instead of actually opening it. I tried opening the garage door myself once, but it was too heavy.

He strode back, jumped into the driver's seat, and drove us into the garage. It wasn't possible to get out on the passenger side because the garage wall was too close. I slid over and got out on Dad's side as he held the door open.

We climbed the wooden cellar stairs into the kitchen. My dad turned on the kitchen lights and opened the refrigerator door.

"Hmmm, what is there for us to eat, Dolly? I saved you some meatloaf from supper. Do you want a sandwich from that?"

"Yes, please."

He made me a sandwich on an onion roll with leftover meatloaf, lettuce, mayonnaise, and salt and pepper.

"I know meatloaf is your favorite, so I made sure I saved you a lot." He put the sandwich on the table with a glass of milk.

I looked at the clock—9:45. *Wow. Everybody else must be in bed*, I thought. *Even Mom. I was out late. I could have gotten locked in at the library. Next time, I better be careful.*

My dad made a call.

"Hey, Jim. She's okay. I found her. She was a sight for sore eyes, I'll tell you that. I was worried sick."

Jim was Father McAvoy. Strange, but I was happy that Dad was worried about me.

"Yeah, she was at the library. I'm a dumb klutz for not thinking of it. So long, Jim, thanks for your help. I owe you one."

My dad joined me at the dining room table and sat next to me as he read the paper. Once in a while he would glance up as if to make sure that I was still there. He had this funny look of appreciation on his face, an almost smile accompanied by sparkling gray eyes behind his glasses. "You are going to grow up to be a looker, Dolly. And you're smart, too. Where did you get those good looks and brains? From your old man?" He smiled that conspiracy-like smile of his, and his bright eyes danced with his own joke.

I spoke to him. "Mr. Wilson, a teacher at school, told me that the Irish and the Italians are known to have the best looking children. Do you think so?"

My dad continued our conversation with, "I know so. You're Italian and Irish and look how pretty you are." I blushed. We both silently admired me for a minute or two. I was glad Dad thought I was pretty, and I was almost sure he wasn't bluffing. Aunt Rosa said that my dad kissed the Blarney Stone. He did bluff and joke a lot but I could usually tell when he was kidding. Tonight, he was not bluffing.

"Wait for me, Dolly. I'm going to lock up, and we'll go to bed."

I stood by the stairs as he locked all the doors and shut off the lights. The locks clicked into place, promising me safety for tonight.

"Do you want me to tuck you in?" he asked, as we reached the top of the stairs.

"Yes."

"Get ready for bed and call me when you're ready. I'll be right out here," he said, and sat down at the top of the landing. Unlike my mean mother, sister, and brother, my father was one of those kinds of people who would never barge into someone's room, but I undressed in the closet anyway just in case. I never knew when my mother might be lurking around. I peered out of the closet. My dad was still on the landing looking off into space in the opposite direction. I put on my nightgown, got into bed, and lay stiff and still with my hands at my sides. I knew he would not budge until I called him. That's how my dad was. Somehow he knew how to behave around a girl even if you didn't tell him what to do.

"Dad, I'm ready," I called as softly as possible so as not to wake anyone.

He came in to the room, still dressed. He had waited. I could see his face by the hall light while, in total concentration, he tucked the sheets and the blanket in at the bottom of the bed and folded the top of the sheet over the blanket carefully. He took both his hands and with kind of a sliding motion he went all around my body, tucking the sheet all around me until I felt like an Egyptian mummy. I didn't move so as not to disturb the warm feeling the blanket made around my body.

I didn't tell Dad about Judy and me. I wanted to, but I knew better. My dad was a quiet man, not shy, but quiet. When I was with him, a sense of peace usually came over me, and when you know a peace like that with someone, you hold on to it with all your might. I knew Dad would not say anything, and neither would I. The subject was closed.

Still with his arms around me and the mummy case, he said, "I don't want you to be out alone at night again, okay? I'm going to call Blue Sky Taxi in the morning. Hal Robbin works for them. Do you know him?"

"Yes, he's Barbara Robbin's dad. He gives us rides sometimes for free in his taxi."

"Well, tomorrow, I'll open a charge account with Blue Sky. When you need a ride home and you can't find me, you can call Blue Sky. It's an easy number to remember, Exel 8-2000. They will give you a ride home and bill me. The only thing you have to remember is the telephone number and to have a dime with you wherever you go to make the call, okay?"

I nodded ever so slightly so as not to disturb my mummy case.

Dad moved in order to put his hand in his pocket. "Here's your first dime. Keep it with you, and use it to telephone when you need a ride. Okay? Promise?" He tucked the dime into my book, in the envelope where the library card goes and replaced the book on the nightstand.

"Now, what's the Blue Sky Taxi phone number? Are you smart enough to remember it?"

"Exel 8-2000."

"Perfect. How could I even think you wouldn't remember it?" He gave me one of his "you and I are the two smartest people in the world" looks.

Dad smelled good as he kissed the only part of me outside of the make-believe mummy case, my face. He kissed me once on my forehead and once on each cheek. Three kisses in all, the most I'd ever gotten at once.

"See you in the morning," he called softly as he turned out the hall light and went into his own bedroom.

I looked out the window by my bed, said good night to the star that was Monk. Miss Roberts said that the brightest star in the heavens was the North Star, but I didn't think so. The star that I saw was Monk Webber, smiling down on me, his friend, Dolly. "Good Night, Monk," I whispered and went to sleep.

I went to church on Sunday and noticed for the first time, that Judy sat in the back corner of the church together with other colored people.

My mother had done her job well. Judy's mother had been told. Judy and I looked at each other and said goodbye.

I never played with Judy again. We did sneak into the back of the library from time to time, but no one ever knew. She liked me to show her what books to read. Her favorite author was Charles Dickens. Sometimes we would see each other on the playground, each alone, but we didn't speak. And—I dearly missed the fat Negro lady with the big white teeth and the beautiful little tan girl who were my friends for a day.

§§§§§§

It was an odd coincidence that less than two weeks later, Mrs. Coleman invited me to accompany her daughter, Sue, and her to a musical play on Broadway. I'd never been to something like that before. They invited my mother first, who was Sue's tutor, as an appreciation gift for my mother's lessons, but my mother didn't want to go.

Mrs. Coleman and Sue picked me up at home. They came in a huge black car, and they had a colored chauffeur who was all dressed up in a black suit, white shirt, and black bowtie. He opened the car door for me, and I slid in next to Mrs. Coleman and Sue, who were both dressed in red.

"Good evening, Dolly," said Mrs. Coleman. Sue giggled as I answered, "Good evening, Mrs. Coleman, thank you for inviting me." This was a phrase I had rehearsed. Mrs. Coleman wore a red silk dress, high heels, and a long black mink coat. Sue had on a red velvet dress and a bunny fur jacket, which felt soft under my hand. I wore a gold taffeta dress that my grandmother made me. I didn't like it because my sister had one just like it and Brenda looked fat in anything. Sue chattered all the way to New York even though her mother asked her several times to be quiet. I knew why she couldn't be quiet because I was just as excited and could hardly sit still. I was just too shy to talk as my heart pounded along with Sue when we pulled up to Radio City Music Hall amidst all the gleaming Broadway lights.

The inside of the theater seemed to be all red and velvet. There was red carpet everywhere as we followed an usher in a red coat. My toes kept slipping to the front of my shoes as I tried to negotiate the downward sloping aisle. The red velvet drapes on the stage were closed, yet alive with anticipation. The usher took us to seats in the second row, right in front of a huge hole in the floor with an orchestra in it. The sounds of their tuning, which I loved, echoed in the still mostly empty theater.

We each were given a program. On the first page, I read *South Pacific* starring Mary Martin and Ezio Pinza. The room began to fill up with people chatting in their seats, which, sadly for me, muffled the sounds of the orchestra. I contented myself with watching even though I couldn't hear as well.

The conductor arrived, and then the music really called for my attention. I was transformed into a being that saw and heard nothing except the show. I didn't see the show. I walked into it. I floated into a dream with music everywhere around me and the beautiful people on the stage right in front of me. I liked the song "Honey Bun" the best, with the funny man on stage all dressed up in a grass skirt, wearing coconuts that bobbed around as he danced. They were tied to his hairy chest with clothesline and it looked like any minute they'd fall right off him. I was fascinated by Mary Martin trying to wash her hair on stage. I searched and searched for the source of the water that cascaded down her back as she sang, "I'm gonna wash that man right out of my hair." I was full of music and warmth and good feelings for the men and women on the stage as a story unfolded, about people loving each other even though they had different color skins and backgrounds—some were colored, some were white, and others were French. Everyone was different from everyone else, and it didn't seem to matter when it came to love.

When the show ended, we applauded and applauded as the performers skipped across the stage for one bow after another. I clapped as hard as I could because I wanted them to come back again and again, but all my clapping couldn't keep them. The curtain came down for the final time, and there were only the voices of the people behind me. The palms of my hands burned from clapping. I didn't care. I would have clapped forever to keep them on the stage.

Sadly, I left my dream world, as Mrs. Coleman took my hand and urged me up the aisle. I wanted to ask Mrs. Coleman something I really needed to know.

We reached the top of the red ramp and went into the lounge. I held on tight to her hand and asked, "Mrs. Coleman, do you think that people are born with a dislike for colored people?"

Mrs. Coleman suddenly looked down and directly at me. She seemed angry. "Dolly, I'm Jewish, and I know first hand the wrong that prejudice can do. And we are *not* born with prejudice. Intolerance is learned, just like the song in the show says—you have to be taught to hate. It's a terrible thing to dislike someone just because of something they can't help—their religion or color."

Finally, I actually found a grownup who agreed with me. Encouraged, I looked up and answered. "Well, if such a lesson is taught to me, I just won't learn it. When I grow up, I'm going to travel all over the world, make friends with anyone I please, and no one will stop me." I was in quite a brave mood.

Mrs. Coleman softened and squeezed my hand, "You know, Dolly, from what I know of you, I'm sure you will do exactly that. When you grow up, it will be a far better world thanks to nice girls like you." She gave me a long, thoughtful look that I didn't quite understand. We all three waited for the big black car lost in our own thoughts.

It wasn't long before the colored man, Mrs. Coleman's chauffeur, pulled right in front of the theater, got out on the driver's side, walked around the back, and opened the door for us. He leaned a little on the door and asked, "How was the show, Mrs. Coleman, ma'am?"

"It was lovely, Walter, thank you. Dolly was enraptured," Mrs. Coleman politely responded.

He looked at me and smiled. His teeth were bright white, too, just like Mrs. Davis.

Mrs. Coleman sat between Sue and me, smelling of perfume as the soft fur of her coat warmed me on the long quiet ride home. Sue was quiet, too, as the sound of the cars on the highway lulled us to sleep. The show music played softly in my ears, and I watched the beautiful show-people in my mind's eye all the way home.

8

"Money talks...but does it always tell the truth?"
Herb Cohen

My mother's entire family thought my brother was an adorable child and I inadequate because I was a girl. Being born a girl was like being born with the plague. George was older, and that, plus being a boy, gained him a lofty position in the family. My low station was clear from the beginning. Eldest sons are kings. Eldest girls are slaves.

All my mother's sisters, seven in all, came to visit George, the only begotten son. He was a small boy with pigeon-toed feet and dark unhappy eyes. The aunts admired him, planned for him, dreamed for him, and pooled all their money so that he could go to college. As we got older, they gave us pocket change. They gave George two quarters—they gave me one. No one questioned that, even me. George was not deceived. He paid little attention to any of it, except to make fun of them. Mocking them always, he cocked his head, and with a brief nod up to Heaven, he'd say, "Will you listen to that?" as he eavesdropped from his perch on the steps over the living room.

My dad built us a new house the year I was born. George had his own room, the only room where pictures were allowed on the wall. Dad didn't allow anyone to nail anything to the wall because it spoiled the plastering job that he did himself. George had a picture of the Virgin Mary on his wall, the only exception. There were candles by the picture and a kneeling post.

No one was allowed in George's room except my mother. She went in to pick up his laundry and stuff. Sometimes, there'd be an exception to the rules. He left his socks under the bed and my mother couldn't bend down so I had to go in when she called me to pick up his socks.

One day, as I searched under the bed for a wayward sock, I saw a pile of comic books hidden way over in the corner. We were not allowed to read comic books. I didn't say anything. Getting George in trouble might have been fun, but if things went as they usually did, I'd be the one punished. I'd be rewarded for my efforts by beatings from both George and my mother. Besides, I wanted to come back and read them. I picked up the sock and handed it to my mother without a word, frightened as usual that she'd see the look on my face and question me.

Later, I returned more than once and read whatever new versions of the comics were under the bed. I sneaked into his room and looked around on the afternoons when no one was home except me. I read all his books, too. He had a set of *Hardy Boys* books that my aunt gave him. He had all of *Bomba, the Jungle Boy,* and I read those, too. I found a bunch of pictures of naked women in a small tunnel in his closet that connected to the bathtub pipes in the next room. Just holding those pictures scared me, not just because of the possibility of being caught but also because of seeing what I shouldn't be seeing. There were some pencil sketches of a nude woman on tracing paper. I recognized the pose from drugstore magazines, which my brother probably traced himself. It was Marilyn Monroe lying on a red velvet bedspread.

Terrified of being caught, I didn't stay long, but I was drawn to the closet every day. I went back when the coast was clear to get another look and, then, another. I found some more pictures and comic books. Every week, I read *Brenda Starr, Batman* and *Superman* until I had them all memorized. Then I waited for the next week and another batch to appear, the next best thing to having my own newspaper stand.

Thus the time-laden days of my life were lessened a little by George's closet. I never got caught and got used to being a champion sneak and liar.

Uncle Joe built a golf course in the back yard for George. He was a man who knew about the things that are necessary to succeed in business, for he had connections with the Mafia. That's something important and meant that the family followed his advice, about anything and everything. So, when he said that George needed a putting green to succeed, of course, they built one.

Uncle Joe collected nine empty tin cans and washed them. He trimmed the edges and smoothed each can's rim. He dug holes in the backyard to fit the cans, specific distances apart, which I helped him measure. He was fat and could not bend too far, so it fell on me to put the cans in the holes and sow the grass seeds around them. His shiny black white-tipped shoes were small compared to the large stomach protruding over them. There was a gold watch on a long chain in his vest pocket. The chain jiggled on the top of his belly as he moved around the yard. His pinkie finger swelled around a diamond ring, and he smelled of cologne and unwashed body odor. This distracted me some, but I managed to concentrate enough to get the job done. My uncle checked this homemade maze of tin and said that it was excellent because each hole was a measured distance from the next, for perfect putting practice. He leaned his chubby hand on his knee to get up and groaned with relief as he completed the effort to become upright. I heard a noise that I knew I should ignore as he passed gas. The golf course task was, all-in-all, a painstaking effort, and George, as usual, did nothing. In fact, he wasn't even there.

As the grass began to grow around the holes, no one was allowed to step there except when playing golf. Being a girl, I was not expected to like golf, so I was not allowed to walk on the grass. George sometimes caddied at the country club where my uncle played, but George and his friends never played golf in our putting green. They didn't like it. The putting green just sat there with beautiful green grass everywhere. When Dad mowed the grass, he gave me the job of trimming around the golf holes. He said the cans were dangerous; he didn't like them. My dad hated when things are poorly done, especially in his backyard. He was right about the cans, which were terrible. I trimmed as Dad muttered that he was going to have to dig them all up. After a while, they got so rusty that we did dig them up, and I filled in each hole with soil.

Dad wasn't keen on my Uncle Joe either. He said that my mother's whole family was crazy. "Her family wants what they want, and they don't care who they hurt to get it," my dad had told Charlie Malone when they didn't know I was listening.

§§§§§§

It wasn't long before Dad and I had a new project. Soon after, I was sitting on the back porch steps reading, when Dad drove a truck over the grass and poured a whole pile of red clay dirt in the middle of the yard. He looked up at me, smiled an impish grin as his great eyes twinkled. "I bet you're wondering what I'm doing. Perhaps I'm not quite right in the head dumping large quantities of red clay all over the yard?" He circled his forefinger around his head in a gesture indicating that he was crazy.

I laughed. I knew he wasn't crazy. He and his Irish friends were always pretending they were totally nuts.

He took a large cylinder with handles down from the truck and started rolling it around the yard. He said, "Come over here, I'll show you a neat trick."

He let me roll the cylinder around.

"This is a rolling drum. What do you think of it? Pretty light, right?"

I didn't think it was so light, but I could push it.

"Now, watch this."

He rolled the drum to a specific position and showed me a hole near the top of one side.

"See, I'm moving the opening to the top on purpose." He pulled out the small rubber plug. It was wet. "Bring me the hose over there, Dolly. I need an extra smart person over here to help me out."

I uncoiled the hose and pulled it over to him. He stuck the end into the cylinder. "Now, hold this, Dolly, right there. Don't move."

I held the hose into the drum while he went to the faucet and turned on the water. I felt the hose jump and almost dropped it as the water pushed its way to me.

Dad watched a while, turned the hose off, and said, "Good job, Dolly. Now let's see if you can roll it."

I pushed. The heavy drum wouldn't budge.

He smiled and took the handle from me. He inserted the plug. His muscles tensed, and he smoothed and smoothed the large square of red clay soil flat as I admired his power.

He knelt near me and with his arm around me he explained, "See, it's the weight of the water that exerts the pressure to flatten the clay. Pretty clever, your old dad, don't you think?"

I agreed. My dad and his friends were always having fun over how clever they were.

He rolled the spout to its bottom most position. When he opened the spout, the water ran out.

"See, Dolly. Do you get it? When the cylinder is full, it's heavy and I can flatten the soil. When the cylinder is empty and light, you can easily push it back into the garage until the next time."

I really did think it was pretty clever. Each day for several days, I rolled the empty cylinder out of the garage; Dad filled it with water and rolled the court. When he finished, we both emptied it, and I rolled it back into the garage. While my dad worked, I waited on the porch steps and read or did my homework.

When he wanted me to help, he'd call, "Hey, Dolly, come on over and help me. I need another genius to help me figure this out." I had to satisfy myself with the job Dad gave me of pushing the empty cylinder into and out of the garage each day before he filled it and after he emptied it. But even with only that small job I felt pretty important being my dad's chief helper.

The best part was at the end of each day.

Dad looked up at the setting sun, wiped his brow with one of the clean white handkerchiefs I ironed, and said, "Hey, Dolly, let's call it a day." We put everything away and sat on the porch steps together. He put out his arm. "Hey, look at those muscles will ya'? I got a few more today, don't you think? Go ahead, feel them, Dolly. What do you think of your old man?"

I felt the muscle in his arm, smiled my approval, and moved over a little closer to him. He put his arm around me, and we sat there watching the birds dancing on our basketball court near the bird feeders we had all over the yard. My dad liked birds, and I liked the way he smelled even when he was hot with sweat covering his face and arms. He smelled clean. He always smelled clean—any time, any place.

He went inside to get himself a large pitcher of water and me a Coke poured over ice.

"Here, Dolly, just like you like it. Warm coke, on the rocks. This will soothe your tired beast." My dad was quoting poetry again. He loved to quote poetry. He changed the words when he felt like it.

He handed me my glass, and we sat on the steps drinking the cold drinks, quoting poetry and admiring our handiwork—just Dad, the setting sun, and me. The beast was soothed. My mother and George were forgotten—if only for a moment—as we talked and laughed about anything and everything.

In the corner of the yard, much too close to the basketball court for comfort, was one of our other projects—my favorite stone. It was a huge, perfectly slanted boulder that angled up in a way that was meant for lying on in the sun. I lay on it in the spring and the fall, and it felt warm on my back. It was my favorite rock and my favorite place to be on sunny winter afternoons because of the heat of the stone. My dad and I built a beautiful fireplace that leaned right on top of one side. The stone formed one side of the fireplace while the other side was made of bricks layered one on top of the other. The rock and the other side of bricks together held two iron grilling shelves. We grilled out there from time to time. It was a great fireplace, and I was glad to see Dad making sure he left plenty of room around it when the basketball court went in.

Soon, a wooden backboard on stilts went up on the red square, complete with a basketball hoop for George. Our job was done. I was sad that the lovely task was over because I knew Dad would go back to his household chores and I'd be alone again.

"Not bad," my dad said to me as we perched on the porch steps. "Not bad at all." My dad was a quiet person, not shy, but quiet. There was a peace when I was around him. His quietness comforted me and made me feel wanted.

The next few days, I was alone again as I watched the boys from my spot upstairs near the bathroom window. They didn't let me play with them, and I didn't care. Dad and I had built that basketball court—the far better part was mine and I knew it, even then.

§§§§§§

On Saturdays, the uncles came to take George to the baseball game. Uncle Ted was married to my mother's sister, Aunt Margie. Uncle Ted had a brother, Ralph Branca, who was a professional baseball player and a pitcher for the Brooklyn Dodgers at Ebbets Field. He wore the number thirteen. I asked my mother why he wore the number thirteen because to me it was bad luck, but my mom said it was St. Anthony's Feast Day and so it was a lucky number after all. We called Uncle

Ralph "Big Ralph," because he was tall with huge shoulders.

One Sunday afternoon he came to visit. Usually rumors walk, but his one flew. All the boys knew a major league baseball player was at our house. When Uncle Ralph climbed nimbly out of his car and, before he even was able to step up the walk to the house, he was surrounded by droves of boys on bicycles who seemed to come out of nowhere. Obviously prepared for his arrival, they pulled beat-up looking autograph books out of their pockets and thrust them at him all at once. I walked down the hill and stood next to my uncle. He noticed me and singled me out with, "Hey, Dolly, you're looking as beautiful as ever," as he took another book in his large hand. He was my uncle, well, almost my uncle, and that made me as proud as he was tall.

My almost-boyfriend, John, flipped the pages of his autograph book, pointing to a place for Ralph to sign. Ralph had the pen ready in his right hand. I knew Ralph was a right-hander, the uncles talked about that all the time. His hands were bigger than I ever imagined. They were like Eugene Gant's hands in *Look Homeward, Angel.*

With his large fingers around the pen, he paused and asked John, "Are you a Yankee fan?"

Oh dear, I knew John was indeed a Yankee fan. In fact, I didn't understand at all why he came to see Uncle Ralph. John was always arguing with my brother about how awful the Dodgers were compared with the Yankees.

John looked surprised and answered, "Yes, but how did you know?"

"I saw a picture of Mickey Mantle as you were turning the pages of your autograph book for me to sign."

I was mortified. I expected Ralph to refuse to sign the autograph book, but, he signed it anyway.

The afternoon rushed by as I admired "Big Ralph," the major league pitcher, as he enjoyed lasagna, laughing and jesting with my dad. I loved baseball. I wanted to be the first girl in baseball. I joined the school team and begged to be the second baseman. I chose second base because of Jackie Robinson. He was the first colored person in baseball, and I figured that he probably got in because second base is the easiest position to play. Uncle Ralph handed my dad some tickets for the game Saturday and strode down the hill to his car, all the while, waving goodbye to me. The boys were still hanging around outside, and boy, were they jealous.

Saturday's ballgame was at Ebbets Field, and I wanted to see Jackie Robinson. I hoped one of those tickets was for me. Perhaps I could even get his autograph. George had autographs of all the Dodger players, but I just wanted Jackie Robinson. It seemed to me that I deserved one turn to go to a game.

I asked my mother if I could go just this once. "George can't even play baseball. Why can't I go instead? I'll be good, I won't say anything." I really wanted to see Jackie Robinson play. I really did.

"Please, Mom."

"No." She was folding clothes, and I was unimportant.

"Please, I'll keep score for the men. I know how."

"I said no. You stay home and spend some time with your mother." *No* was her favorite word. She spoke it

like a soldier, stiff and sure that she was to be obeyed—
no questions allowed.

Later, when my mother finished folding the laundry,
she saw me crying. She sat down next to me with this
funny look in her eye and said, "Some day you're going
to be very proud of your brother."

Those words were a death sentence. It meant that I
would never have anything to do in my life except be
proud of George like my mother was—a life with no
achievement of my own, no life. I was doomed to the
sidelines with my mother, staring at him with her idiot's
grin forever. I cringed. I hated her. I hated him. Why
did she get that funny, starry-eyed look when she talked
about him? She never had that look for me. I tried to be
proud of him, but I couldn't think of a reason. He got
terrible grades, and he hit me every time he passed me
in the house, usually saying, "That's for nothing. Do
something and see what happens." I had to get out of
there.

Sunday, I found a miniature baseball in the living
room with all the Dodger players' autographs. George's
pigeon-toed feet were alongside of me as I looked sadly
at his baseball—Ralph Campanella, Gil Hodges, Ralph
Branca, Pee Wee Reese, they were all there. One by one,
I memorized each signature. George laughed that mean
laugh of his and leaned over to glare at me.

"Well, look at you, now," he said as he cocked his
head to the side and rolled his eyes up to his friends in
Heaven. He knew it broke my heart, and I hated that he
knew. I didn't mind a broken heart; it was him knowing
about it that was so hard. I turned my face away and left
the room.

I made up my mind that I would spite them and be
the first girl in baseball. I practiced every day with

Colleen Wetherford. She was a good player and could hit grounders to me while pitching to herself. She threw the ball up in the air and hit it right at me, and she would coach me as we went along.

"Bend your knee, Dolly. Put it in front of the ball. Otherwise the ball goes through your legs. See. You missed that because you didn't use your knee." She came out on the field and demonstrated in frustration as I missed the ball again and again.

Even though Jackie Robinson never smiled at me or handed me an autographed baseball, I loved him. He was the first colored in baseball and therefore one day there would be the first girl. My mother even liked him. She surprised me one day when she said that he was a gentleman and that was more important than the color of his skin. He was quiet on the field in spite of all the jeering he sometimes endured and the names he was called by lesser men. He must have really wanted to play baseball, and if he was gentlemanly enough to impress my mother—well, he had to be a real king.

I did finally go to one game. Uncle Ted taught me how to better keep score. He let me keep his scorecard. I loved to make the big K's the best. They were fancy K's.

One of the men looked over my shoulder, "Hey, she got that double play exactly right, Ted. Six to four to three."

Knowing how to score that play was really no feat of genius. It was easy, actually. Pee Wee Reese to Jackie to Gil Hodges. They did that a lot.

"Of course, she's right," my dad piped up, "she's smarter than all of you put together."

Uncle Ted became too busy to discuss it, but he nodded assent as the Dodgers came up to bat. He pointed to my scorecard. "We're right here, Dolly. Pay attention because your man, Jackie is leading off. Get your pencil ready, he'll get a hit off this guy, watch."

My Uncle Ted turned to my dad, "Hey, Spence, take that cigar out of your mouth, will ya, for Christ's sake." The other men nodded assent.

My father answered, "I can't, Ted, it's my good luck piece."

"Yeah, right, like that Cookie Lavagetto double. You almost turned up your toes that time, Spence," cracked Charlie Malone.

"Nah, just a little pause in my breathing."

Everybody hee-hawed those deep throated laughs that men laugh when they forget there are any women present. Men have a lot of fun when women aren't around. I wasn't at the game they were talking about in 1947, but it was a big story at my house. It was the day Cookie Lavagetto hit a double in the ninth inning to win a World Series game against the Yankees and my dad swallowed his cigar. According to family folklore, he turned all blue until Charlie swatted him a huge swat on the back and the wet cigar came flying out of his throat.

"You owe me," Charlie said. "You could be dead right now if it weren't for me."

"Yeah, how much do I owe ya', Charlie? If you're trying for that one-hundred dollar bottle of champagne in my closet, you ain't gonna get it."

My dad and Charlie started boxing with each other and laughing.

"Will you guys pay attention, we're gonna win this game and you're gonna miss it with all that yakkin'. " Uncle Ted was intent on the field.

"Dolly, we're lookin' at a possible grand slam, here, get your pencil ready."

I was more than ready. I had marked the movement around the bases while pretending not to listen to my dad and his friends. If I pretended not to listen to grownups, they would forget about me. I got to hear a lot of conversations that way.

That was my one and only day at Ebbets Field, but I'll never forget Uncle Ted. He really believed I could keep that scorecard as well as anybody.

Shortly after that, during the week of my thirteenth birthday in October 1951, there was an important game against the Giants, called the Pennant Race. Everyone except my mother and I went to the Polo Grounds to watch the last pennant playoff game. The teams needed to win two out of three games for the best of three, and the Dodgers and the Giants were tied, one game each. My mother didn't let me put the radio or television on when my dad wasn't home, so I was riding around on my brother's old bicycle. It had been given to me when he received a new bicycle for his fourteenth birthday in August. I didn't like the bicycle because it was a boy's bicycle and I wanted to have a girl's style bicycle, but it got me around. I stopped in the Woolworth's Five and Ten Cent store. The store cashier was broadcasting the game on the store's amplifier. The door to the store was open, and several people paused on the sidewalk to listen. It was the ninth inning. I heard the announcer say that it was four to one, Dodgers. We were three outs from winning the pennant, but Don Newcombe, the Dodgers pitcher was tiring. A run scored, making it four to two. They announced a relief pitcher: right-hander, Ralph Branca—Uncle Ralph.

Bobby Thomson, the third baseman, was up, followed by the bottom of the batting order. It looked easy, and I was confident. The radio announcer talked about the crowd as it started to leave in order to beat the traffic after the game. The store cashier went back to her cash register. Several people started walking again.

"It's in the bag, The Bums' have finally won a pennant, " I heard one man on the sidewalk say to his friend as I took my leaning bicycle from off the brick wall. I started to throw my right leg over the seat and take off when what I heard next caused me to freeze, my leg in mid air.

The radio announcer's voice stopped me dead. "Bobby swings, a long drive to left field!...Going...Going...Gone! And the Giants win the pennant!" The bicycle and I skidded to an off balance stop as in the last of the ninth, three outs from a Dodger victory, Bobby Thomson had hit a home run. The announcer screamed, "The Giants have won the Pennant. The Giants have won the Pennant," over and over again, loud and clear on the Woolworth's radio amplifier.

I bicycled slowly home, dejected. The men walked up the walk in single file, not a word was spoken. My Uncle Ted waved silently to me, but that was all. The house was a morgue. The next day, October 4, my dad and I were reading *The New York Herald Tribune* together, as was our habit, and he handed me the sports section.

"Here, read this, Dolly," he grumbled. "We're witnessing baseball history." He walked out of the room shaking his head from side to side as if wondering how it all happened right before his eyes and he couldn't do a thing about it.

I put down the comics and read, "Now it is done," the sports writer, Red Smith wrote, "now the story ends. And there is no way to tell it. The art of fiction is dead. Reality has strangled invention. Only the utterly impossible, the inexpressibly fantastic, can ever be plausible again."

The words stung. I looked at the newspaper picture of a huge man, Uncle Ralph, walking off the field in front of Jackie Robinson, shoulders hunched, his body radiating indescribable defeat, and the all too evident huge number on his back—thirteen. In three days I would be thirteen. Saint Anthony had let us down. It was not a good omen.

Ralph Branca had pitched to Bobby Thomson, and they both made baseball history. Bobby Thomson hit Uncle Ralph's pitch and earned himself a home run with two on and a bright place in history. The Dodgers lost the pennant. No one was going to remember Big Uncle Ralph for his twenty-one game wins in 1947 or for his total of sixty-eight wins and only forty-seven losses. They were going to remember him for being the goat in "the shot heard 'round the world." I was inexpressibly sad.

The next baseball seasons after that home run were dull. No one went to the games much any more, even George and Uncle Ted. My mother said Uncle Ralph had done okay for himself anyway because he quit baseball and married the Dodgers owner's daughter. I saw that as little comfort.

There were a few diversions like baseball for me, but mostly George just made my life miserable. I longed for brothers like Huw had in *How Green Was My Valley*. Huw's older brothers loved him. They helped him because he was younger and smaller than they. I wished that George and I were orphans together and we'd help each other, like in *Oliver Twist*. I longed for a real brother.

George never helped me. Instead, he came into the bathroom when I was on the toilet and pointed at me and laughed. I asked Mom if I could lock the bathroom door sometimes. She said no. She liked to come in too. She came in a lot to empty the hamper and would stare at me with this look of disgust and usually said, "It stinks in here." I wished that they would both just stay out or knock so I could say don't come in. My girlfriends at school had mothers who knocked on the door before they came in, even just someone's bedroom.

Sometimes George came into the bathroom fast, pushing the door as far back as he could so the bathroom door hit my knee, which hurt a lot and made my knees black and blue. I tried to remember to always sit sideways on the toilet so the door didn't hit my knee.

When George came home in a bad mood, which was often, Brenda and I could tell, because he knocked on the door of the house—loudly. I knew I had to go and open it because we were required to let him in. It was my job to answer the door because I was older than Brenda. This time, he knocked again, louder and louder, on the window of the front door—bang, bang, bang. The window was going to break, and I hurried. It was dark in the house. When I opened it, I opened it as fast as I could. I was ready to move back as soon as he started to push on the door because if I didn't, he'd push the door really fast in order to catch my body between the door and the wall. It hurt terribly when the doorknob went right into my stomach if I was not able to move fast enough. I had learned to be quick. If I dodged the crush of the door, I was safe because, once free, I could run a lot faster than George. And most of the time he didn't bother to run after me. I could jump out of the way before the door slammed against me and then run, but not always. Sometimes I wasn't fast enough, and my stomach became black and blue from the doorknob. Usually, after he entered, he stopped short with his big feet pressed down fast and wide apart kind of like the giant in the story, *Jack and the Beanstalk*. He wore those white "fruit boots" that were popular with the boys in school. His large, turned-in feet were more menacing than usual in those big white shoes. He stalked around the living room looking for someone to hit. That's when Brenda usually got hit hard. My sister was younger and fat and just not fast enough to get away from him. So if he was out for her, she was dead meat. Once he smothered her with a pillow. Her body was jumping so frantically under him, and then all of sudden, it just went limp. When he took the pillow off her face, she was all blue and wasn't moving. I ran to the neighbors and told the neighbor lady, Mrs. Grant. She hurried back to the house with me, but by the time we got there, Brenda was sitting on the floor playing with her dolls and George was gone.

Mrs. Grant called my mother that night. I heard my mother say the usual, "Dolly over-dramatizes everything. Everything was fine when I got home from school."

There was a pause as I guessed she was listening to the neighbor.

"Everything is fine. I'll speak to her. There must be some mistake."

Another wait.

"Dolly is emotionally immature. She's like this at school, too. She gets upset over nothing. But thank you for letting us know."

That's how it always was. No one ever listened to me except the neighbors and the teachers, and then Mother always talked them out of believing me. I hated her, and I hated George. I just kept filling up with hot hate. I went out to the backyard to torture ants. I put them in a pan of water, and then I poured them back and forth into a second pan and watched them race for safety. I was mean. I couldn't help it.

9

"You can do anything you want to, if you want to badly enough." Katherine Hepburn

Aunt Theresa lived in Long Island with her husband, Steve. She was my mother's favorite sister and best friend. I never saw my mother yell when my aunt was around. When Aunt Theresa came to visit, my mother had a softness around her eyes that I never saw with anyone else, even my dad, and her face was full of love. Aunt Theresa had no children because she had rheumatic fever as a child and her heart was weak. This made me sad because her husband, Uncle Steve, was nice and I felt that he make a good father.

About once every month, early on Saturday morning, my mother and I went to Long Island in the car to pick up Aunt Theresa and bring her back home to visit for the day. My mother saved socks for us to darn and dresses for us to hem.

Aunt Theresa knew exactly what she was doing as she placed Dad's black sock over the wooden darning ball and wove a smooth pattern over each hole. I was terrible at darning socks. Aunt Theresa's darned socks ended up smooth while mine were filled with knots and bumps. I just couldn't get it right. At hemming, I wasn't much better. My stitches showed right through to the other side.

"That's better, Dolly," Aunt Theresa said as she looked over my shoulder one day.

I knew it was terrible but since whatever I did seemed to make her happy, I didn't say anything. I just kept trying to do better. I don't remember ever succeeding but I do remember all the love I felt while I sat next to her at the kitchen table. The house was quiet when she visited, but it didn't have the sad tense quiet that usually permeated our house. This silence was peaceful and full of love.

One Saturday I was invited to stay at Aunt Theresa's house in Long Island. I packed a small suitcase and my mother drove Aunt Theresa and me to her house on Primrose Lane. George and Brenda were not allowed to go because Uncle Steve felt that they were too unruly. I was his only niece who was well behaved and quiet enough to be able to stay with Aunt Theresa without being a strain on her heart.

Their house was the coziest house I had ever known. It was a Levitt house. All the houses on the block were like little dollhouses, exactly the same, with each front entrance opening to a small living room. Their living room was all done in blue with an open L-shaped dining room that led to a pretty yellow kitchen. On the left of the living room was a staircase that turned as it wound upstairs. They slept in a beautiful double bed with an afghan that my mother crocheted. The wooden, attic-like ceiling slanted onto the headboard of the bed where there were reading lights for two. Next to the bed, in a small alcove, was Aunt Theresa's sewing room. It was there she taught me how to sew, but the best part of my visits was how much Aunt Theresa and Uncle Steve liked me. They asked me where I wanted to sit, what I wanted to eat, and, they were polite to me, as though I was an important being.

When my mother left me with Aunt Theresa, we were standing next to the car, and Aunt Theresa said to both of us at once, "Dolly is a better tonic than all of my heart medicines put together."

We dusted furniture and set the table, waiting for Uncle Steve to come home from work. My own happiness at being with Aunt Theresa was even better than hers. In the evening, we sat out on the small cement patio. Uncle Steve sliced salami and put the pieces on a small wooden cutting board with some crackers. Aunt Theresa sat in the big chaise lounge with the afghan that my mother had crocheted for her on her lap. Uncle Steve and I sat on small white stools at her feet. We all just barely fit on the small patio, so we were warm and cozy, close together. I knew "You are My Sunshine" by heart, and we sang every verse. I sang the last verse by myself because Aunt Theresa and Uncle Steve didn't know it.

"Let Dolly sing solo again, Steve," Aunt Theresa exclaimed. "I like it when she sings." That probably wasn't true, but I didn't care.

Since Uncle Steve was an amateur photographer, we took a break from singing and he took slide pictures. "She's peaches and cream," he said as he turned the camera every which way to get a closer shot. I took off my glasses and turned my head, to make sure he took the side of my face without the crooked tooth.

When Aunt Theresa got tired, she said, "Steve, I'm tired, let's go upstairs, now," in the softest, gentlest voice.

Uncle Steve was in the furniture business, and he had a Hide-A-Bed from his store in the living room where I was to sleep.

As I helped him pull out my bed, he said, "Choose a book, Dolly. You can leave the light on for a little while. Aunt Theresa and I will be upstairs if you need us."

"Thank you, Uncle Steve." He kissed me goodnight and turned on the floor lamp.

"Not too long now," he warned. "We are just at the head of the stairs and the light will keep your aunt awake. But a few minutes is okay because we read a little, too."

I became lonesome again as Uncle Steve and Aunt Theresa went upstairs to sleep.

I looked around. There were lots of good books on the shelf. I chose *Rebecca* by Daphne du Maurier, and with the peace and quiet that gently enveloped me, I became completely engrossed in my book.

Uncle Steve called down. "It's getting late, Dolly. You need to turn off the light because Aunt Theresa is ready to sleep."

As quietly as possible, I switched off the light. I felt badly. I had taken so long with my reading that Uncle Steve had to ask me to turn off the light. I hoped he wasn't angry. I loved them both so much that I didn't want to be the cause of any discomfort. If someone as nice as Aunt Theresa was kind to me, I certainly didn't want to mess it up.

In the morning, I folded the bedclothes and pushed the Hide-A-Bed back in its place. Everything looked clean and neat after the bed was back in its socket. The lack of chaos that normally pervaded my mornings felt good. I was sitting and reading *Rebecca* when Uncle Steve came downstairs to go to work. He smelled as good as my dad. Again, I regretted that he could not have children.

"You made the bed yourself? You're a lovely guest Dolly. What are you reading? Oh, *Rebecca*, that's Aunt Theresa's favorite book. How do you like it?"

"I like it so far," I answered. I wanted to say that I was sorry that I left the light on too long, but I didn't have the nerve. It was always hard to talk to grownups. I never knew if I would make them angry or not.

"Well, good, enjoy it. I'm off to the store. Take care of your aunt and call me if you need anything."

He showed me, as was his habit, exactly where his phone number was tacked to a small bulletin board on the wall.

Aunt Theresa and I listened to her show, *Radio Grand Slam* on her Stromberg-Carlson radio, a small one on the kitchen counter. We listened carefully because Aunt Theresa sent in entries. She played from home. To play from home, she made up five song titles. These song titles were also answers to five questions, which Aunt Theresa also made up. She sent both the questions and the answers to the radio show on a postcard. If her postcard was chosen, Aunt Theresa played against the radio audience guest. If the person on the radio missed three out of five questions, we won. If the radio guest answered three out of five questions correctly, the radio guest won. If the radio guest missed all five answers we won *Grand Slam*, which was a better prize.

Each day we addressed as many postcards as we could make up. Then we'd listen to the radio.

And today it happened. "Dolly, did you hear? Listen, it's our entry."

I listened, and we won. The radio announcer said, "And to Mrs. Stephen Maguire of New Hyde Park, New

York, we'll be sending a set of Samsonite luggage. Congratulations, Mrs. Maguire."

Aunt Theresa was happy when my mother came to pick me up to go home. "Dolly brought me good luck. I've never won the whole *Grand Slam* before. I gave her the luggage. You can save it for her for college. Steve will send it to her when it arrives. When can she visit again? Steve loved having her, as usual."

Just as we were leaving I saw Aunt Theresa waving from the window.

I alerted my mother as I said, "Aunt Theresa wants us to go back."

My mother turned the car around as Aunt Theresa walked slowly down the sidewalk. She never walked fast because of her heart.

"Theresa," my mother said, "go inside. It's too chilly out here."

"Oh, just for a minute, Anne," she answered.

She handed me *Rebecca*. "Dolly," she said, "I want to lend you my book. Uncle Steve said you didn't have a chance to finish it. Bring it back the next time you come. Okay?"

She turned to my mother. "She likes to read, Anne. She takes after me."

"We should be so lucky, Theresa," my mother answered.

"You *are* lucky, Anne," Aunt Theresa said looking right at me with her sweet smile.

We said goodbye again and I waved to her as she stood in the doorway.

This was great. I could go visit more often. My mother liked anything that made Aunt Theresa happy. If she thought that I was good for my aunt, I'd have lots of chances to visit.

I didn't know that the great day was to turn into a black, black night.

§§§§§§

A few weeks after we won the luggage, a year after Uncle Ralph lost the Pennant for the Dodgers, I was awakened in the middle of the night by a telephone call. I didn't really hear the telephone, but I knew it had rung as I woke up.

"Spence, Theresa's—dead."

Then, all the night sounds went dead. I heard nothing except the loudest silence I had ever known. I puzzled and puzzled. *Why isn't Dad saying anything? Is he still asleep? Maybe it's a dream.*

To test if it was a dream, I took my small statue of the Virgin Mary from my night table. I put it under my pillow. If it was there in the morning, I would know I hadn't been dreaming. I looked out my window at the sky and the bright star that was Monk Webber.

Please, Monk, make this a dream. I prayed to St. Anthony, the Patron Saint of Miracles, to make it a dream.

The next day, my birthday, was a sad day. I was fourteen, and my luck was bad, like Uncle Ralph. St. Anthony had failed me. When I woke up, the statue was exactly where I had placed it, under my pillow. After that, I didn't pray to St. Anthony any more.

My mother limped heavily into our bedroom and woke my sister with her footsteps. She looked almost majestic as she stood next to Brenda, like a commanding saint with news from God, Himself. Her breasts heaved with her pronouncement. "I have sad news. Aunt Theresa died last night."

Brenda started crying and thrashing wildly about. She grabbed her hair and a big clump fell out. I thought, *Brenda is so crazy that she will drive us all completely mad some day. Will she ever stop bawling?*

My mother looked at me. I couldn't cry. I tried but I couldn't. I wanted to cry for my mother. She looked alone without Aunt Theresa. I could see it in her eyes. If I could cry, maybe she would see how alone I was too.

I could see she was angry with me for not crying. She could get angry with me when no one was around, but at other times, if anyone was looking, she acted like she was the best mother in the entire world. Often, before we went out together, she instructed me as to what to say to people. She'd tell me to say that I was close to my mother—that I tell her everything. But about family business, well, it was always, "Keep your big mouth shut." Family business was anything that might make her look bad, which was just about everything that ever happened between her and me.

Later that night, she talked with Grace. "Steve is upset. He punched two holes in the wall of their bedroom."

My heart broke. I couldn't believe Uncle Steve would break the beautiful and peaceful silence of Aunt Theresa's bedroom by punching holes in the walls. That would upset her. I was angry with him.

§§§§§

Everyone went to the funeral in Long Island except me. My mother didn't want me to miss school. Mr. Emerson was coming to the eighth grade to administer aptitude tests, and there was no make-up day.

"And, besides," I heard her tell Aunt Grace, "Dolly gets upset too easily. She oughtn't to go."

I stayed with a classmate, Rosalee, at her house overnight. Rosalee was beautiful, had a large, wide smile and a lot of marvelous clothes. She had a full figure and large breasts, something I did not envy. She was the first in our class to have her period and to wear a bra. I envied her clothes, but not her breasts.

My mother was her usual sweet-as-pie self as she talked with Mrs. Freidman and arranged for me to stay with Rosalee.

"She's a sensitive child, Mrs. Freidman—I think it better if she doesn't go to the funeral."

There was a long pause.

"Thank you," my mother said. "That's kind of you. You're right. These are hard times."

I didn't have any black clothes to wear to school. I wore a gray skirt and faded pink sweater. The pink sweater was so faded that it could pass for gray. I wanted to go to the funeral to say goodbye.

The guidance counselor, Mr. Emerson, came into our homeroom class. In all the commotion, I had forgotten that today Mr. Emerson was giving us aptitude tests to see what we might like to do in the future. He placed the first section of the aptitude tests on each child's desk with two sharpened pencils. We were not allowed to look at the exam paper until he started the timer. I had to try hard not to look. This was my first aptitude test, and I was curious.

"Everyone put his first and last name at the top of the first page," he said. I noticed that he used the pronoun his with everyone. I remembered that from English Grammar class, although it seemed as though only teachers used the pronoun that way.

"Do not open the exam booklet until I tell you to start."

After he was satisfied that we had all finished writing our names, he said, "Everyone put his pencil down. When I give the command to start, you may begin."

He started a timer and said, "You may pick up your pencil, *now*, and begin."

I turned the page of the exam booklet. My mind went blank as I looked at the questions. The arithmetic problems seemed overwhelming. All I could hear was the click of Mr. Emerson's timer and the scratching of the other pencils on the test papers.

I did finally manage to forget the timer and was engrossed when Mr. Emerson said, "Everyone put his pencil down, *now*, and stop."

I quickly put the pencil on the desk, although I was still trying to figure out the last question.

Each new exam booklet got a little more interesting, and I was soon ready and waiting when Mr. Emerson set the timer and said, "You may pick up your pencil, *now*, and begin."

It was kind of like a race to see if I could finish all of the exercises before he said, "Everyone put his pencil down *now*, and stop," and came to collect the exam section.

I liked the spatial relations exam the best. When I got to the last one, I was stumped. I eliminated three of the five answers, but I couldn't choose between the other two. I was wracking my brain when Mr. Emerson picked up my paper from under my pencil. I hadn't heard him give the command to put the pencils down. He smiled at me as I looked up, startled. He said kindly, "Sorry, Dolly, time's up."

He handed me the next test, which was easier—verbal skills. We had to match words with their meanings. I was fast at this one and finished before the time was up. I was obediently waiting with my pencil on the desk when Mr. Emerson gave the command to stop.

After lunch, he called each student into the principal's office to explain the results of the tests.

"How did you enjoy the tests, Dolly?" he asked.

"I liked them, but I missed the last one on the spatial relations test. I couldn't choose between the two answers." I didn't say I was sorry that I missed the cue to put my pencil down, but I wanted to.

"Well, you did well on everything. Here is your chart." He showed me a line connected by dots going up and down over a solid line on graph paper.

"See the dark line across the middle of the page? That is the average line. You are above average on everything. Look at your verbal skills. See how high that line goes. You are at the absolute top of the ratings in verbal skills."

He looked at me and asked, "What would you like to be when you grow up?"

"My mother wants me to become a teacher like her. She went to New Paltz."

"Yes, but what would *you* like to be? Your occupational skills set show that you would make a good lawyer or a journalist. Do either of those interest you?"

"I'd like to be a journalist, or a writer."

"Well, according to these tests, you can be almost anything you want, so make sure you choose something wonderful for yourself. I'll be sending these results home to your parents. Have them call us if there are any questions. Dolly, you have a good aptitude for any curriculum you choose. Good luck."

He stood up and walked around his desk and opened the door for me to leave. He was a nice man. I was happy he told me all that. *A journalist or, maybe, even a writer. Wow.* I didn't want to be a teacher. I didn't want to be like my mother. I wanted to be anything but a teacher. I wanted to be different than my mother in every way. I knew that it wasn't going to be easy. My mother was going to mold me, and if she had her way, I would be exactly what she wanted.

Dinner at Rosalee's was wonderful. We all sat around the kitchen table in casual fashion. I saw a dining room, but it did not look as though they used it much. Everything in the kitchen was peaceful and white and gleaming clean. There was a paper towel holder hanging near the sink and a box of tin foil close by. This was a sign of extra money to me because my mother never bought such luxuries as disposable towels or paper cups.

I was hungry, but I tried hard not to eat too much. Mrs. Freidman would offer me things, but I was afraid to say yes. I looked at the string beans. They looked really delicious in a white bowl, long and dark green. Mrs. Freidman saw me look and offered me more string beans. I felt like such a dope for making it so obvious that I wanted them.

I answered, "I don't like string beans." Maybe she would not see how badly I wanted them.

To my total embarrassment, I remembered that I was never supposed to say I didn't like something, but it was too late. They all looked at me. I was a dope. I managed to get through the rest of the dinner, but I was mighty embarrassed.

We got into a discussion about what our career choices might be. Rosalee's father and mother sat around with us to see what we'd like. Mr. Emerson had told Rosalee that she would make a good nurse. That was right for Rosalee because she wanted to be a nurse, and she was happy with the results. I wasn't as happy because my mother was planning for me to be a teacher, and I didn't want to be one. I didn't tell anyone what Mr. Emerson told me. I just said that my mother wanted me to be a teacher.

"But, what would *you* like to be, Dolly?" Mrs. Freidman actually seemed to think what I wanted was important.

"Anything but a teacher," I answered emphatically. I didn't know how I was going to accomplish it, but I wasn't going to be a teacher. I had made up my mind.

Mr. Freidman got up from the table. Rosalee and I helped her mother clear the dishes and then we followed Mr. Freidman. We crossed a dark room with velvet drapes and velvet over-stuffed armchairs that looked like no one ever sat in them and continued through into a marvelous room—the sun porch. This room was bright and beautiful with clean, white wicker furniture with blue cushions and blue and yellow curtains across a large window that ran the length of the room. Rosalee and I sat on a love seat, and Mr. Freidman sat in a large easy chair. Mrs. Freidman had not followed. I could hear her doing the dishes in the kitchen. I wanted to offer to help, but I was too nervous and tongue-tied. After my performance about the string beans, I thought it best if I just kept quiet, before I made things worse. I felt selfish watching television while Mrs. Freidman was in the kitchen, but soon she joined us. She didn't seem to mind that I didn't help her. I felt relieved. We watched *Kukla, Fran and Ollie* on television in the sun porch. It was Rosalee's favorite show. Her dad seemed to love watching with us. It was strange to see a house where the child was allowed to choose the television show. At first, I thought her parents acted interested because I was a guest and they wanted to show off. But, Mr. Freidman knew all about *Kukla, Fran and Ollie.* He discussed it with Rosalee as the show went along. It was clear they watched the show, which Rosalee herself chose, every evening. I was jealous, again.

I slept in a beautiful, clean, white bed next to Rosalee. The next morning, after breakfast, I made sure that I thanked Mrs. Freidman because I would not be returning. After school I was to go straight home.

Mrs. Freidman said goodbye and smiled, "Dolly, tell your mom Mr. Freidman and I enjoyed our day with you. You're a lovely girl."

"Thank you, Mrs. Freidman," I answered as politely as I could.

I walked to school with Rosalee. It was easy to get to school because Rosalee lived right down the block. I wasn't sure if Rosalee liked me. She was popular and had many other people to choose as friends. I really didn't know even if she had wanted me at her house, but I felt proud to be walking with her. She had so many friends. I wanted to be like her. I had so far prayed to St. Jude, Patron Saint of Hopeless Cases, and to St. Anthony, Patron Saint of Miracles, for almost two years to be popular, but they seemed to be ignoring me.

As we walked to school, Al, a boy who liked Rosalee, came out of his house as we passed and called out to her. He had obviously been waiting for us to pass.

"Hi Rosalee, did you watch *Kukla, Fran and Ollie* last night?" He ran down his walk to catch up with us.

Rosalee answered with a big smile, "Of course we did. It was great." She had a beautiful smile with bright white teeth. She said "we" with a sense of belonging that I had never felt. I envied her again.

Al joined us, and Rosalee asked him how his science project was going. I studied Rosalee to see why she was well liked and I was not. One of the things I noticed was that she seemed to find something to ask everyone on a subject that they liked to discuss. I vowed I would try to ask a question of someone and see what happened.

No time like the present, I said to myself as I took a deep breath, turned, and looked directly at Al across Rosalee.

"I saw you working on your project in shop class. How did you make the miniature windmill?" My voice sounded scared and soft, but Al did not seem to notice as his eyes lit up. He launched a long drawn out explanation of windmills and how they work. Rosalee and I both listened intently. Rosalee asked a couple of more questions as we turned and entered the walk to school.

As for me, I was delighted with my new skill for making friends. With a little thank you prayer to St. Jude for the idea and another little prayer to St. Anthony, I vowed to try the technique the next chance I had.

When I returned to my own home after school, I didn't tell my mother much about what the guidance counselor said because my aunts and uncles came to our house from Aunt Theresa's funeral and she was pretty busy. That night, I did tell my friend, Monk Webber, from *The Web and the Rock*, about it. I remembered how hard he had worked to be a writer, and I was willing to do the same. He must have gone to his mailbox a million times only to receive rejection letter after rejection letter. And yet, he had prevailed, and I would too. I looked out my bedroom window up at his star and quietly wished.

"Monk, I want to grow up and go to work, but not as a teacher. I want to be a writer, like you."

The Samsonite suitcases that Aunt Theresa and I won came a few weeks later. Uncle Steve sent them to me. My father took them out of the corrugated boxes. There was an overnight suitcase and a smaller square cosmetic case, complete with a marvelous mirror inside the cover. They were different shades of beige and gold in a kind of mosaic pattern. All the trim was gold and there was a small lock on each case with little gold keys hanging from the beige plastic handles. It was the first brand new luggage in the family. I liked them, and they were mine.

"Spence," my mother said, "put it up in the attic. Theresa wanted Dolly to have it for college."

I helped Dad pack it up and carry it up the ladder into the attic. And then I went to my room to read. I didn't want the luggage. Not without Aunt Theresa. I picked up *Rebecca* from my night table and hugged it to my heart.

I brought the book into the closet and shut the door tight. I put my knuckles hard into my teeth to stifle the sound. With my left arm, I held on to *Rebecca* with all my might. I was alone again. I had no one—again. Aunt Theresa was dead. I felt so alone that my stomach hurt. There was a big gaping hole where love should be. The knot in my stomach broke, and like water finally having a chance to break through a dike, a thousand tears burst forth.

When it was all over, I took my fist out of my mouth, and in the darkness of the closet with only the brilliance of truth to light my way, I raised my fist to God and added yet another sin to my list of sins: blasphemy. I would never ask forgiveness either. God deserved everything I said to Him and then some. I dared Him to come down and explain why He, with all of Heaven at his beck and call, had to take Aunt Theresa. I called Him selfish. I called Him a coward. I simply wasn't going to count on God anymore. My mother took Rosamarie, Father McAvoy, and Judy away from me, and now, God had taken Aunt Theresa from my mother and me. I could count only on myself.

I stood up to leave the closet. When I tried the door, it was locked. I knew George had locked it, but instead of praying to God to help me out, I simply fell asleep. George may have been trying to drive me crazy, but he wasn't going to succeed. I knew that my mother would be up to get me as soon as she needed help with supper.

She arrived as expected and woke me up as she opened the door and said, "Why do you insist on staying in the closet? You know George will lock you in every chance he gets. Don't look at me to protect you. I can't do anything with him. Come downstairs, I'm waiting for you to set the table."

"Mother," I said, as I was getting the silverware from the kitchen drawer. "I've decided to change my name. I don't want to be Dolly anymore. It's too babyish. I want to go by my nickname, Dee."

"What do you think this is, Miss? That you're suddenly an adult just because you declare yourself one? You're only fourteen, and you'll do as your mother says and be called as your mother calls you. Stop trying to be a grown up. You'll have time enough, Dolly."

"My name's Dee," I shouted it right at her.

She hit me. "You're stubborn and willful. I'll call you what I want."

"My name's Dee."

"That's not quite right, Miss Queen Bee, and I'm your mother and I'll call you what I please." Her arm rose to hit me again, and she did.

"Dee," I countered again.

She slapped my face, my glasses flew off, and I fell.

From my hands and knees I saw her blurred face. I returned her vicious look with one of my own. "Dee!" I screamed, this time with force.

"Dolly," she said and kicked me. I didn't care what she did.

I protected myself, my arms around my head and against the floor, screaming all the time. "Dee, Dee, Dee. It's my name."

My brother flung the door open. "Call her Dee, Ma, what's the big deal?"

"Because she's stubborn, like her father. It's the Irish in her. She's got too much of the drunken Irish Morgan family in her. And she doesn't appreciate her mother. All that I do, I do for my children and she refuses to cooperate."

I took strength from George's alliance and stood up. "Mom," I pleaded, "I just want to be me, to have a little fun." She turned her attention to her beloved George, and I quietly disappeared into the living room, where my sister was cowering in the corner.

"Why didn't you just give in, Dolly?" she asked.

"Dee," I corrected her, "my name's Dee."

"Okay, Dee," she answered.

"I didn't give in because she wants me to do everything she wants and I'm not going to. That's why." I had made up my mind. And as for God, and all that turning of the other cheek, well, I'd had enough of that too.

My mother followed me to the living room. "I talked with George, and we agree that it's okay for you to use the name Dee at school. But here at home you're my daughter, and your name is Dolly."

I knew more about my mother than she realized. I moved closer, my face right up to hers and answered, "I don't see why George should have any say-so about my name, and if you hit me any more about my name, I'm going to tell everyone—Aunt Grace, Father McAvoy, Dad, the teachers at school—everyone. And one day, I'm going to grow up, write a book, and tell the whole world."

Her eyes filled with anger and so did mine. She raised her hand to hit me again. For a moment, we were like two cats facing off. We were both monsters, and this monster was not going to give way. As I moved my face closer in defiance, she hesitated, turned her back, and walked away.

As she was leaving, she turned again. "You think you're smart, don't you? Well, let me warn you. You're not one-half as smart as you think you are." She strutted back into the kitchen.

I was still shaking, scared to death. I didn't feel smart at all. I felt scared. But hesitation had entered her anger-filled eyes. She wasn't sure how much she could get away with. The tables were turned. I had found a weakness. She didn't want anyone in the world to know about her hate for me any more than I wanted the world to know about my hate for her. Her secret was safe with me. I was much too terrified and ashamed to tell a soul. But—I had made her unsure of what I would do. I was taking care of myself—without God. And—I had gotten my way.

10

"I cannot fiddle, but I can make a great state from a little city." Themistocles

I was in my bedroom reading when my mother called from the kitchen, "Dolly, come down here." I didn't call back. We always had to go and see what she wanted. She didn't like anyone to yell.

The slices of eggplant frying smelled good as I joined her in the kitchen. "I want you to walk to the train station and meet your dad's train so he won't be late for dinner. He doesn't come straight home unless you go and get him, and I don't want him to miss the eggplant parmegianna we're having for dinner."

I didn't need to hear that command twice. I ran upstairs, stashed my homework in the closet behind the shoes for later, and ran out the door before she could change her mind.

"Dolly, come back here," she called. My heart sank as I went back, sure I couldn't go after all. She shook a finger at me. "Remember, Dolly, no bars. Don't let your father start drinking with those Irish firemen. He'll be there all night."

"Okay."

"Okay, Mother," she reminded me.

"Okay, Mother."

I ran the three miles to the station. I flew by the storekeepers as they waved and called out, "Hi Dolly, you meetin' your old man again? He's a lucky guy."

I waved to everyone but kept on. If I was late, Dad might not wait since I was never sure when I could meet him. Sometimes, my mother wouldn't let me, other times she said it was okay.

Mr. Robbin pulled up alongside of me in his taxi. "Hi Dolly, need a ride?"

"No, thank you, Mr. Robbin. I'm almost there." I was afraid he might charge my dad for the ride. The charge account with Blue Sky Taxi was only to be used in an emergency.

I kept on with my run to the station.

The train was just pulling in to the platform as I, breathless, mounted the stairs from the sidewalk two at a time, relieved as I saw my dad swing off the train steps. He was dressed in his blue seersucker suit and straw hat with the Wall Street Journal, as usual, under his arm.

He saw me, smiled, and waved. "Hi, Dolly. You're right on time."

He handed me a small package from his pocket. "Don't tell your mother," he cautioned.

I smiled and assured him I wouldn't as I opened the small box of Fanny Farmer's butter crunch, my favorite candy. I started to eat immediately as my dad looked down at me. We were conspirators; I wouldn't tell.

My head began to hurt. My braids were too tight again. They were always hurting—they were always too tight. I started to complain to Dad, but then thought better of it because I knew he wouldn't do anything about it anyway. My dad didn't like to upset my mother. We always kept peace around George, Brenda, and her.

He took my hand as we crossed the street. We were heading right for the bar. This didn't upset me even though my mother had warned me against it. I had already learned that Dad would not stay long if I were with him. That's why she sent me. I think she knew he would stop at the bar regardless, but with me along, it would only be for a drink or two. If I weren't there, he would come in as late as three in the morning, and she hated that.

The squeaky door to Whitey's Bar and Grille opened to welcome us, letting in the warm spring air and letting out lots of laughter.

"Hey, Charlie," my dad greeted his best friend.

"Hey, Spence. So that pretty daughter of yours is meeting you again, huh. You're a lucky jerk. How did an ugly mug like you get such a looker of a daughter? Come on in, I'll buy you a drink."

"Okay Charlie, but only for a minute. I gotta go. The wife's waiting. Besides Dolly here is much too pretty and much too smart to waste any time talking to you. What makes you think we'd hang around with a dumb klutz like you anyway?"

"Yeah, she's smart, Spence. She was reciting the multiplication tables one day while she was waiting for the train. I'm too dumb to even know if she's right. Is she right Spence? Does she know them tables?"

"Of course she's right Charlie, I ain't even listenin' and I know she's right."

"She's gonna be a looker, Spence. How did you get so lucky? I want to know."

"The luck of the Irish, Charlie. You've heard about us."

"I'm gonna marry her, Spence, not yet, when she's older."

"Charlie, I'm tellin' you, don't get your hopes up. She's much too smart for the likes of you. And anyway, what would your wife say about it?"

My eyes moved back and forth between the two men. Charlie Malone was my favorite friend in the whole world. I saw to it that he got the biggest slice of pizza when the firemen played poker at the house.

"Spence, don't worry about my wife. She'll be too old and gray by then, and I won't want her."

My father's eyes twinkled a bit now as he launched into the teasing humor of which he and his friends never seem to tire.

"Right Charlie, what are you selling anyway, the Brooklyn Bridge? Are you forgetting that you'll be old and gray too. In fact you're lookin' a mite old right now."

"Who me, Spence? You and me? We're gonna be young and handsome like we are now, forever. Right Dolly?"

Charlie reached down and swung me up, almost over his head. I felt the strength of his arms even while I worried about the cigarette package that was about to fall out of the turned sleeve of his T-shirt. I felt safe with him and all of my father's friends. I sure would like to marry Charlie, I thought. But I knew that he was only joking. People only marry once. I learned that in church.

Charlie put me gently down on the bar. "Bring me a Coke on the rocks, will ya Whitey. Put it on my tab."

"Is that Spence's daughter with you, Charlie? Yes, it is. I recognize her. The coke is on the house. Hi Dolly." He winked at me from behind the bar.

Whitey, a winking man, came over, winked at me again, and poured the coke. I sensed the taste of the warm coke being poured over the ice. I was getting really thirsty, but I knew not to be rude. I waited until it was handed to me. He smiled directly at me and moved the coke closer to me. "Go ahead, Dolly, it's yours. How's that Dad of yours? Does he appreciate that you come to pick him up every night? I bet you walked all the way again. He's a lucky man, your Dad."

"Hi Whitey. Who said you could talk to my daughter?" Dad brought his own drink from the other end of the bar and settled down on the other side of me to talk with Charlie and Whitey. They talked about things I didn't understand, and I didn't really listen. I just liked the sound of their relaxed voices, and once in a while Charlie looked over and smiled at me as though he and I were the only two people in the world.

My dad got up to go as I, too, suddenly remembered my mother's orders.

"See you later Charlie. We got more important things to do than sit here chewing the fat with the likes of you."

I was pretty sure his friends knew that he wanted to stay. He was obvious about his preferences, and his preferred company was definitely not my mother. I waved goodbye to my friends who knew that Dad would not want me to stay too long in a bar with them. My mother was right. He was cornered. She knew he wouldn't ever come directly home, but when I was with him, he came home a lot faster than if he were alone with his friends. This arrangement was good for all three of us.

"See you tomorrow, Dolly. If you come early, I'll buy you a Coke."

"What! Dolly never buys Coke in here," argued Whitey. "Her drinks are always on the house. Come whenever you want to Sweetheart. You don't need money when you're a friend of mine. And I'd rather see you than these lugs any day."

I was quiet the rest of the way home, knowing Dad didn't like me to interrupt his thoughts. My dad was such an important part of this town, sure of his place, his part in it as solid as stone, with the absolute knowledge that he belonged. It was great to be his daughter. Automatic acceptance anywhere I went, and that was enough for me. And when he was around, my mother's punishments were significantly less. Friday night was the worst because he stayed out all night whenever he got the chance. Sunday nights were the best because he was always home, watching TV and making us sandwiches for school the next day. His sandwiches were great with tons of mayonnaise and salt and pepper.

As we walked, hand in hand, Dad greeted the shop owners one-by-one, most of them sitting outside on the sidewalk.

Today was certainly a good day.

11

"Few men have virtue to withstand the highest bidder."
George Washington

I heard lots of stories about Uncle Vincent from my Aunt Rosa. Vincent was the youngest brother, and the sisters were proud of him. He was ill as a child, born with a convulsive disorder. Sometimes, it helped him to sit in hot tubs of water, and each of the sisters had a part in taking care of him when he had a seizure. When an attack was coming on, his eyes crossed, and everyone rushed to get the hot water set up. They dipped him up and down in it until he quieted.

After an attack, he felt so ashamed, that he would cry for hours and swear that he would never do it again. Aunt Rosa told me how he persevered and studied in spite of his poor eyesight to become a dentist. He accomplished the first profession in the family. They talked about his achievements endlessly. He kept an office in their home for a while, and then he worked so hard and became so successful that he rented his own office down the street in an elevator building. Aunt Rosa said that my uncle was generous because he did all the children's teeth for half-price.

Every six months I went to Mount Vernon, where Uncle Vincent had his dentist's office. I took the train by myself, which to me was a really big deal. I enjoyed the trips by myself, but I hated my uncle. He was the worst man in the world, and he had terrible bad breath. Because he gave my parents my dental work for half-price there was no going to another dentist. There was no doubt in my mind they were getting gypped, but I didn't tell them. It wouldn't do any good. We were not even allowed Novocain because that was extra. Without money, dentistry was hard to get at all, much less with a dentist other than my uncle.

The train rumbled through the usual stops as the fat-bellied conductor hollered each station in turn: Larchmont, New Rochelle, Pelham and, finally, Mount Vernon. I got off the train as his pudgy face smirked. He saw my fear. I was afraid of the train steps. They were steep with big spaces in between, and I was afraid that I'd slip in between them and get my foot caught. If no one noticed, I might be stuck there when the train started up again and lose a foot.

There were several close calls as my feet got caught and I tripped. There were other times when I was too afraid to get off, and I'd end up going to 125th Street. My mother admonished me before each trip. "Watch out for your daydreaming because Dad will get mad if he has to pay extra when you carelessly miss a stop." My dad seldom got mad at me, but my mother was always sure that he would. In some ways, she seemed afraid of him. She acted as though he was always going to punish me, but he never did. "You better pray that your father doesn't hear about this," was one of her favorite threats.

Finally, I made it down the steps okay and proudly pranced down the hill from the train station, happy to be on my own, even for this. My feet strained to keep me from walking too fast with the steep slope of the hill. I crossed the street. There was a lot of traffic and no cross walk, but I dodged a few cars and made it across okay.

Inside the dark hallway of my uncle's building, the tile floor looked cold as the dusty door creaked open. I passed that same old fat man who was always in the hall of the building. I wondered if he had a job. *He must never go to it*, I thought. *He always looks at me so funny.* Sometimes he got in the elevator with me, and his paunch took up all the room and forced me to back up into the corner to avoid touching that big belly.

Entering the ever-so-small elevator, I pushed the button for the second floor. Nothing happened. I looked around and saw that the door had not properly closed because the iron inside gate of the elevator was partially open. The elevator didn't move. The fat man reached in and pulled the iron gate shut for me, chuckling and looking at me as if he saw a total moron, which was about how I felt. The elevator rose and stopped. My stomach stayed up longer than the elevator, which missed the second floor by a couple of inches. That happened all the time. It was almost impossible to get the floor even with the elevator floor, and the door wouldn't open if I didn't get it exactly right. I kept pushing buttons. Once too high, then too low, my stomach constantly got left behind as the elevator moved up and down. Finally, the gate opened, and I got out, a little dizzy from the ride.

My footsteps echoed in the dark, silent hall as I approached the door with the frosted glass panel.

Vincent M. Esposito, D.D.S.
Ring Bell Walk In

I could smell his office even outside, and I hated the smell. I rang the bell and waited. I didn't want to walk in by myself, and I hoped that someone would come to the door. No luck.

Having no other apparent option, I opened the door and entered the waiting room. There was no one in sight. There was no music, just the stillness of a dreary office and some dusty magazines. My uncle never seemed to have any patients. He came out slowly and looked at me. He was never glad to see me. Mom said it was because he was busy and had his mind on a lot.

He wore his short-sleeved shirt and was drying his hands on a small white towel. The hair on his arms frightened me. I hated the hair on his arms. When he leaned on me, I could feel the skin and the hair and the clammy sweat. I liked it better when he wore long sleeves. Even though it still hurt a lot when he leaned on me, the shirtsleeve nylon fabric was not as sticky as his skin.

"I'll be with you in just a minute," he spoke like the fancy doctor he thought he was as he dried his hands over and over again with a white towel. I saw more hair on his arms and hands.

I sat in the waiting room for a few minutes until he returned. The magazines were lined up on top of the radiator, but I never bothered to read them because they didn't look interesting. I worried more that they were a fire hazard on the radiator. My father would never stand for anything on the top of radiators. He said plenty of fires started like that.

"Come in," he said, like I was a total stranger.

I followed him, and he motioned me to the chair, which always looked like an electric chair.

"Sit down."

I climbed up on the chair, and he put out a paper cup in the little saucer. I held on to the arms of the chair and prepared for the worst.

I knew that there was an end to it, and I kept reminding myself of that. I knew when he finally said, "Rinse out," it meant he was done. I would really like to rinse out more than once, but he never said to, so I just waited with my mouth full of gunk. I fixed my eyes on the light and waited for "Rinse out." The room was as hot as the lamp. The heat was so dry that it parched my throat and every time the drill began, I felt sprays of cold water wetting my face and lips. The noise of the drill in my head was like a thousand street drills, banging and hissing.

His elbows dug into my developing breasts, and his nicotine breath smothered me as he leaned on them to drill the cavity. It seemed like forever. I was afraid to move for fear of his anger. I was glad I had small breasts because he didn't always land on them. My mother had a friend, Mrs. LaRenteria, who went to Uncle Vincent for dentistry, and she had huge breasts. I wondered what happened to her breasts when he leaned on her.

My hand, trapped between the chair and his leg, hurt. I kept my eyes on the light, an ugly light with a cloudy glass pane over it. I concentrated on that light until I lost track of everything in the room. The buzzing of the drill ended, and the worst was over.

Big tubes of cotton went in and out of my mouth. It seemed that he was concentrating so much that he must not have noticed that he was crushing my hand again. The clamp for holding the filling silver in place was digging into my gum. The stuff in my mouth was choking me.

His hands flew apart in a similar fashion to my mother when she was angry, wide away from his body, an all-encompassing gesture of frustration. They flew out again all over the place as he threw the clamp to the ground and yelled, "God dammit!"

He grabbed everything out of my mouth. The cotton went flying, and then the clamp wrenched itself away from my gums, which began to bleed. Finally, with one swoop, he knocked everything including the cup of water to the floor.

"God dammit. Your mouth is too small, it's impossible to work on you."

He threw his instruments to the floor, stormed into the next room just like my mother. I waited. He was calling her.

"It's impossible to work on her; her mouth is just like her grandmother's."

There was a pause while my mother said something.

"This will take longer than I planned. I'll call you when she leaves."

He came back, picked up the instruments from the floor and began again. I fixed my eyes on the light.

Please God make my mouth bigger so he can finish without getting mad again. I opened my mouth as best I could. God answered. Time ceased. God was here, and children are safe with God. I started to think about the train ride home, the billboards blurring by, the trees, the apartment houses, and the children playing in the street as the train goes rumbling by them with me in it, on my way home.

The hurt from the cuts in the corners of my mouth brought me back to his office as I heard the words I needed, "Rinse out." Finally, the words which meant that it was almost over had come. My mouth was throbbing, but it was over. I couldn't wait to get on that train. I knew the cuts at the corner of my mouth would heal in a few days.

He said, "You can go now."

I rinsed, got up, said thank you, and left. I think he grunted a goodbye, but I really didn't hear—I was just glad to be out of there.

I hoped there were no more visits, but I was sure there would be because the last appointment is the cleaning. And he hadn't done that yet. Later, he'd call my mother and tell her how many cavities I had.

I waited for the dreary elevator, managed to get the floor even with the door, passed the grimacing fat man, and walked quickly up the hill to the train station. I checked for my ticket, which, thankfully, was still in my pocket.

I went straight to my room when I came home because I didn't want my mother to ask me how it went. I was reading *How Green Was My Valley* when she stomped into the room and sat on my bed. I hated when she sat on the bed. She was always too close, she smelled awful, and the bed tilted way down so my body was forced to lean into hers. I could feel her fat, dirty flesh. She could take her right arm and swing it back at me at any time.

She had that I-am-the-perfect-mother look on her face as I tried again to avoid touching her body.

"Mom, I think that Uncle Vincent had one of his attacks today. He started throwing stuff all around the room, and he scratched my gum when he pulled the clamp off my teeth and threw it on the floor. It hurts. My gum is still bleeding at the bottom."

She thought a long thought, took a deep breath and said, "Your uncle is a good man and generous. Sometimes he just has a hot temper."

"I can't go back there any more. I just can't." I was desperate.

"Oh, yes you will, young lady; as long as you live under my roof, you'll go to your uncle for dentistry and appreciate his kindness. Besides the fact that he is your uncle, he charges us half-price, which is a wonderful gift. Don't look a gift horse in the mouth."

She got up to leave. She had her that's-that look on her face.

"Well, I'm not going and that's that." I yelled at her as she started to leave the room.

"Yes, you will, as long as you live under my roof and I feed and clothe you."

"No, I won't."

She turned around, gave me one of her haughty looks, and answered, "Stop talking back to your mother, Miss. Some day you'll grow up and appreciate all that I have done for you."

That word, appreciate, was everywhere. It was too much. How was I supposed to appreciate something that I didn't want in the first place? He terrorized me and the sores in my mouth hurt from him. I just couldn't keep quiet any longer. I got off the bed and stood tall. "No, I won't. Some day I'm going to grow up and get out of here. That's what I'm going to do." My mouth burned with pain.

I started to cry. I looked down at my feet. I was in for it.

"Well, Miss, that will be a very long time from now. In the meantime, get your nose out of those books and come downstairs and set the table for dinner. Your father will be home any minute. As for your silly dreams about writing books about your mother, I wouldn't tell your father any of that nonsense if I were you." She stuck her nose up in the air and stalked out of the room. She was short, and when she stuck her nose up in the air like that it seemed as though she was trying to be as tall as possible and touch the sky with her nose.

"Wait," I muttered to myself, "just wait."

"What did you say, Miss?" She turned back as if to hit me.

"Nothing."

"It better be nothing."

I remained, kicking at the bed for a while. I hated her.

Why couldn't they understand? Why couldn't anyone see? She's getting gypped by that dentist; she doesn't know it. Alone in my room, I turned back to my friend, Huw, in *How Green Was My Valley*. He grew up and became a writer. *It's not just a foolish dream to grow up and be somebody*, I told myself. That was a great book. I cried again.

I looked at the inviting stack of books I had just signed out of the library, and I chose a grayish blue fat one, *The Count of Monte Cristo*, by Alexander Dumas, which Miss Roberts had told me to read. She said that I would like it.

My tears cleared, and I was engrossed when I heard my father open the front door. Instead of going downstairs to greet him, I waited. I needed his habit of looking for me every day. He called only for me, every evening, and it made me feel loved.

"Spence, is that you?" My mother asked.

"Yes, where's Dolly?" Those were always his first words.

"Upstairs, Spence, daydreaming—on the moon, she lives on the moon."

I imagined my dad smiling as he turned her remark into a joke. "Hey, Moonbeams, come on down. I'm home".

That's what I was waiting to hear, and I went to the head of the stairs.

"Hey, what're you reading, that English guy again? Lives on that little island, doesn't he?"

I laughed. "No, I finished that a long time ago. I've already read two books since then."

"Well, what's next on the agenda?"

"I finished *How Green Was My Valley,* and I just started *The Count of Monte Cristo.*"

"Oh, that's a good one. He was the count who waited and waited and got all that revenge."

"I don't know yet. I'm not finished. Don't tell me the end." I walked downstairs to join him.

He put his hat on the top of the closet, took off his jacket, entered the living room, and rolled up his sleeves. He turned on the television set and sat down on the couch. He put his arm over the back of the couch. That was my cue. I sat next to him, and his arm came around my shoulder as we settled in for the news.

I told him about Uncle Vincent.

"That whole family is crazy. They're all nuts," he responded.

"Do I have to go back, Dad?"

"Your mother will insist on getting her way about this." As much as I loved my dad, and I did, I knew that he could be bought. Half-price dentistry was the price of my soul.

My mother called us for dinner, and we didn't talk during dinner. It was clear that the subject was closed.

No point in getting Dad mad at me, too, I said to myself as my aching mouth accepted the sentence of life imprisonment with Uncle Vincent. Still, in the back of my head was that little voice, tiny, but sure—*you'll be eighteen sooner than they think, and then, you'll do whatever you want.*

After dinner I cleaned up the kitchen and went back to the living room. I took my place next to Dad on the couch, under his outstretched arm, which folded over me.

At 7:30 exactly, my mother told me to go to bed. I reluctantly left the couch, and Dad went to his armchair in front of the TV. *He never sits on the couch with her. That's for him and me.*

From my bedroom, I heard them talking, and it sounded like I'd be going back to the dentist. I heard them say that I had thirteen cavities.

Uncle Vincent came to the house the following Sunday for his usual Sunday visit. He pulled a trinket out of his pocket. It was a pink plastic star with a little silver monogram of "D," my initial. He handed it to me.

"I made it for you. The letter D is made from the silver that goes in the fillings, and the pink star is from plastic when we make dentures."

"Thank you." I hated it. I could taste that horrible silver stuff, and my mouth hurt again with the memory of it. The pink stuff made me even more ill. I had seen those dentures, more than once, covered with saliva as my grandmother removed hers at night. I thought I was going to be sick right there.

As if that wasn't enough, he knelt down next to me, singing to me, his foul breath blowing right at me. It was annihilating me, but I stood still, forced to show respect or get a beating. He continued singing right in my face and tapping the air with his hand, to teach me the notes.

> Toyland, Toyland,
> Beautiful girl and boy land,
> Once you pass its borders, you
> Can never return again.

This went on for a while as I tried not to breathe in the bad air from his mouth. His voice went up high to make the last note. Just like he thought he was a great dentist, he also thought he could sing.

"That was Rodgers and Hart. How do you like it?"

"It's okay."

"Do you want to help me wash the car?"

"Okay." Anything was better than his singing concerts.

His Cadillac was big and black with tons of chrome and white walls on the tires. I liked to make it shine, but I didn't like to ride in it. I got carsick because the cigar smoke really stunk. I did like washing the car, though, and the polishing was the best. Uncle Vincent applied the Simonize in little circles, and I polished it off. He did the roof because I couldn't reach. I whitened the tire walls because he was too fat to bend down.

He liked what I did, I could tell, and after I finished he gave me the usual shiny quarter. Uncle Vincent would get the quarters from Uncle Carlos, a banker. He looked at the car; we were both smug and satisfied—we had done it exactly right.

That night, I went back to the reading and the waiting. *The Count of Monte Cristo* and I have some waiting to do, and preparing. Four and a half years to go—a long, long, time, but, if Count Edmond Dantes could wait fourteen years, than I would wait too.

12

"I only ask to be free. The butterflies are free." Charles Dickens, *Bleak House*

It had been a long time, almost a year, and yet death remained fresh in my mind. My mother gave me some of Aunt Theresa's clothes. Usually I hated any hand-me-down, but I liked her clothes, even if they were second-hand. I tried on a gray felt skirt with a pink short-sleeved angora sweater, but finally chose a red wool plaid skirt with a red plaid matching vest. I ironed a white long-sleeved blouse for underneath. The outfit tapered at the waist, which made me look grown up.

I was engrossed in admiring myself in my long mirror when my mother shuffled up the stairs, her footsteps heavy under the burden of the large basket of laundry for me to fold. She handed me the laundry basket and sat down on the bed, breathless from her climb. I started to fold the sweet-smelling sheets and towels. My mother's laundry always smelled fresh because she hung everything outside on the clothesline, even in winter. This old habit, leftover from her childhood days, of hanging laundry late at night in any weather came from her family situation. They used to take in laundry. It was lowly employment, and they hung it out to dry at night, so the neighbors wouldn't know of their difficult circumstances.

I stood near the mirror as I folded, since I couldn't resist continuing to peek at my outfit in the mirror. That sweet scent carried me back to one day during the previous winter when the clothes froze right on the line and looked stiff and funny, like winter scarecrows, and yet they smelled even better frozen. I helped take their cold, stiff bodies down from the line, pushing on them to make them fold into the laundry basket.

I glanced again in the mirror at the outfit I wore and wondered if my aunt might be a bit cold in her dark place in the ground in Long Island. I hoped not. She didn't deserve to be cold.

There hadn't been much fuss made over my birthday the year before because of Aunt Theresa's death on the exact same date, October 7, but this birthday promised to be better. Grandma Morgan was coming to town. The ballroom dance class was having a formal ball at the end of the month. All the girls were to wear long dresses, and the boys were to wear dark blue or black suits. I didn't see my father's mother much, but she had promised to make me a long dress for my birthday to wear to the ball, which was only three weeks away.

My mother cut in front of me and looked in the mirror. I didn't protest. Yes, it was my bedroom, but my mother saw all of my things as primarily hers first. I moved behind her. I didn't dare ask about the dress my grandmother promised or even seem to want it. When I asked for things, I didn't get anything.

My mother adjusted her girdle and glanced again in the mirror. "You know, Dolly, I was not as pretty as you when I was young. Your father married me anyway. I like to think it was because he saw the beauty inside of me. It's more important to be beautiful on the inside than on the outside." She patted her hair and grimaced as she examined the circles under her eyes.

"But, Mom, I think the picture of you with Aunt Theresa is pretty," I protested. I pointed to a picture of my mother and my aunt that was kept in my bedroom on the night table. In it, they were visiting Washington, D.C. at cherry blossom time, sitting under the trees. My aunt was smiling in an impish way, and my mother more serious, sat peacefully next to her. They wore black skirts and blouses with black and white saddle shoes. They both looked happy, young, and full of love for each other. My mother turned from the mirror and glanced at the photo. She looked a lot better then than she did now. She was younger—and happier. She never once looked like that with me.

She made an effort to look away from the photo, walked away from the mirror and sat on the bed. "Thank you for the compliment, but I know I'm not pretty. You are, though. The Irish and the Italians have beautiful children. Both you and George are good looking." Sitting on the bed with her hands primly folded in her lap was the signal for me to sit down because she was going to launch into some type of lecture. She crossed her legs at the ankle and continued. "I'm not pretty, but I was a good dancer. You inherited your dancing ability from me."

I sat down on another bed across from her. I tried to avoid sitting next to my mother as much as possible. At the same time, I had to be careful because she could get angry if she thought I was avoiding or rejecting her. It was her idea that a child must always love a mother and do whatever a mother tells her, no matter what it is.

"Is that why you don't like to have your picture taken? Because you don't think you're pretty?" I moved a bit, feeling that I would just as soon avoid any conversation that might end in anger.

She tilted her head to one side in thought. This was the we're-having-a-conversation-now pose. I was expected to listen and agree with her. "I just don't like to pose for pictures. I know that I'm not photogenic. Uncle Steve has mentioned it more than once. Some of his slides of you are lovely." She nodded her head up and down agreeing with herself.

I felt awkward, as usual, talking with my mother, but I obliged her with conversation as best I could.

"Am I a good dancer?" I asked her.

I didn't think that I was especially good, although I loved to dance. I danced in the living room when no one was home. I especially liked the waltz and the polka. We had an old phonograph with some records that my Aunt Rosa had given us. No one played it except me. I was allowed to play the records if I promised to be careful, which I was. We had mostly Strauss waltzes. I really liked Strauss, especially "The Blue Danube." It was such an easy waltz—the tempo all but told me when to step, when to slide, and when to step—one, two, three, one, two, three—it was the perfect waltz music, and it made me admire Johann Strauss because he made such beautiful music right out of his head.

I couldn't figure out why my mother was being this nice. I thought it might be because we would be in public together and she was trying to make us look good. She did that a lot. "Yes, you're good. Mr. Appleton said you're an excellent dancer, that you have a good sense of rhythm and are graceful."

I was surprised. Although both George and I went to Mr. Appleton's ballroom dance classes, I never felt like anything but a total klutz. Mr. Appleton was tall and thin. He looked like Fred Astaire. His wife was thin, too, with beautiful, blonde hair. She looked like Ginger Rogers. I wondered if maybe Mr. Appleton said good things to everyone's parents because we paid for the lessons. But my mother didn't mention George. If Mr. Appleton had said George was a good dancer, my mother surely would have bragged. The fact that George was not mentioned made me appreciate the possible truth in Mr. Appleton's comments.

My mother continued, "I was a good dancer. I won a Charleston contest more than once."

"Really, when? Would you teach me?" I couldn't help myself. I stood up to try.

My mother didn't move. "It was before I met your father. I used to go to a lot of parties before I met your dad. I was popular."

"I'm not popular." I sat down again. It didn't look like there'd be any dancing. I wanted to try the Charleston.

My mother stood up and went back over to look again in the mirror. She puffed her hair up a bit and looked rather proud of herself. "Oh, but you will be. College is where you'll blossom out. That's what happened to me. No one even noticed me in high school, but in college I was a cheerleader, a dancer, and I was the first Italian girl allowed in the girls' dorm." She patted her hair again, adjusted her girdle, and glanced in the mirror. It was clear she was remembering better days. "In fact, I was the first Italian allowed to teach in the elementary school here in town. Mr. Collins, who was just a principal then, made sure I got the job. He liked me and saw that I would become an excellent teacher. He's a superintendent, now. He chose many good teachers for your school."

As she started out the bedroom door, she thought a minute and turned towards me. She got a proud look on her face and said, "Come down to the living room, and we'll try the Charleston while we wait for your grandmother and your father. They should be here soon with your birthday cake."

There was no mention of the dress. I followed her as she descended the steps. Her limp was more noticeable when she went up the stairs. The sound of it coming up the stairs at night was scary. The limp wasn't as obvious when she went down the steps and not as scary in the daytime. All the same, I made sure I walked down behind her, as slowly as she did, so as not to call attention to her problem.

No one was around as we entered the living room. My mother sat me on the couch with herself standing in front of me.

"Okay, here's how it goes."

She put one foot in front of the other, but she moved her feet back and forth, each in a different direction. She was singing the tune as she moved her feet, slowly at first to show me. "Charleston, Charleston, da da da da Charles...ton, Charleston, Charleston raagggg..." The singing and her movement went faster. When she forgot the words, she just hummed. As she picked up speed, she kicked her leg way up. I could see her garters and her girdle and her fuzz peeking out, but she didn't seem to notice. She was really enjoying herself. She knelt down. Her hands went back and forth over her knees. Her hands were moving in a way that made her legs seem to be switching places at the knee. All the while she was singing, matching the beat of the music to the movement of her feet. She moved so gracefully that I forgot all about her limp. It seemed to disappear.

She sat down on the couch, winded. "Do you want to try it? Stand up and I'll show you."

I stood up in front of her, and, anxious to please, started to kick as I had seen her do.

"No, not like that. It's not just a kick. It's the way I move my feet. Watch."

She turned her feet in and out but didn't kick at all, and I saw that the kicking had nothing to do with the movement.

"Now, try it like that, but don't kick."

I tried it myself without the kicking. It took a few minutes, but my feet were soon turning in and out as I moved them up and down and my mother sang.

"That's it, you've got it. Now do it faster." She sat down on the couch and watched as I tried it. I was moving my feet on the floor as she had showed me, when suddenly my feet took off and I realized that I was doing the kick as a follow through of the dance step. I understood. I danced a little more while she sang.

She stopped singing and sat down, flushed. I sat down next to her. "We didn't learn that dance in class."

"That's too bad. A lot of dancing teachers just can't do it. I could teach if I wanted to. I'm that good."

I was sure she was right. I looked at her. She looked back at me. It was a long look, full of pain, and suddenly, she had her arms around me. She was hugging me very hard and awkwardly; her breasts were big and in the way. Awkwardly again, she turned away as though she didn't want me to see her face. I had already seen it. It was too late. Her face showed such terrible pain, and I didn't know why. I loved her at that moment, and I was infinitely sad. I didn't understand, and yet I did.

There were parts of my mother that she couldn't help, parts of her that were a lonely mystery, both for me and for her. Her determination to mold me was foremost in her mind. It consumed her. She would control me in any way that would work—manipulation, threats, rewards, beatings, it all had one goal: to form me into what she believed best. Leaving her was going to be an impossible task, and yet, I knew I had to. She was a hen, and I was her best-laid egg, trapped under her wing. She wanted me to conform to her plan for me, to take after her, to be a teacher, to live at home, to marry, to buy the house next door, and take care of her in her old age—they were all her dreams. Maybe, they weren't even bad ideas—they just weren't mine. I wanted to be me, to make great decisions, to have my own opinions, to grow up, to have thousands and thousands of friends, to speak every language, to travel, to dream, and most of all, to live.

After that moment, time moved like a block of cement as we waited for Grandma Morgan to come. My mother hadn't said a word about the dress. If Aunt Theresa were here she would have made me one; I knew that. Perhaps I was to be ignored again. I was preparing myself for another disappointment when I saw my dad's car pull up outside. In the passenger seat was Grandma Morgan. Dad helped Grandma out of the car. She was carrying a cake from the bakery. No dress.

I still hoped that by some miracle my father would take a package out of the trunk of the car. He didn't. He helped my grandmother up the walk and up the two porch steps to our door. The only package they were carrying was the cake box from the bakery. At least there was a cake. Last year, I couldn't have anything because of Aunt Theresa's death. I accepted the sadness my birthday caused. I was getting used to it.

My mother took her coat and said, "Hello, Mom how was the ride?"

My mother didn't kiss Grandma. When she said "mom," it was awkward. She never kissed anyone except Aunt Theresa, and Aunt Theresa was dead. The term "mom" for my dad's mother was more polite than meaningful.

Grandma Morgan looked at me. "My, you're getting big."

"Hello, Grandma." I stood up and got ready to kiss her. She was a fat, stern looking woman, standing there expecting a kiss. One thing about all my relatives; they expected kisses no matter what was going on. It didn't matter whether the relative was fat, ugly, dirty, or smelly. Kisses were expected, and required.

My grandmother walked casually around the house, inspecting everything. She spoke to my father, "You did a good job building the house, Spence. You should let your Uncle John move in here with you and your family. He's alone and needs a place."

My dad didn't say anything. He had heard this request before, but my mother said no. Uncle John was another one of my grandmother's brothers who lost all his money in the stock market crash. Uncle John drank, and there was no room for him in our house. My brother had one bedroom, my sister and I had the other, and my mother and father had the third. There was no place to put him. George's bedroom was too small for two. I would have liked to have him. He was funny and played the concertina while I sang Irish folk songs with him. I thought we could find some room.

There was still no package except for the cake. My heart sank. I was not to have the dress. My grandmother was still waiting for her hello kiss. My dad looked at me. He knew. My secret was out. Everyone must have known how much I wanted a dress, and the humiliation was going to be too hard to bear when I didn't have it. I couldn't stand it. I just didn't want to be disappointed in front of all these people.

Evidently, my father couldn't stand the cruel joke either. He went over behind the couch and, with a grand gesture, pulled out a huge box wrapped in pink paper. "Here it is, Beautiful," he said. "I've had it since last week. This is just your grandmother's idea of a joke." He put his arm around my waist and gave me a little hug as he handed the package to my grandmother. She sat down in the Windsor chair and reached out to hand the package to me. She always used the Windsor chair. She liked the straight back. She didn't sit back in it. She sat on it as though perched, her large belly protruding almost touching me.

"Happy Birthday, Dolly."

Grandma got her kiss as I took the huge box from her. She laughed. She got a certain chuckle out of torturing me, I guess.

"Mom, you shouldn't play jokes on her," my mother said. "She's a serious child." My mother didn't much like anything Grandma Morgan did. It had nothing to do with me. It would just give her something to talk about on the phone with Aunt Grace tonight.

I was waiting to open the package. Nothing, even my mother's approval, seemed more important.

"Go ahead, open it," my grandmother finally commanded.

I opened the box to the most wonderful long, deep pink dress, an absolutely beautiful color with tiny white roses embroidered all along the collar, the sleeves, and the hem. It felt smooth and made a swishing sound as I pulled it out of the box.

"Those are cap sleeves," she explained as I touched the beautiful flowers. "The dress is taffeta. That's the style now." She looked more at my mother when she spoke.

Stylish or not, I didn't care; I loved it.

"The color is fuchsia, Anne. That's the shade of pink that's in style now."

Again, I didn't care. I was in heaven. I had a long dress for the dance and a most beautiful one at that.

"All the girls wear taffeta now," my grandmother continued explaining. "Fuchsia is *the* color. Dolly will look absolutely beautiful in fuchsia. I chose the A-line skirt style because with Dolly's slim body and long legs, that's clearly the best choice. It will accent her graceful figure."

I was happy to hear she thought of me as thin. I was afraid I was fat and didn't know it.

"Dolly, you're going to be the most beautiful girl at the class ball," my grandmother announced. She was proud of the dress she made. So was I. Nothing she had made before compared with this. This was the first dress that was for me alone. Usually she made my sister and me matching outfits. When I looked at my sister in the same dress, she looked so fat that it scared me to death. A nine-year-old kid with a fat butt and even fatter stomach was awful. I was afraid that I had the same figure and just didn't see myself in a true light.

Today, at least, I didn't have to look at Brenda making every dress, no matter how lovely, seem ugly. This dress was mine alone.

For once, everyone in my family was in agreement. Brenda gaped as I went upstairs to change, and even George took a second look as I re-entered the living room amidst the swish, swish, swish of the taffeta. He knew too. I was pretty, the dress was pretty, and I was smart, too. And I looked great in that dress. My dad's unrelenting look of appreciation told me that. My mother's face softened when she looked. It was the softest I had ever seen it except when Aunt Theresa was around.

"When is the ball?" my grandmother asked.

"Three weeks from Saturday," I answered as I smoothed the dress, felt the silkiness of its material, and admired the sleeves again and again.

I was thrilled. I would be going to the dance in a long dress.

In the three weeks before the dance there were many tasks to accomplish. The very next Saturday, Aunt Grace came to take me shopping in her Pontiac. She hurried up the walk, opened the front door, and let herself in. "Hello, Anne. I'm late. Is Dolly ready?" My mother's jealousy sneaked out as she answered, "I don't know, Grace. All I know is that she spends hours in front of that mirror admiring herself. It can't be good for her."

"Oh, let her be, Anne. She's only young once."

I rushed down the stairs, not wanting to be the cause of any lateness. We said our goodbyes and hurried into the car, and Aunt Grace drove to Altman's, smoking in the car as usual, lighting one cigarette after another from the hot, glowing car lighter. We were planning to buy black patent leather shoes with leather soles. Mr. Appleton told us all to find leather soles because it's easier to dance with leather soles. I chose the patent leather part because the bright black shiny toes of the shoe would look just right as they peeked out from under the fuchsia long dress and its hem, embroidered with little flowers. I asked for nylon stockings but my mother and aunt both said that I was too young. We bought white cotton socks. That was the only damper.

While we were in the shoe department, Aunt Grace tried on two or three pairs of shoes. "What do you think, Dolly? Which do you like?"

"I like the blue and white ones, the ones with the high heels." The front part was on a white platform, and there was an open toe.

Aunt Grace said, "Mmm, if I buy those I'll need nylons for sandal-toed shoes, too."

She chose the blue and white ones.

The following Saturday we went back again. This time, we bought a long white cotton half-slip for the A-line dress and white cotton gloves. Aunt Grace bought sheer-toed stockings for her open-toed shoes. I tried once again for stockings for myself, but no luck.

As we drove home, I reminded myself to take small steps so the other girls would not see that I didn't have stockings. I knew Alice Simpson would have stockings because she already wore them to school. I was pretty sure by taking small steps less people could to see that I had white socks on.

I waved goodbye to Aunt Grace as her new shoes carried her gracefully down the walk to return home. I went straight upstairs to try on the dress with all the new accessories. I took another admiring glance in the long mirror. There was no doubt that I was wearing the most beautiful dress that I had ever owned, made for me, and only for me. I was ready and now—there was only one Saturday to go.

"Dolly, stop admiring yourself. Come and set the table." It was my mother who had eyes in the back of her head and knew from the kitchen that I was admiring myself. She seemed to know everything.

I began placing the silverware at each place on the table. My mother handed me the bread as she said, "You spend too much time in front of the mirror. I think you were better off when all you did was keep your nose in a book. At least you were learning something."

I did everything my mother wanted for the next to two weeks, except to keep from admiring myself. Every chance I got I tried on the new dress, swished around in front of the mirror, practiced all the dance steps, and just plain had a great time. I even allowed Brenda to admire me. She watched constantly from her bed. The pink dress crackled as I waved the skirt in front of her. Brenda's eyes were practically popping out of her head. "Let's kiss like movie stars," she requested one day.

I obliged her. Brenda loved to kiss like movie stars, meaning on the lips. I found it dumb, but this week I was a charitable older sister.

Exactly one week before the dance, the printed invitation from the dance school came through the door slot into the vestibule. My parents were invited. Brenda was not invited, thank goodness. She was going to have a baby sitter for the first time. It was a big decision, but Mr. and Mrs. Appleton made strict rules that this was a grownup dance and nobody's little sister or little brother was welcome. That Sunday, I was bubbling over with excitement as I walked to church with Mary Alice. We talked and talked about nothing except the dance and the new formal dress and Monday, things started to move fast. Saturday was only five days away.

Aunt Grace arrived Thursday afternoon to do my hair. She gave me a Toni Home Permanent. I hated permanents but wanted to look my best, and the other girls had curls. My aunt talked my mother into it. Aunt Grace had influence with my mother.

"Just a body wave, Anne," she said. "It's mild."

My mother was occupied across the room peeling tomatoes for sauce as I sat at the kitchen table near to the sink with Aunt Grace behind me. She handed me the rollers, small little white papers and rubber bands each in separate compartments of a cardboard box, and instructed, "Dolly, each time I say end-paper, hand me an end-paper, each time I say roller, hand me a roller, and each time I say rubber band, hand me one of them."

She took about an inch strand of hair and swabbed it with an awful smelling white lotion. I kept the little packages on my lap.

"End-paper." she said.

I took one small piece of the special papers out of the little packet. She wrapped the inch of hair in the piece of tissue, swabbed it again with lotion.

"Roller."

I handed her a roller. She placed the pink plastic roller on top of the end paper. She rolled the curler up tight to my scalp. It hurt.

"Rubber band." Aunt Grace was in deep concentration, tilting her head back and forth as she surveyed where to put the rollers.

I handed up a rubber band to her. She tied the curl from one end to the other with the rubber band. My hair got caught and it hurt again as the rubber band snapped into place.

After all the rollers were used, I waited in that same spot at the kitchen table with a towel around my shoulders. The cold lotion dripped on my face, which I constantly wiped with a sticky piece of cotton that seemed to only spread the goo around. The odor coming from the goo stung my nostrils. The rubber bands continued to hurt. Aunt Grace set the timer and tested one curl every five minutes. It was all I could do not to shriek with the gooey lotion all over my face and the pain of the rubber bands getting caught in my hair. Each time she tested, I hoped we were finished.

Finally, she said, "Anne, come here, what do you think? Is this curly enough?"

"Whatever you think, Grace," my mother turned towards us as she rolled some meatballs and tossed them into the hot sauce. "You know better than I about those things."

Aunt Grace turned to the sink and ran the water, testing for warmth. She turned on the spray attachment as she motioned to me to stand at the sink. "I don't want too much curl. A body wave is much gentler for someone young. I'm going to put the rinse on. It's time."

She rinsed once with the curlers in. Then she yanked and pulled all the rubber bands and curlers out until my whole head throbbed. Finally, my scalp felt relieved of the pull of the rollers, as the soft wet curls sprang back, free of their shackles.

Aunt Grace applied the second rinse. I put my head in the sink, and she put a white creamy cold liquid over my hair three times.

"This will set the curl, Dolly," she said.

After the special rinse, she doused my hair again with warm water, which felt wonderful on a scalp that still smarted from being pulled apart by rollers and rubber bands.

Aunt Grace cleaned and wiped the sink and gave me a clean towel to pat dry my hair. "Pat your hair dry, Dolly, don't pull," she instructed as she poured herself a cup of coffee and headed for the dining room for a cigarette and coffee before she left. I hated for her to go home. I was getting nervous and her leaving meant the dance was getting closer. My hair was still wet, so I had no idea how it would turn out.

I sat with Aunt Grace as she smoked. She told my mother. "She's beautiful, Anne. You've done a good job. She has a bright future."

"She's a natural-born schoolteacher, Grace. She's going to be like me."

"Aunt Grace, I don't want to be a teacher," I said softly so that my mother would not hear me.

"Oh, Dolly," she answered, "just forget about it for heaven's sake. It's a long way off. Just forget about it." She gave me a little hug, lit another cigarette, and walked down the path to her car.

But, I didn't want to be a teacher. I didn't want to be like my mother. I wanted to be like the men. I wanted to go to work and come home from an office. I wanted to earn my own money, but not as a schoolteacher. Mr. Emerson said I had the ability to be whatever I wanted to be. I was going to find a way.

I waved goodbye to Aunt Grace from the porch and went upstairs to my room. I wish I had never looked in the mirror. But there I was, in the frizziest hair I'd ever seen. It was awful. I was so ugly; I didn't want to go to the dance. I'd rather stay home. I took a scissors and

starting cutting. Before I even noticed there were piles
of curls in the bathroom sink. I kept cutting. The ugly
curls never seemed to go away. I cleaned up the sink as
best I could and went to bed. Some things are better put
off until tomorrow.

Friday, my mother was furious as she called Aunt
Grace first thing in the morning. "She cut off all your
beautiful work. Now it's half curly and half I don't
know what. She looks like a little pickaninny."

There was silence. I felt bad that I had messed up
Aunt Grace's work, but it was just too ugly.

More silence. Then my mother talking, "Yes, I can
do that. Grace. I'll have to take her to Arturo's; maybe
he can do something with her. I can't have the whole
town see her like that." Arturo's Beauty Salon was the
beauty salon where my mother went every week. Her
hair never looked great, but that didn't matter. She liked
Arturo. He was Italian, and I knew I had to go. I didn't
want to go anywhere. I wanted to go to sleep like Rip
Van Winkle and wake up with long hair.

My mother raved as she hit me and tried to drive
too. She swerved as she screamed at me, "You are the
most unappreciative child in the whole world. After all I
do for you and look how you act. You ought to be
ashamed of yourself. You don't deserve a beauty salon,
you deserve to go like that to the dance. If it weren't for
your Aunt Grace, I'd make you go to the dance looking
just like that."

My mother dropped me off, admonished me again,
and handed me three dollars. "I don't know how much
Arturo will charge you because he doesn't usually cut
children's hair, but remember not to tip him. It's not
proper to tip the owner of the salon. It is okay to walk
home if it is not dark. If it is dark, call me and your

father will come for you." I didn't care if it was pitch black, I hated her; she was cruel. I wouldn't call her no matter what. I'd find my own way home.

When Arturo saw me, I expected him to laugh, but he only just smiled and went to work. He cut and pushed and stuck me under the hair dryer for what seemed like hours.

He looked over once, while he was working on another lady. His dark eyes smiled at me. "Be patient, Dolly, it's hard to be beautiful."

My face was as hot as it had ever been, my head hurt, my eyes dried from the hot hair around my face. When Arturo finally got around to me and brushed me out, I have to admit my hair looked really good.

"You look much better, Dolly. How do you like the bangs on your forehead? You have a large forehead, and bangs soften it."

"Thank you, Arturo," I took the hand mirror, and Arturo swirled the chair around. I looked at the back. It turned under in what Arturo called a "page boy."

"It was easy, Dolly. You are beautiful, and I like to work on beautiful young women." He said "beautiful" with a long "o," "boootiful." Arturo began sweeping my hair from under the chair. "Anything I would have done couldn't take away from your dark Italian beautiful eyes. You will be beautiful all your life, no matter what style hair you have. Have a good time at the dance," Arturo talked with an Italian accent. It sounded beautiful. *Maybe some day I will learn Italian, travel to Italy, and have an audience with the Pope.*

I walked slowly to the cash register as I peeked at myself in the mirror. I looked really nice.

"How much do I owe you, Mrs. Castagnolo?" I tried to act like my mother.

Arturo called from the back of the shop. "No charge, Dolly. I consider it an honor to have a chance to have such a nice young lady in my shop. Have a good time at that dance. I wish I were going so I could have a dance with you." He smiled again, his dark eyes looking devilish. "Believe me, if I were one of those boys, your dance card would be full from the first minute." I guess Arturo was the perfect hairdresser. He said such nice things to me. He cheered me on.

As I walked home, I saw Mary Alice cross the street towards me. "Hi Dolly," she looked twice as she noticed my new hair cut. "Hey, your hair looks great. I like you in bangs."

I laughed, "You should have seen it an hour ago. I cut it myself and messed it up. Arturo had to fix it."

Mary Alice looked around the back of my hair. "He put you in a page boy—he did a great job."

"Thank you, Mary Alice. I better get home. I have to be home before dark."

I stopped as I looked up into the tree where Mary Alice and I used to have the tree house. I grabbed Mary Alice's arm. "Shh, look, there's a cardinal right on the branch where we had our tree house. It's a male."

Mary Alice quieted down and looked as she whispered, "How do you know that it's a cardinal?"

"Aunt Theresa taught me. She had cardinals in her back yard in Levittown, and I saw them every morning."

Mary Alice was interested, "You know what my grandmother says?"

"No, what?" I was curious.

"She says," Mary Alice whispered, "that when people die, their spirits take the form of birds so they can watch over us for God. They peer in our windows and report back to God if we're good."

"Do you think that's my Aunt Theresa watching over me?" I asked her.

"Maybe".

"Hey, there's another one. It's a little browner. That's the female. Aunt Theresa told me that cardinals always travel in pairs."

"Good, then, your aunt must already have found a new friend in Heaven."

The cardinals remained perched on the tree limb right where the tree house used to be, just looking at us.

"It must be true, Mary Alice, look how they're watching us." We sat down as quietly as we could on a tree stump near the corner. There was no sound except the rustle of a few falling October leaves as we watched and waited for some sign that they knew us. But there was none. They just sat on the limb and watched and watched. I was afraid to breathe for fear they'd fly away.

But soon I realized that I had wasted much too much time. It was getting dark. "Mary Alice, I've got to go," I whispered. "I have to be home before dark."

We took one last glance at the birds. They sure were pretty. As we moved, they both flew right past us in perfect harmony as if to say that they'd be back to see us again, as though they were going to be our friends forever. Soon they were gone over the horizon, unconcerned with the world below them.

I ran down the steep hill to home. The breeze of autumn felt cool on my face after the burn of the dryer. It's nice to have a birthday in October. I liked the weather, the falling leaves, and the quick darkness in the late afternoon. My favorite author, Thomas Wolfe, died the September before I was born. He led a sad life, too. If he had lived, he would have been my friend because we were just alike. Perhaps it was Thomas Wolfe who had made friends with my aunt, and now, they were traveling around as cardinals together.

Thomas Wolfe's books were about his sad life, and I knew his characters as well as myself. I had made quick friends with Monk Webber, of *The Web and the Rock*, my favorite story character. I even talked to Monk at night when no one was listening.

The autumn sky dimmed. The gravel road gave way under me. I ran faster. I wasn't afraid of the dark, I was afraid of the dance tomorrow night. *Please Monk Webber, be my friend at the dance. Bring Aunt Theresa to watch over me. I have no one except you.*

13

"The kingdom of God is like a mustard seed that someone took and sowed in the garden; it grew and became a tree, and the birds of the air made nests in its branches." (Luke 13:18-19)

It was the Saturday of the dance and things were pretty bleak. I had made everyone angry when I didn't like my hair. My mother hardly spoke to me all the next day. I would rather stay home and skip the dance because nothing I did went right.

I took my bath at exactly four o'clock. For the first time, I was allowed to bathe by myself—no fat Brenda next to me and no mother to wash me. I washed myself. It was wonderful. I was careful not to get my hair wet. If I messed up my hair again, I'd be in for it. I would have liked to stay in the tub longer, but I had to make the shower available for George and my dad at five o'clock. I stepped out of the tub on to the dry bath rug. A dry bath rug was a luxury to me because normally I used the rug after Brenda, who made it quite wet first. The rug felt warm and good under my feet as I dried, and I checked my body in the mirror. It was neat to be in the bathroom alone. I could stare at myself all I wanted, although I knew better than to stay too long.

I called to my mother, "Mom, I'm done with the bathroom."

I heard her tell George, "Son, you are next in the shower. Call your father when you have finished. We need to leave by 6:30." There was no answer from George. He didn't much like to shower.

As I lay out my underwear, socks, the long half-slip, and gloves on my bed, I thought of the approaching dance at seven o'clock. I was a bit disappointed that I still had only an undershirt and no bra. Most of the girls had junior bras. I didn't like the white socks either. I would have liked to have nylons, but both my mother and Aunt Grace said no.

As my mother came in to my room, she handed me a purse that belonged to Aunt Theresa. It was black patent leather with gold "T" for the clasp. I put a white handkerchief in it and laid it on the bed. I didn't see the point of a purse. I didn't need a handkerchief and the initial wasn't mine. I hoped no one would notice.

Then, everything went on, piece by piece, until last, the dress. I was staring at myself in the mirror when Dad left to pick up Mrs. Moreno, who was going to baby-sit for Brenda.

When he returned, everybody was ready. I came downstairs and turned the corner into the living room. Dad stood up.

"Wow," he said. That's all.

I blushed.

"Is she ready, Spence?" My mother called from the kitchen.

"Yes, she is, and she's a looker. The question is, not if she is ready, but, are those boys ready for her? There's no boy in this town that I know who's got looks and brains enough to even come close." He was staring straight at me. I blushed again. He smiled and put his hands in his pockets. He kept smiling and looking all the while. I was happy that I looked okay.

When my mother saw me, she stared. It was a look of jealousy that I was used to. She was not happy with me most of the time. Every once in a while she was proud of me, and I liked that look better. Not tonight. She hesitated a minute and gave me a look of appraisal.

"You must walk carefully. Pick the dress up a little bit with your right hand, not too much or you will look clumsy."

I tried it.

"No, not like that. Pick up only a bit of the skirt, not the whole skirt."

I tried again.

She accepted that time, but I felt she was disappointed in my lack of grace. She thought a moment and went upstairs. She came down with Aunt Theresa's bunny fur jacket out of her closet.

"It's a cool evening, Dolly, wear this." I put it on. I loved the feel of it, the beautiful soft fur. My mother looked at me and the jealousy was written all over her face. I was sad.

My dad pulled the car out of the garage and waited, holding the passenger side door of the car like a private chauffeur would do.

As I stepped up to get into the car, my father helped me pick up the end of my dress, which was trailing behind the car before he shut the door. I checked, worried that I may have gotten mud on it. It was okay.

"Shall we?" he said as he smiled directly at me, and with a sweep of his arm equal to the best performance of any real chauffeur, he shut the car door. He walked around the back of the car to the driver's side. My mother got into the back seat, and George sat with her.

This was the first time I had ever been in the front seat of the car when George was around. For once, I was the star attraction.

We parked right in front of the church, and my father opened the door to the church gymnasium. My mother and I went in first, with Dad and George walking respectfully behind. Mr. and Mrs. Appleton had decorated the gym, and there were fresh flowers and streamers everywhere. In the middle of the room was a shiny ball made of small chips of mirrored glass reflecting light on the ceiling and the walls. There was a semi-circle of chairs for the boys, and opposite the boys' chairs was another semi-circle of chairs for the girls. Each chair had a pink ribbon on the back and what seemed to be a pink flower on each seat. I felt like I was in a movie. If Gene Kelly walked out of *Singin' in the Rain* and came up to me and asked me to dance, I wouldn't have been a bit surprised.

The gymnasium doubled as an auditorium and there was a stage set up front. Father McAvoy was in the front on a platform. He gave me a welcoming wave and a smile, but went quickly back to his work of trying to get the Public Address System wired to the phonograph. The Public Address System belonged to the church parish school. It was up to Father McAvoy to make it work with Mr. Appleton's phonograph.

"Ohh," I heard the sighs from some of the women who had turned to look at me. It was true. I was Dee Morgan and I was pretty and this was a beautiful fuchsia A-line taffeta dress. The women who sighed made it all true.

"Welcome," Mr. Appleton said to each of us, one by one. When he got to me he paused a moment to admire my long dress.

You look lovely, Dolly," he said as he took my gloved hand and bowed a small gentlemanly bow. Most of the grownups still called me Dolly. The kids knew I didn't like it and they had all changed to call me Dee, but the grownups followed along with whatever my mother wanted. I didn't have much to say about anything yet, but it was just a temporary setback. I had made up my mind. This was one argument my mother was going to lose. I was forever going to be called Dee, with or without her approval.

"May I take your coat?" He took my bunny fur coat. I struggled a little to get out of it because he was tall and the sleeves were too high. He handed my coat to Mrs. Appleton who went into the back room with it. My mother followed her with her own coat. They were chatting together.

I heard, "It's a lovely evening, Anne. How are you feeling tonight?"

"I'm adjusting, little by little, Fay," my mother answered. The town knew that my mother was still a little sad because of my aunt's death last year.

George and I entered the circle where folding chairs were reserved for the class. People continued to watch me as I walked to one of the seats. For once, I was glad to have George around. He never hit me in public, and having George was like having a boyfriend. I didn't have to walk in alone. He was shy and most girls didn't like him, but he was a boy and for this function, it almost seemed like I had a date. As I sat down, I picked up the beautiful pink flower on the seat. There were white satin ribbons tied to it and some type of wristlet around the back. I was puzzled. I picked it up and placed it in my lap.

My dad went to the makeshift stage to talk with Father McAvoy who was looking around with a worried look on his face. Soon, my dad took his jacket off, rolled up his shirtsleeves, and peered at a bunch of wires with Father McAvoy. The gymnasium was quiet. Mr. Appleton looked worried.

I heard my dad say, "Hey, hold it, Jim, I think I see what's wrong." He looked behind and underneath the phonograph and tilted his glasses up on the top of his head to look. Father McAvoy's cassock, which already was dusty along the bottom, brushed the floor again as he joined Dad and they discussed what might be wrong. Dad switched the wires around and a loud noise came crashing out of the Public Address System. Father McAvoy ran over and turned down the volume on the phonograph. He looked at my father with relieved appreciation as my dad happily explained the crossed wires. The phonograph was working.

"You certainly are a useful man to have around, Spence. You can do anything." Father McAvoy was pleased.

My dad laughed. "Make sure you recommend me to the man upstairs, Jim. I'll need a reference." Both my dad and Father McAvoy enjoyed the joke. They laughed a couple of loud guffaws as the rest of us sighed in relief. My dad saved the day.

I looked for some recognition for my dad from my mother. She was still chatting with the ladies. It seemed to me that my mother was not as proud of my dad as she should be. He was a real genius. Everybody knew it except her.

Jenny Whitcomb rushed to sit next to me, and whispered. "I'm so glad that you wore a long dress. I didn't want to be the only one."

I looked around. She was right. I hadn't noticed, but she and I were the only ones with long dresses. Jenny wore a black, strapless dress with a net shawl. It was a grown up looking dress. There was no doubt that she had on a strapless bra underneath. She wore makeup, stockings, and earrings. I recognized that my dress was not as mature looking, but I honestly thought I looked better. There was something about the simplicity of the A-line dress I was wearing that seemed just right for me. I wasn't the make up type, and I definitely didn't want size C breasts like poor Alice. They were always bobbing up and down and getting in the way. *Please, body*, I said to myself, *Size A is as big as I want to be. Just a junior bra will do, not more.*

"Don't you want to wear your corsage?" Jenny picked it up and handed it to me. I saw that Jenny had her flower on her wrist.

"It's a wrist corsage. You wear it on your left wrist if you're right handed and your right wrist if you're left handed." She slid hers off and slid it back on to show me how. I made my hand small and pushed it through the elastic ribbon to my wrist. It looked so beautiful next to my skin.

I looked up and caught Mrs. Appleton smiling a broad smile. She mouthed the words, "your first corsage." right at me, and I beamed back. I had a corsage. I think Mrs. Appleton was glad that I was happy with it because she kept looking at me and smiling. I sat down and tried not to look at the corsage too much, but I couldn't resist. The delicate pink carnation surrounded by shiny pink and white satin ribbons on my small wrist next to my white glove placed me right in the middle of a movie again.

The music started and so did the torture. The boys began to cross the room to the girls of their choices. I looked down at my feet. I knew I wasn't supposed to do that, but I couldn't bear to watch as the boys passed by me to other girls. I just kept looking at my feet. A couple of small feet in black shiny shoes came close to my own. I was afraid to hope, but the shoes stopped right in front of me. Before I knew it, a much bigger pair of dusty brown loafers with rubber soles joined them. There were now two sets of feet in front of my surprised self.

Both boys spoke in unison, "Dee, would you like to dance?"

I looked up. One boy was Avery Steerforth, probably the most popular boy in school. He was short but handsome, and I couldn't believe he was asking me to dance. He never ever even noticed me.

Next to him, stood Bruce Johnson, a tall, gangly boy, the tallest boy in the class, almost six foot three already. My mom called him an early bloomer, and my dad said he was cut out to be a star basketball player. He was a quiet boy, shy, and as I looked at him, his pimpled face turned a beet red. He had been slightly ahead of Avery and did not realize he had set himself up in competition with the most popular boy in school until it was too late. His fate was sealed. Red as red can be, he turned to walk away.

Then I did the unthinkable. I knew just what Bruce was feeling. He was just like I was and embarrassed easily. My heart went out to him. Avery was forgotten for a moment as I said, "I'd love to, Bruce, thank you." I stood up and faced him, almost pushing Avery aside.

Avery smiled a confident smile, "Next time, Dee," and turned quickly to ask Jenny to dance. My loss was Jenny's gain as she gushed, "I'd love to, Avery."

Bruce was still recovering as he put his right arm at my waist and held my right hand with his large left for the box step. My own hand was encompassed by the size of his. He was so tall that I barely reached his chest, and it was awkward. I had practiced with him before, so I expected the usual conversation from him.

"Hey, Dee, how's the weather down there?" That was what he always said. He was awkward, as awkward as I, maybe worse, but I loved him for trying so hard. I wracked my brain for conversation. Mr. Appleton said it was the boy's responsibility to lead and the girl's responsibility to follow, but poor Bruce could hardly shuffle out the box step. He was doing it all wrong. His rubber soles squeaked along the gymnasium floor just as Mr. Appleton said rubber soles would do. I followed the best I could, avoiding his ever so big feet, so he would not step on me.

"Ooops," Bruce said as he did exactly that. It hurt, but I didn't cry out. I didn't want to embarrass Bruce.

"It's okay, it didn't hurt." All the practice lying to my mother assisted me here as I cheerfully lied yet again. We struggled on together as I hoped he hadn't scuffed my shoe when he stepped on it.

The music dragged on forever, until at last I heard, "Thank you, Dee," from Bruce almost before the music ended. He was as glad as I that it was over.

I answered exactly as Mr. Appleton taught us. "It was fun, Bruce, ask me again any time." The champion liar spoke again. It seemed I was always lying—lying to my mother, lying to my friends, lying to boys.

Bruce walked alongside of me to my seat and turned quickly away.

I am such a dope.

Jenny's dress rustled over next to me, and she whispered, "Why the heck didn't you dance with Avery? At least he can dance."

I didn't answer. I was asking myself the same question. Was the whole night to be a series of my usual mistakes? I looked at the clock. It was only five minutes after seven. The dance was only just beginning, and I had already made a total fool of myself.

Another boy came over to ask me to dance, and then another, until there were more and more boys crossing over to me, and I began to be able to look up without total fear. Mr. Appleton announced all the dances, and we showed the parents all that we had learned: the fox trot, the waltz, the jitterbug, the polka, and even the Virginia Reel. There was a special dance for the parents, and we all sat while they danced. My parents were dancing what I recognized as a modified box step. It wasn't exactly a box they formed, but the step was similar. I was surprised to see that my mother was leading my father. Mr. and Mrs. Appleton insisted that the girl must never lead the boy. Still, I had the feeling that if my mother didn't lead Dad, nothing was going to happen. I hoped Mr. Appleton would understand.

We had a dance where the girls danced with their fathers and the boys danced with their mothers. I liked that because I danced with Dad.

Dad looked a little sheepish as he took my hand and said, "I'm not good at this."

I didn't say anything. I didn't know what to say because I didn't care if my dad could dance or not. I felt warm and soft to be held by him. He was gentle and kind and handsome, but I didn't know how to say that to my father so I didn't say anything.

I saw George out of the corner of my eye, and he, poor thing, was still short enough to be almost smothered in my mother's big breasts. He looked miserable.

Mr. and Mrs. Appleton went around making sure to dance with everyone because some of the students didn't have both parents with them. They made sure they danced with every student at least once.

As the music ended, Mr. Appleton went to the microphone. "The next dance is a girl's choice," he announced, as his wife asked one of the boys to dance. The girls began to make their choices. The popular boys were smug as they waited across the room—the others looked in torture.

I got up all my nerve. This was my chance. I wanted to dance with Father McAvoy, and I went over to him and asked. It was risky. He and my dad were quite involved in conversation.

They both gave me their full attention as I asked, "Father, would you like to dance?"

"Oh, Dolly, I can't. Priests are not allowed to dance."

I was mortified. How could I have been so stupid? My face was as hot as I had ever known it. I must have blushed bright red. And when I turned to ask someone else to dance all the girls had chosen. I saw Bruce suffering with me. Even Bruce was taken, so there was no one. Now, I was truly in a fix. It looked like I was going to have to stand there mortified throughout the entire dance.

Mr. Appleton walked quickly from the other side of the room. "May I offer myself as a substitute for Father McAvoy, Miss Morgan?"

"Go ahead, Dolly," my father quipped, "but word has it he's a terrible dancer." Father McAvoy laughed, and Mr. Appleton put his nose up in the air, ignored them, and smiled politely as he offered me his arm.

The polka was playing. Mr. Appleton turned to me. "Shall we?" he asked.

On the dance floor, I was self-conscious, and at first I was counting one, two, three as we had been taught. As we moved, I forgot, and pretty soon I was dancing all around the gym in a big circle with Mr. Appleton. He pushed my waist a bit, and I realized that I was to go out in front of him. I stumbled, confused.

"That's okay, Dolly. Let's try it again."

The second time I caught on and it was fun. Every time he pushed my waist, I turned and faced him. In that position, I had to polka backwards as he moved forward. Once I caught on, it was the simplest thing, and I wanted to do it all the time. I tried to go out when he didn't push me, but he stopped me with a gentle jerk on my arm.

"The man leads, Dolly, remember?"

Shortly after he pushed me out all the time, and I was going backward more than was going forward. It was great. I would turn towards him every time he pushed on my waist a certain way.

We started to fly with the music. Soon we were twirling so fast that my feet didn't touch the ground except about every five steps or so. He liked to pick me up, and I sensed how light I must be to him. Mr. Appleton was turning and twirling me, sometimes we were side by side sometimes he went backwards, sometimes I did, and all with gentle pushes on my back. He made me feel like Fred Astaire again, not Ginger Rogers; she was only Queen. I was Fred Astaire because surely I was King tonight.

The others stopped to watch and soon we were all alone on the floor. My dress was flying, my white socks were showing, and I didn't care. I could have danced with him forever.

A tiny little voice inside of me would not give up. *She is your mother, she is talented, and you will be too.*

Now, we all gathered around in a circle and held hands. Mr. Appleton put on the phonograph record, "Good Night Irene." Father McAvoy broke into the circle next to me and held my hand. I was glad he wasn't angry with me for asking him to dance.

The grown-ups sang, "Good Night Irene, Good Night Irene, I'll see you in my dreams."

Mr. And Mrs. Appleton stood at the door and said goodnight to each of us. Mr. Appleton helped me with my bunny fur coat. Again, I couldn't get my arms in the sleeves. Mr. Appleton saw the problem. "Sorry, Dolly, let me lower your coat a little. There, that's better."

"That's a lovely coat, Dolly," said Mrs. Appleton.

"Thank you," I answered. I did so want to tell her it was my Aunt Theresa's, but I didn't know if I should. My mother didn't like me to tell anyone when I wore hand-me-downs. She said it wasn't anybody's business where I got my clothes. But, somehow, this seemed different.

I got up all my nerve and said, "It belonged to my Aunt Theresa. I'm the same size as she was, and I'm allowed to wear her clothes."

Mrs. Appleton looked at me and smiled, "I think your aunt would be proud to have you wear it, Dolly.

You look like peaches and cream with the soft white fur next to your face."

She hugged me a little bit. I felt her girdle against me and smelled the clean scent of her hair. She went back to her other guests as I looked outside. It was raining. I didn't want to get my dress wet.

Mr. Appleton handed me an umbrella. "Keep it, Dolly. You can bring it to school on Monday."

"Thank you Mr. Appleton."

As I walked down the sidewalk to the car, something came over me. I pointed the open umbrella right up to the sky, and I started dancing and singing, just like Gene Kelly.

"I'm singin' in the rain, I'm singin' in the rain, what a glorious feeling, I'm happy again." I hopped on and off the curb as I sang just like he did in the movie.

My mother called from the car, "Dolly, stop jiggin' around and get in the car."

Mr. Appleton saw me dancing and hurried out, stood next to me and chuckled, "Hey, Anne, she's just singin' in the rain." He took the umbrella and sang with me. "I'm singin' in the rain. I'm singin', just singin', in the rain."

He waved the open umbrella with one hand and held mine with the other. We danced down the sidewalk together. Mrs. Appleton joined us and then some of the others jumped in. One of the parents, Mr. Jackson, grabbed a rake from behind the church hedge and danced with it, twirling and dipping with the rake as his partner. We were quite a spectacle in front of God's House, everyone singing and dancing to his own tune and having a great time.

My mother called again from the car. This time she spoke to Mr. Appleton. "John, send her here, the babysitter is waiting." Mr. Appleton didn't hear her, and I didn't go. I knew I'd be in for it, but I just couldn't leave. We kept dancing until my father got out of the car and opened the back door.

"Hey, John, over here."

Mr. Appleton caught on, bent down, and picked me completely up, depositing me in the back seat of the car, all the while grinning at my dad and singing.

"Thanks, John," said my father still smiling, as he shut the door and jumped into the driver's seat.

I just didn't want to leave. I thought I was going to cry right in front of everybody. I bit hard into my lip.

My mother turned to scold me, but thought better of it, as Father McAvoy came to the open window. "Don't worry, Dolly, go with your family. They'll be plenty of other dances for you. God bless you darling. Good Night." There was Father McAvoy, helping me as always to do the right thing. And always, my mother, with the familiar strange looks in her eyes.

My family—I had a family tonight.

My heart was as big as all outdoors as we drove home silently, Dad and Mom in the front seat and George with me in the back. For once, George didn't poke me in the ribs. The dress confused everybody I guess. We were a family tonight, a real family.

The car slipped silently down the steep narrow driveway to the basement garage as the darkness of the back seat engulfed and comforted me. I put the beautiful memory of the dance into the far reaches of my head to keep it safe. My father left again to drive Mrs. Moreno home, and I went quickly to my bedroom and, happy to find Brenda asleep, pressed the wrist corsage into the book Aunt Theresa gave me, *Rebecca*. I put everything between the mattresses for safekeeping. I had to squeeze them a little to get them into the middle of the bed where my mother would not notice.

As I dreamed the night away, the memories locked themselves away even deeper, into the safest part of my brain, as though they were a thousand tiny pink wrist corsages, safe from all tears and beatings.

Aunt Grace telephoned the next morning and my mother told her the news.

My mother was pacing back and forth with her own excitement. "She has a natural sense of rhythm. Spence was pleased as punch."

Was my mother talking about me? Herself? In my eyes, my mother was the best dancer, not me. I might be a good dancer too. Maybe it was in the genes.

Can Hope grow from one dance during one night? Yes, indeed. She was small, a little mustard seed, a timid guest—just a tiny light—Hope. She was born in me last night, like the mustard seed in one of Father McAvoy's parables. She was just a glimmer, but she was there, and stubborn, too, for she would prove herself a mighty opponent for my mother, refusing to be crushed. And some day, bloody but unbowed, Hope would grow into a great big huge tree and lift her leafy arms right up to the sky.

14

"You do the best you can with what God gave you, and then, you leave the rest up to Him." Susan Healey

When I entered ninth grade, I had no idea how much my life was about to change. The J. T. Collins High School sat on the corner of Linden Avenue and Sycamore Street inviting me in each morning. Becoming a freshman in high school did not feel like much of a change since the eighth grade was in the same building. Each day I was more and more lonesome. I had few friends. Every time I tried to make a friend, my mother interfered. She listened in on the phone and seldom allowed me out of the house except for church. I was not allowed to make telephone calls because we were on a "message unit" limited telephone system, and any extra calls were expensive. There was no slumber party for me, no afternoon gossiping with the girls, no cherry coke at the corner drugstore—a bleak existence.

Did Ninth Grade put me on the verge of something new? Or would life just strike me yet another blow?

My classmates talked of the cheerleading tryouts six weeks away and as I heard them I became interested.

Colleen had been discussing it since the first day of school. "Why don't you join me?" she excitedly asked me one day. I agreed to try.

Six weeks seemed like a long time, but there were things to do to prepare. Saturday, Aunt Grace arrived in her maroon Pontiac to take me for the saddle shoes we needed to wear. As she got out of the car and came up the walk, I saw her clearly. She walked gracefully, in a blue shirtwaist dress with blue and white high-heeled shoes. There was a pocketbook to match her shoes on her arm. I loved her style—crisp and clean. "Hi, Spence," she called to my dad who was working in the yard.

"Hi Grace," came back my dad's equally pleasant response. My dad didn't like my aunts and uncles, except for Aunt Grace. He met my mom at the time he was dating Aunt Grace. I wondered a lot how my life might have been if my dad had married her instead of my mom. I wished for Aunt Grace as my mom. She was kind and never hit me.

"Hi, Anne." Aunt Grace opened the screen door without knocking.

"Hi, Grace," my mother called from the kitchen. "How about a cup of coffee before you go?"

"No, thanks, Anne, we have a lot to do, and I want to get to Bloomingdale's as soon it opens. The parking is easier and the crowds are less." She handed me a package. "Here are a couple of skirts and blouses for your cheerleading tryouts. You can try them on later. You'll have to hem the skirt."

I opened the brown paper bag. There were two blue skirts, one black skirt, and a blue blouse, the regulation school colors. There was a black sweater vest similar to the one the cheerleaders wore.

My mother came into the living room wearing her apron full of cooking stains. There was the aroma of bacon and coffee from the kitchen. "I don't know if she can hem the skirt, Grace. She has not done any sewing since Theresa died."

Aunt Grace turned to me, "Do you think you can hem the skirt, Dee? I can help you mark it."

"Yes, I remember how. It's not hard at all," I answered. I acted a lot more sure of myself than I felt. I never hemmed anything without Aunt Theresa sitting by my side watching, encouraging, and suggesting.

"Well, Anne, we better be going. We'll be back after lunch."

My mother came to the door and waved goodbye as we got into Aunt Grace's Pontiac. She lit a cigarette from the car lighter. My dad looked up from his gardening, "Remember, the best sale is when you don't buy anything. That's when you save the most money," came his usual unsolicited advice. He chuckled to himself as he returned to caring for his beloved lawn.

I had never been to Bloomingdale's to shop for myself before. Sometimes I went with Aunt Grace to buy her another pair of shoes as she nonchalantly added to the boxes and boxes of shoes already in her closet, lined up in neat rows.

Once, my dad teased Aunt Grace about all the shoes she was wasting money on. For the only time that I've ever known, she was angry. "Well, Spence, if I'm perfectly capable of earning my own money. I guess I'm capable of spending it."

My dad didn't tease her again. I, for one, completely agreed with Aunt Grace. If ever I was lucky enough to earn money, I would spend it any way I wanted and no one would have a thing to say about it. I promised myself again, that one day I would earn my own money.

As we drove, Aunt Grace chatted and lit cigarettes. We parked on a small side street near the Thom

McCann shoe store, shaded by the tall buildings around us. Aunt Grace put some money in the meter and held my hand as we expertly navigated the crowd towards my shoes-to-be. I liked the way the name Thom McCann was written in script on its storefront sign. The letters looked neat, clear, and classy.

Regulations for the cheerleading tryouts required black and white saddle shoes. Aunt Grace and I knew exactly what to get. As usual, I followed Aunt Grace's cue to sit down in the small brown chairs lined up on the wall.

A salesman stopped and asked, "May I help you?" He looked directly at Aunt Grace.

"Yes, please. I would like to see some saddle shoes for my niece." My aunt liked Thom McCann shoes. She said they were the best quality.

"Would you like navy and white, red and white, or black and white?" He looked at me.

I answered easily, "Black and white." He took off my right shoe, put my foot down upon a cold metal platform, and told me to stand up, and then he pushed a wedge next to the ball of my foot. I was glad I remembered to wear clean white socks. Aunt Grace looked at my feet approvingly.

"Size 7 M," the salesman said as he strode to the back of the store to get the shoes.

I thought that seemed big, although I didn't mind because it was the same size that Aunt Grace wore, and I liked to be like Aunt Grace. She was pretty and had wonderful clothes. She had once told me that because her legs were beautiful, she could do stocking ads. She had not tried, but she was sure she could if she wanted. I agreed with her.

We didn't talk much as we waited. I was so happy to be there with Aunt Grace that I had nothing to say. I just drank in the love and happiness around me as the other people shopped together. There was a mother with her daughter, two young girls giggling together, a man alone, and lots of people having a good, good time.

The salesman's hands warmed my heels as he inserted them into the shoes with the help of a tiny shoehorn. I loved them instantly. I looked just like Maggie Hunter, the co-captain of the cheerleaders and the shortest one in the cheerleading line. Since the cheerleaders were arranged starting with the tallest person in the center until the two shortest people were at each end. I liked the end position because you had to run more to get out and back. Maggie had one of the end positions. She always wore the same ponytail with a blue and black ribbon that bounced as she cheered.

I walked around in the shoes, and the man poked the toes with his thumb. He said, more to Aunt Grace than to me, "They fit fine."

Aunt Grace said we would take them. I thanked Aunt Grace because I knew they were a gift. My mother didn't have money enough to pay for them. Whenever I wanted something special, one of my aunts offered to buy it for me and give it to me as a gift. I was lucky that way. My aunts liked me.

The salesman put the shoes back in the box, and put them aside. "Is there anything else?" he said to both of us.

"No, thank you," answered Aunt Grace, and the salesman packed the shoes. He handed them to me and smiled. Aunt Grace took my hand and we headed for our next stop, Bloomingdale's and of course, the shoe department.

A salesman asked Aunt Grace, "May I help you?"

Aunt Grace answered, as I knew she would. "Yes, please, I saw a pair of red platform shoes in the window. Could I try them on?"

The salesman measured Aunt Grace. She was wearing stockings without reinforced toes, the kind she liked best.

The red platform-open-toed shoes had high heels, and I loved them, as did Aunt Grace. She kept walking by the mirror and admiring herself. I knew she was going to buy them. She smiled at me, and then, to the salesman, she said, "I'll take them."

The salesman packaged the shoes, and Aunt Grace paid him. She looked down at me still smiling, "Well, where next? I think the lingerie department for underpants for you and new stockings for me."

I agreed with my eyes. I needed a special pair of underpants that were black and would hold tightly to my hips when I jumped. I didn't really like the underpants—they seemed made of some type of rubber and they would probably be tight. Aunt Grace looked at them, and then me and said to the saleslady behind the counter, "Do you have an extra small size?"

The saleslady said yes, went behind the counter, and brought back another package of the black shiny underpants, which looked to be even tighter. I was worried about being able to jump in them.

Aunt Grace turned to me. "Those are what you need, Dee. We'll get them."

Aunt Grace asked about stockings for herself next. The saleslady showed them by putting her hand inside of one. She had sharp red nails. I was afraid she was going to run the stocking. I didn't like them, but Aunt Grace did.

Next, Aunt Grace took a doggie collar in black and white to match my shoes from a rack on the counter. She smiled, "I've seen these on the girls at school. Would you like one to go with your shoes?"

I never thought that I would be able to have a doggie collar since it was a real luxury item with no purpose. The girls wore them around their ankle socks for decoration. "They're not practical. They're just a decoration."

She grimaced at me, "Do you *like* it? That's the question, I'm asking, not if it's practical. Do you like it? Tell me the truth."

I caved in. "I love it."

"Sold," my aunt smiled again as she handed the doggie collar to the saleslady who was also smiling and looking at me. She placed it in a paper bag.

"She has beautiful eyes," she said to my aunt as she handed the small parcel to me.

I carried our packages as we passed by the shoe department on our way out. Aunt Grace looked around as I followed her. Then she looked at me and laughed, "I guess we have enough shoes for today." She took my hand and we stopped at Fanny Farmer Candy Shoppe. Aunt Grace bought me my favorite butter crunch candy to eat in the car as we drove home.

As soon as we got into the car, Aunt Grace lit a Pall Mall with the car lighter and I settled down comfortably enveloped by the plush gray seats. Because the Pontiac was a big car with large seats, Aunt Grace looked small when she drove it. She had a special pad added to the driver's seat so that she could see out the window better as she drove. I envied her high-heeled shoes on the gas pedal and admired her legs. Then, I carefully opened my candy so as not to spill anything in the car.

As usual, we soon got around to talking about Gene Kelly.

"Dee, there is a Gene Kelly movie in town. How about we go together?"

I answered, "Yes," quite quickly. "What is the movie?"

"*Singin' in the Rain,* with Gene Kelly and Debbie Reynolds. It's in Technicolor."

Technicolor—I wasn't sure what that meant. The idea seemed to please Aunt Grace.

I was happy that day.

When we arrived home, Aunt Grace sat down in the living room for another Pall Mall and a cup of coffee, and I tried on everything to show my mother. I made a big fuss about it all because my mother insisted that I always "show appreciation." Aunt Grace really didn't care. She wasn't as big on "appreciation."

"Everything fits beautiful-ly," Aunt Grace told my mom. Aunt Grace was fussy about adverbs. You could not say beautiful when you meant beautifully.

"She's an easy fit."

This was meant to explain that, unlike, my sister, Brenda, I was thinner and easier to fit. They did not say that but they meant it. Brenda shopped in the Bloomingdale's Chubbette Children's department for her clothes because she was fat. She could not wear any hand-me-downs because they didn't fit her. I, of course, being "lucky" enough to have an easy figure to fit, never bought a single dress in a store.

I asked Aunt Grace about her Pall Malls. "Why do you smoke such long cigarettes?"

"It is less cancerous to use long cigarettes because it takes a longer time for the smoke to get to your lungs."

I was glad about that. I did not want Aunt Grace to get cancer.

Aunt Grace and I hemmed the skirt I chose. I stood on the dining room side chair and Aunt Grace marked the hem with the marker. She pushed a little ball at the top of the marker and a squirt of powder came out to mark the spot where I was to turn the hem.

"Dee, I think this hem will be about two inches. You will not need to cut it, if you put a ribbon on it. Do you know how to do a ribbon around the hem? You'll need pinking shears."

"Yes, I do."

"That's wonderful. I remember the green gabardine dress you and your Aunt Theresa made for you. You looked quite beautiful in that dress." I never liked that dress. I didn't say anything.

Aunt Grace stayed to watch as I turned the skirt up at the mark, ironed it down, and put a ribbon on it with the sewing machine Uncle Steve had given my mother after Aunt Theresa died. I hemmed as Aunt Theresa had showed me. I was careful not to make the hemming stitches either too large or too small. Too big and they would not hold the hem, too small and there would be too many stitches to see on the front side of the skirt. I took the smallest stitch possible to the outside. I ironed the skirt again and tried it on. Aunt Grace totally approved, finished her coffee, and got up to leave.

I said, "Thank you Aunt Grace for the help, the shoes, and the clothes."

"Oh no. Dee, Thank you. You're wonderful company. I'm lucky to have a niece like you. We will do it again soon. Don't forget that next Saturday we will be going to the Gene Kelly movie. She smiled brightly, "In TECHNICOLOR!"

She laughed again, took her own shoebox and went into the car.

I missed her even before she left.

I carefully put away Aunt Theresa's sewing materials and sat down right away at the dining room table to write a long thank you note to Aunt Grace. It freed my heart to write to her. I told her I loved her, missed her, and wanted to live with her. She always wrote back. And, I would make sure as usual, that I gave my letter directly to my dad to mail.

I wore the underpants and the saddle shoes a couple of times when I practiced to make sure I would be able to jump in them. With all the preparation and the practicing and the worry, suddenly five weeks were gone and there was only a week to go. My heart pounded constantly. I couldn't concentrate on anything except the upcoming tryouts. My classmates and I talked of nothing else. No one seemed to expect me to win. I didn't either. I was certainly going to try my hardest anyway. I figured if I didn't try, I would never know whether or not I could really win a spot on the squad. As long as I was willing to try, then it might happen. Without trying, there was nothing.

The rule was that you could try out in your freshman year and if you made the squad you would be a member of the squad until you graduated high school—three years! As a first year member of the squad, you would be eligible to be Captain of the Squad in your Senior Year. Bessie Barnes was a Senior and Captain of the Cheerleaders. She was also full of conceit. When she passed me in the hall, she looked right through me, as though I simply didn't exist. In a way, it was true. I didn't exist to many of my classmates.

Bessie thought she knew everything, which was really strange because she was flunking out of school. She had a boyfriend, Gilbert, who was a huge football player and equally without smarts. They joked together about flunking out of school. They were planning to marry as soon as they finished high school. I couldn't help wondering what it would be like to have a boyfriend. I definitely didn't want Gilbert.

I prayed to St. Jude for help with cheerleading. I was pretty sure I could not make the squad. My childhood dreams of being a second baseman like Jackie Robinson really never had a chance. I was easily intimidated by the other players and usually afraid of the ball. The cheerleading squad was a possibility because of my ability in gymnastics and dancing. I was usually the first one to scramble up the rope as we warmed up.

That thought reminded me of Mrs. Selbourne, the gym teacher, who had suggested cheerleading to me one day when I was again the last person chosen for the baseball team.

As I sat on the bench dejected by the humiliation of being the last chosen, Mrs. Selbourne looked at me and smiled, "Dee, don't take it so hard. You worry too much about baseball. You are athletic in your own way. You are light and agile. I think you might try to be a gymnast or a cheerleader."

After that day, Mrs. Selbourne chose me to help her demonstrate gymnastics and dancing in gym class. We demonstrated the cartwheel, the polka, and the dosey-do of square dancing. One day, while we were demonstrating the polka, we were flying so fast that I hardly touched the ground.

She chose me to help her with the Angel Float. She lay on her back and put her knees up with her feet flat. I jumped on, took her hands, and she pushed me up with her legs. I let go of her hands and held my hands out, as an angel flying.

She lectured to the class as they stood around watching. "See how Dee uses her strength to push herself up. I'm on the bottom, but it's not an effort to hold her on top because she is using her abdominal muscles, which are strong, to hold her up. My part is to be a firm base."

We switched places and she showed how I could carry her on top of my legs even though she was much heavier. As I pushed her lower abdomen with my bare feet I felt the power of her stomach muscles engage.

"It has little to do with the strength of the bottom person. It is the strength of the top person that is the secret."

She was right. With a little push she was on top of my feet while I had made only a small pushing effort. I simply followed her body. I knew that she was much heavier than I. Her extra weight was hardly noticeable as I pushed. I hadn't realized that instinctively I was doing the same when I was the top partner. I had thought it was simply because I was small and light that people could lift me easily. Here was a situation where I was chosen first to be a partner. Everyone wanted me to be the one on top.

And now, encouraged by the confidence of Mrs. Selbourne's gymnastics classes, I bravely decided to take her suggestion and try out for cheerleading.

I went to all the practices. They were run by Bessie. She had several favorite apprentices, and I was not one of them. She paraded in front of us, exuding the most amazing sense of self-importance. How I wished I could feel like she looked. She made it obvious that she did not much like me, picking on me constantly and insisting I did not do the wrist turn properly. There was a certain way to twist your wrist as you punched out a cheer, that I just couldn't do. The more I tried, the more she criticized. I was demoralized. Colleen, who helped me with baseball, was also trying out for the squad, and she took me under her wing. She came to my house after school each day and worked with me on the cheers. We practiced that wrist turn over and over again in the backyard. Colleen thought she would be able to show me the proper way of the wrist movement. She, too, seemed to think I was doing it wrong. It was odd because I thought I was doing it fine, and yet people were constantly correcting me. Even some of the girls whom I thought could not do it, corrected me. I never said anything back to them. I certainly felt like telling them what was wrong with their own form once in a while.

Alone, after Colleen left each day, I practiced my jump over and over again. Take a small jump, then go down and touch the floor with both hands and then jump up as high as you could. The jump was in every cheer—little jump, touch ground, and jump. I had a feeling I could leap high because I could tell by the way the others looked at me that there was something unusual about the way I vaulted that surprised them. They didn't say anything, so I wasn't sure and didn't ask for fear that I was wrong.

Thursday afternoon, I went to the office to put my name in for the tryouts. The list was on a high counter that I could barely touch. I knocked the clipboard over as I reached.

Mrs. Smith, the school secretary was behind the counter. She helped me pick it up. Embarrassed, I took the clipboard from her and signed in the next spot. There was a long list already. I saw many of my friends on the list: Laura Wherehouse, Connie Green, Colleen, and others. My number was thirty-seven. This year they were to pick three freshmen. Three out of at least thirty-seven. My heart sank.

As I wrote my name, Mrs. Smith smiled at me and said, "Dolly, I wish you good luck. I would love to see you make the squad."

I wasn't sure if she meant it. She was being polite. Why would she want me to win? She did not really know me. Still, her smile warmed my heart, and I was encouraged in spite of myself.

When I reached home that afternoon, I finished my homework as fast as I could and went out back to practice for the last time. It was now or never. Either I learned that wrist turn today or not. George was out in the backyard also, playing basketball with John. George made fun of me. I didn't care. I had to practice and this was the only place I had to do it. Colleen came by, but she seemed to be more interested in George than in me, so I practiced alone. George was no oil painting, but some of the girls in school thought he was cute. I, for one, did not think so. Colleen kept going over to the court trying to get the boys to let her play. I practiced on my own, hoping she would come over and help me. She was more intent on the basketball game. Finally, the boys said okay. She was a good basketball player, but I had other stuff on my mind. I went to the side yard, where I could not be seen, and kept practicing. Friday was almost upon us. The tryouts would be during lunch hour in the school gym, and the results would be posted that afternoon in the office.

My mother called me to set the table for dinner. It had been odd because all week my mother had left me alone while I practiced. I stopped as soon as she called because I did not want to make her angry. She was calm even though I'd been outside all afternoon.

I interrupted the basketball game to tell Colleen that I must go in and set the table. We said goodbye, and Colleen continued her game with John and George. I sensed that Colleen was sure that she was going to make the squad. She was full of confidence in herself, as she weaved in and out and around the boys to dribble to the basket. She didn't express much confidence in me. She did not say this; I just felt it. I agreed with her. There was not a glimmer of hope in sight. I decided that I would be kind to the girls who made the squad. They would never know how much I wanted it. It was always worse, when George or someone knew. I determined that no one would ever know how much I wanted this prize.

Oddly, my mother seemed to know. She kept looking at me wondering how she could get something out of me for herself. She knew, of course, that I had neglected my homework in the last few weeks. My mind just would not work right. I thought of nothing except cheerleading. I'd cheerlead on the way to school, my books in one hand and my other wrist twisting in the air. I'd cheerlead in the bathroom, and I'd cheerlead in my bed at night, willing my wrists to turn the way they should.

I knew that I would not sleep tonight. The rule in our house was that if you could not sleep, you were to lie quietly so as not to disturb anyone. I did this through many nights of worry. Brenda was asleep in the next bed. The house was quiet. Only the hall light was on.

My mother came in and sat her huge body on the edge of my bed. The bedside creaked under her weight.

UH-Oh. What had I done.

She looked at me and spoke, "Are you worried about tomorrow?"

I lied as usual. "Not too much, a little."

"Well, you haven't asked for my opinion. I'll tell you anyway. I think you will make it. You are agile and full of pep. I have no doubt about your upcoming success."

I wasn't reassured. *Well, she's my mother, I guess she has to say I'm good.*

My mother kept talking. "You know, I wasn't always this fat. I was a cheerleader in college. I was small, like you and full of vigor. I bet you never thought that, did you?"

She was right. I certainly never guessed that those big breasts could ever jump off anything, no less the ground. I didn't answer.

She smiled a small curving of her lips. Not a real smile. My mother *never* smiled. There was just this tiniest pursing of her lips like she had just tasted a lemon and was pretending it wasn't bitter.

She paused. "Tell me Dolly, can you truthfully say that you have practiced and worked to your best?"

I answered, "Yes." I was sure I had tried and tried and tried. There was nothing left to do except be a good loser.

"Well, then, tomorrow I want you to go out there and do the best you can with what God gave you. Then, leave the rest up to Him. Good night, Dolly. Go to sleep."

Do the best you can with what God gave you, then leave the rest up to Him. The idea felt good. For the first time since

Aunt Theresa's death, I turned all my problems over to God and fell fast asleep.

§§§§§§

Tomorrow came in a minute. The school was noisy with the prospects for the cheerleading tryouts. We were to meet in the gymnasium at 11:50, after our eleven o'clock classes adjourned. We would try out our routines, and the judges' decisions would be posted that afternoon in the principal's office. We all received special permission to be late to our classes if necessary. My class was Shop with Mr. Woodstock.

When I told him I might be late, he offered a huge smile, "So, Dee, you are going to be a cheerleader. Great! Good luck!" He had a lot more confidence than I did.

We would have more than one chance. When Mrs. Selbourne called my name, I was to join a team of two others. We would cheer together, each taking a turn at leading the other two. After all the three person teams cheered, we each had a three-minute final solo, which included anything we wanted to do. Not everyone had a three-minute solo planned. Those of us, who wanted to, gave our names to Mrs. Selbourne. When Mrs. Selbourne called my name for the three-minute solo I would have the whole gym floor to myself. I had practiced my solo routine secretly, each morning before school started. I didn't want George or Brenda to laugh at it, especially when I lost.

I was the first contestant to enter the gym, having learned from *The Count of Monte Cristo*, the power of being on time. He always entered right at the stroke of midnight. Colleen came in next and gave me a big confident smile. I tried to smile back. I don't think I did. I just took my place on the bench in the front cheerleaders row.

"I'm so nervous," Laura whispered as she ran to sit down next to me and squeezed my hand. I didn't answer. I was too nervous to speak. Soon the benches were full of excited girls.

The teachers who were to be the judges entered after we all had taken our seats. There were seven teachers in all, most of whom I'd had in class. Miss Roberts with her warm encouraging smile was there. Mr. Wilson came in last; his ever growing paunch made his history as a U. S. Marine seem far away. He was a fabulous teacher, capable of great innovation. As the teachers assembled, my mind wandered back to Mr. Wilson's eighth grade history class and current events. The current events were the best because Mr. Wilson was an ex-soldier who admired General MacArthur. He had us read the newspaper every night and draw maps of the Korean War progress, which set my mind on fire. Every evening I rushed to my dad's newspaper with my colored pencils. My maps were bright—as I marked our progress from South to North Korea and learned that a troop was not a group—it was one lonesome soldier on the ground fighting for me. These troops moved forward each day, and I got really excited when we crossed the 38th parallel. I raced to class to show Mr. Wilson. He was as happy as I was that day. The others made fun of me and called me "teacher's pet" and "brown-noser," but I didn't care enough to stop. I loved those colored maps, so neat and clean with a sense of our army always moving forward.

Mr. Wilson and I were both pretty upset when retreat came, for different reasons. I worried about how to show the retreat over the colored penciled patterns on the map. Mr. Wilson worried about the soldiers on the ground in Korea retreating. One night, I figured out a way to show the withdrawal. I cross-hatched No. 2 pencil lines across the parts of the maps where the troops had withdrawn and arrived at school the next morning to show my maps. Mr. Wilson was glad for an excuse to talk about something that so touched his own heart. He had me come to the front of the class and demonstrate my crosshatched map. He filled in with war stories about friends of his whose lives had been lost in war and in training for war. He talked about his friend, who was an ex-Navy man who captained a PT Boat in the Philippines. I really liked those PT Boats. They were small next to the big submarines they torpedoed, but a PT Boat made up for its small size in quick movement and bravery. The whole idea of that big submarine made me think of my mother. She was as large as any submarine and just as mean. Her oddly calm moments didn't fool me. She was like a submarine covering itself with ocean water when it submerged to hide. Given any chance, she would mow me down.

I'm like a PT boat, small and fast, always taking a chance that I could win the next battle against the huge submarine that was my mother.

I didn't really understand in eighth grade, that lives were being lost—I saw the war as a colorful drawing on a piece of paper. In high school, now, I was much older. I knew about the ugly, unwanted monster, Death, first hand because of Aunt Theresa, and I understood the quiet sadness in Mr. Wilson's eyes.

I came out of my daydreams because Mr. Wilson waved to me when he entered the gym and joined the other judges on the top back row of the bleachers. Mrs. Selbourne, the gym teacher, stood in front of us, her large muscular body alive with energy, ready to call the names of each pre-specified cheerleading team.

My name was on Team Six with Laura and Connie.

Mrs. Selbourne announced us, her notepad in hand, "Will all the teams begin, please." We ran out with all the other teams and lined up behind Bessie, who began the first cheer.

"T–E– and a LOUD A–M!" I watched Bessie closely. I wanted to cheer exactly like her.

"T–E– and a LOUD A–M!" I followed again. I was self-conscious about the wrist movement. I cursed my awkwardness.

We sat down and each team was called separately until, finally, I heard "Team Six." I ran out with Laura and Connie with Laura leading first. As we cheered, I forgot my self-consciousness, and a funny thing began to happen—I felt on my own, as though I was in the backyard practicing and no one was there to worry me or to laugh at me.

The first jump and here we go. I lost contact with the floor. Jumping was easier on the gym floor than in the yard.

"With a T–E–A–M yaaaay, team." I was enjoying the yelling. I had never yelled before for fun. I never dared make a peep at home.

I led now and completely forgot where I was and who was there. It just didn't matter any more.

At the second jump. I thought I would never come down. I was flying. I jumped, I turned, I yelled, I jumped again. I yelled louder. I saw Connie and Laura out of the corner of my eye—they were with me. We were together, and yet I felt alone as though I was the only one on stage. I was flying across the gym floor accompanying myself with the loudest yelling you could ever imagine. I had never been as noisy in front of anyone. It was great fun. Yelling and yelling, just for the fun of it.

Hurt, hate, anger, frustration, and fury all rolled themselves up in a ball and helped me yell. We yelled and we yelled and we yelled. Out came hate, out came fury, and out came anger, all happy to be free at last.

"T–E– and a LOUD A–M!"

I yelled some more just for good measure. And away I went again, jumping with all my might. I thought that I would reach the sky. Up, up, and away. Like Superman, without need of a cloak. My feet refused to stay on the floor.

"Come on Collins. Support your men."

Now, we all turned left and skipped across the gym. My feet took on energy of their own. Down, up, down, up, we flew together, my feet and me connected by hate, anger, and even fear, who himself was no longer afraid. We were friends all of us, and each had a part to play today.

"T–EAM, yaaaay team, team, yaaaay team."

There was no one telling me to keep quiet, no one telling me to stop jigging around. The more I yelled the more my voice deepened. I yelled and I yelled and I yelled.

And then, behind hate, out of nowhere, came a new friend from deep inside my heart. Her name was joy—and behind joy, came hope, proud to be with me, proud to have found recognition.

Hate surrendered to joy and hope, and we took over the show. We jumped, we leapt, we twirled, we spun, and then we jumped and leapt again. All the while, yelling and yelling and yelling, over and over again. Everyone was on fire, including me. We ended together and ran to our bench and sat down. I perched forward anticipating the next routine.

"Laura Wherehouse." It was Mrs. Selbourne. She was calling for the solos. Laura would go in front of me, then me, and then Connie. The final cheer, three minutes of our own routines. If we went over three minutes, we were automatically disqualified. I had practiced and practiced to keep my routine within the three minutes. I had a cartwheel planned at the end. I hadn't asked anyone to time me because I was too afraid they would laugh at my routine. I had to time myself and I was careful to check the mantel clock in the living room many times. I could only hope it was an accurate clock.

Connie and I watched Laura's routine. I did not think she was good. She was too heavy on her feet, and, at the same time, too dainty. She didn't seem to jump high.

I can do better than that.

Laura finished with a small straight jump. It was not spectacular, but when she returned to the bench, I congratulated her and said that I liked her routine. It was a lie. Lies were my specialty.

"Dolores Morgan." Mrs. Selbourne called me next.

I jumped off the bench feeling my ponytail in excited motion. I stopped in the middle of the floor, turned and faced the group of judges. Sixth grade was a long way back, but Miss Roberts's smile continued to warm my heart. And I smiled back, not with my face, with my heart. Beautiful Miss Roberts, there was no one better. Mr. Wilson was leaning back against the bleachers with his hands resting on his stomach, looking expectantly at me.

Mrs. Selbourne clicked her stopwatch and motioned to me to begin. I thought I detected a small smile of encouragement.

> "T–E and a LOUD A–M.
> T–E and loud A–M
> T–E and loud A–M
> Come on Collins,
> Support your men,
> With a T–E–A–M, Yaaaay team,
> T–E–A–M, yaaaay team,
> T–E–A–M, yaaaay team,
> TEAM, (get ready),
> TEAM (jump down),
> TEAM (jump up)."

I let the last one jump itself. My arms took me with them, and up I went, for a moment in time, suspended like a giant eagle. The sky belonged to me. I landed lightly, did one more jump and prepared for my cartwheel. I deliberately ended the last jump across the floor from the judges. I hesitated slightly to get their attention, jumped as high as I could and turned right towards the judge's stand, leapt again, and turned a one hand cartwheel landing in front of Mr. Wilson on one knee. Today, I didn't care if the girls thought I was his favorite or not, I was having the time of my life.

I bowed mostly to Mr. Wilson and Miss Roberts, jumped again, and ran to my seat next to Laura, my ponytail flashing in the gymnasium lights as I heard some scattered clapping.

Laura whispered to me. "That was a beautiful routine, Dee. If I were voting, I'd vote for you. I think you will win."

Mrs. Selbourne looked at her stopwatch and nodded to the judges. I had made the time frame.

I couldn't resist any more. I held both my fingers crossed and put them under my legs and then I did it. I dared to hope. I was *hoping.* I was *hoping* and *hoping.* My new friend hope shined in my brain as I turned to see if Mr. Wilson was looking. I didn't care if the other girls saw me. I had to know. Did I have a chance?

Mr. Wilson looked right at me as though he had been waiting for me to turn around. He gave me a huge smile and a "thumbs up," which was kind of hidden in his lap behind his paunch. I saw it, and I smiled back. I didn't care who saw me. I was just plain full of energy, not the energy of hate this time—it was hope, and joy. Hope and joy didn't want a back seat any more. Not today. Not ever.

For the rest of the afternoon, as the rest of the teams cheered, I tried to concentrate on them, but I was mostly interested in myself. I went over in my head my whole performance, trying to find an error. I had done the best I could with what God gave me. The rest was clearly up to Him.

Oh, please God, please.

There was one more final cheer with all of us together, which wasn't important since we all knew the judging was over. All the girls ended clapping, and we ran back to our seats still clapping. I wasn't even tired. I could have gone on all day. I was back sitting on the bench. Well not exactly sitting, I was perched, more like

a bird ready to take flight again. I had done it. I hadn't
forgotten a move. The world was mine.

The tryouts had ended as quickly as they had come,
and now there was only the excruciating long wait for
the list to be posted.

Mrs. Selbourne thanked all of us for trying out and
explained that the next fall's cheerleading squad would
be posted in the principal's office at three o'clock.
Almost one hour away—forever.

As soon as Mrs. Selbourne dismissed us, I headed
for Mr. Woodstock's Shop class. I was glad it was Shop
because I would not have to concentrate much. I was
building a silkscreen frame, which was easy and fun. I
had been working on it a long time and had gotten
special permission to use it as my class project instead
of the class projects that were simply assigned by Mr.
Woodstock. I was planning to make stationery with the
frame to write letters to my aunts. I planned a frame
and on top of the frame on two hinges rested the inset
for a piece of silk. I cut carefully and measured where to
put the silk. I hammered the silk into the frame with
small tacks. Each tack had a large head that would hold
the silk. Mr. Woodstock walked by me and said, "Good
job, Dee."

I was glad he continued without asking me any
questions because usually, I was totally focused on my
project, but today I was all pretense. I saw only a list in
the office, *was I on it? Oh, please, God, let me be on that list.*
The hammer missed the tack and came down right on
my thumb. Ouch.

I was again engrossed when the bell rang at 2:50,
signaling the end of the last class that day.

I quickly put my project back in its spot on the class
shelf, in a hurry to get to the principal's office. I exited

the class and walked as fast as I could without running. We were never allowed to run in school, and I certainly did not want to be stopped now. I took the steps two at a time, also not allowed, but there are times when there is no holding back a tide. The office was at the end of the hall. I walked quickly while at the same time trying to look casual. I didn't want anyone to know that I was in a hurry. If I didn't win they would feel sorry for me, and I couldn't have stood that. It was hard enough to lose without anyone enjoying your humiliation like George always did.

I was just down from the office now. I could barely breathe. At the door of the history classroom to the right was Mr. Wilson.

"Hello, Mr. Wilson." I smiled and tried to continue on my way. He called me.

"Dee, come here, I would like to speak with you."

I stopped because it would be rude not speak with him even though I was dying to get to the office.

He began with, "Dee, you are an interesting phenomenon. Most of us go to a lot of trouble to display what little assets we have. You seem to be hiding your far greater talents from us. I'm not allowed to say for whom I voted, but I can tell you that my opinion is that you did a beautiful job. I don't know if you won or not, but win or lose, be proud of yourself. You've got brains, you've got talent, and I'm expecting great things from you in high school and then, well, one day you'll write your own ticket. You're a lucky girl."

My mind was on the principal's office wall.

Mr. Wilson figured it out. He smiled. "Go ahead, Dee, hurry and take a look at the list, and good luck."

I was almost running now as I approached the end of the hall. There was a crowd of people in front of the office all straining to see the list. Avery Steerforth, the captain of the football team was coming towards me. Avery was a senior and never bothered with me. He hung out with the Bessie crowd. Except for that one time in Sixth Grade Dancing Class, he had never spoken to me.

Today, he looked right at me with a huge smile on his face, and said, "Dee, you made the squad. I saw your name. Congratulations." He waved as he passed by me.

I gasped. *Avery, talking to ME?* Could what he said be true? *It wasn't true.* He was being mean. Like George always was when I lost at something, sneering at me and laughing his ugly laugh as I was humiliated. I had to look for myself. It was the only way to know. I kept walking toward the office down the hall, this time more slowly, afraid of the finality of knowing.

Another person whom I didn't know passed me and said, "Congratulations, Dee, you made it."

And here again came ever-persistent hope. Dare I hope? Was it true?

More and more people were smiling and congratulating me, some of whom I didn't even know.

Colleen strode towards me, her face set in a menacing grimace. She spoke, hard and mean, "You only won because your mom used to be a cheerleader and helped form the first cheerleading squad."

I was dejected. I didn't want Colleen to be angry with me. She had been kind to me, when the others were not.

"Didn't you get it, Colleen?"

She answered "No, you made it because of your mother. Connie Green made it because her dad is on the school board, and Helen made it because of her dad being in real estate. He owns the whole town."

How could she think of all that stuff?

"I'm sorry. Please don't be mad at me. It's not fair. I wasn't angry with you when you made all the athletic teams and I didn't".

"That's different. You never had a chance to make any of those teams." She sulked.

I was beside myself. "I only became a cheerleader to try and make friends with everyone. I don't think I could stand it, if you don't want me as a friend any more."

Colleen hesitated for a long moment. She looked down at her shoes. "I'm sorry, Dee. You know, I'm really angry because you were good. You never showed me your solo routine. It was wonderful. Why didn't you show it to me before?"

"I was afraid to tell anyone. I thought you would laugh at it."

Colleen finally looked up at me. "It was wonderful, and you deserved to win. Don't pay any attention to my ramblings. I'm just jealous. I know the real reason that I didn't get on the squad. It's because my grades are too low. The teachers consider good grades very important because cheerleading needs people who can afford time away from homework, like you."

"Thank you, Colleen. For what it's worth, I think you were great. And without you encouraging me, I might have been afraid to try. Thank you for being the only person who believed in me." That really wasn't true, but I wanted her to feel better. Aunt Grace, Mrs. Smith, and Mrs. Selbourne had all believed in me. And, I would have tried out no matter how rejected Bessie had made me feel.

"I hope you'll try out next year."

Colleen looked sad as she answered, "Perhaps you'll be willing to help me with my solo routine next year."

I was thrilled. No one ever asked me for help except with their homework.

"I promise I will, Colleen. I can help you improve your grades, too. And, we'll make sure you win." I wanted her to like me. I didn't want anyone mad at me because I won. Cheerleading was my chance to be popular, and already I had almost made an enemy. I wished everyone could be like Laura Wherehouse. She was nice when she saw that I was better than she. And again, I realized how well liked Laura was. I took note. Whenever I lose I must remember to be like Laura. Laura's key to popularity had a lot to do with her style, not whether or not she was the best at everything.

But for now, I still wasn't completely convinced. I hadn't yet seen my name on any list. *Could it be true? Could it really be true?* I ignored the no running rule. I had never run in school before, but I had to know.

And there it was, people crowding around a list that was posted on the glass. I couldn't see over their heads, so I crouched under them and got to the front. Some said, "You made it, Dee." I looked at the list.

My name was right there. All the names blurred except for one, which stood out like a thousand cheers: **Freshman Candidate—Dolores Morgan.** It was too much to bear. I walked straight into the girls' room into one of the stalls and put the toilet seat down and sat on the seat. And then I cried. I cried and cried. I just couldn't stop crying. It was not possible. Did the Lord help me? He must have. Just when I thought He had deserted me He changed my whole life. *Please God, forgive me for thinking you didn't want me.*

I heard someone come into the girls' room and I quieted down as best I could. I used some toilet paper for a tissue and blew my nose and wiped my eyes. I flushed the toilet twice to cover the sounds.

As I left the stall and went to the sink to pretend to wash my hands, Cynthia Nelson, another senior smiled, "Congratulations, Dee, I heard you made the squad."

"Thank you, Cynthia." I didn't smile. I was afraid to appear too proud or conceited.

As I left school for home, I was too thrilled to even know where the ground was. I skipped and ran and jumped and leapt all the way as fast as I could to tell my mother. Several students waved to me whom I didn't know. As I passed Rosalee's house, she waved at me from the window. "I heard you won, Dee, Great!"

I think Rosalee was surprised. Rosalee was a star softball player, the pitcher, and she knew how bad I was at team sports. She saw me agonize every week as she was chosen first and I last. Well, now I had something better. A cheerleader—ME!

"Thank you. I'm on my way home to tell my mother." Finally, I had something to tell my mother. How I envied Rosalee as each day she went home to discuss the day's events with her mother. I wanted her to think that I, too, had one of those kinds of mothers.

"I know she'll be happy for you!" Rosalee shouted back, sure that all moms were eagerly awaiting their children to come home from school to discuss the day's events.

I skipped and danced. I passed Alex Miller's house. His older brother, Thaddeus, was out in the yard, trimming their hedges. I didn't know the Miller brothers well because they went to the Catholic Boys High School, but I saw Thaddeus in church a lot. He was a short, fat boy, with milk white pudgy hands with which he played the organ. Thaddeus was named after St. Jude Thaddeus, my favorite saint. Ted, as everybody called him was planning to enter the priesthood after high school.

"Hi, Dee, what're you so happy about?" questioned Ted as I skipped past him.

Still in my cheerleading outfit, I couldn't resist showing off as I turned a cartwheel on his front lawn and yelled over my shoulder. "I made the squad."

"What squad?"

"The Cheerleading Squad!"

"Hey that's great. Congratulations." He smiled his cheerful smile. "God bless you."

Two blocks of cartwheels later, I entered my own house where my mother was in the living room ironing. She liked to iron in the living room so she could see her favorite TV shows. She and Aunt Grace loved Jack LaLaine and his physical fitness show. I wondered why they just watched because it seemed to me they ought to get off the couch and exercise with him. I often thought of saying that to them, but never did.

Once I tried it myself to give them the idea, but my mother stopped me with her usual, "Dolly stop all that jiggin' around."

Jack LaLaine was saying, "You know it takes more calories to eat a carrot, then they have in them."

I interrupted, "Mom, I got it. I'm on the squad."

Brenda, of course, came down stairs to butt into my life as usual. "Did you get it?" I ignored her.

My mother put the iron down and turned. Her lips pursed as she tried to smile. "I guess you think I should be more excited. But you know, Dolly, *(would she ever stop using that name?),* I'm not at all surprised. I've always known you would make it. It never occurred to me that you wouldn't."

It made me feel proud. She had really thought I might be good at something.

She took a small book off the mantel. She had obviously been waiting to show it to me. It was an old book, with a leather bound padded cover. It looked like a library reference book. On the front was embossed: New Paltz State Normal School, New Paltz, New York.

She turned to a page she knew well. Brenda pushed her head in front of me so that I could hardly see, but I saw enough to be astonished. In a photo, were three cheerleaders with megaphones held high. In the middle of them was a younger version of my mom, a small, thin, woman, completely flat chested, not a breast in sight.

I was stunned. "Is that you, Mom?"

She answered, "Yes. You see that is how I knew you would make it. You take after me."

I was beginning to understand that my mom's life had had some interesting twists and turns. Her rage episodes were only one part of her.

My mother's pain took a back seat right now as I gloried in my achievement. I went upstairs to my room. Hope and Joy were born in me that day and they never left me. I vowed to change. This was my chance to be popular. I started to sing and dance in front of the mirror.

"I'm gonna change my way of living and if that ain't enough,
I'm gonna change the way that I strut my stuff,
'Cause nobody wants you when you're old and gray,
They'll be some changes made today,
They'll be some changes made."

In front of the mirror, I took an Al Jolson bow to the audience of one, me. In the mirror was a girl with a new light in her eyes, the light of hope.

15

In order to achieve anything, you must be brave enough to fail." Kirk Douglas

The phone rang. I wasn't allowed to answer, so I pretended to read. My mother called from downstairs, "Dolly, its Jeff Streeter. He's having the football team and the new cheerleading squad over to his house for a party."

I bolted down the stairs, realizing too late that it was the wrong way to get her to do something I wanted. Jeff was captain of the basketball team, a handsome and popular boy. He had never called me before this.

"Oh, Mom, can I please, please, please, please go?" I seldom begged. It usually guaranteed a no. To show that I wanted something was certain death to it.

"The question is '*May* I please go?'"

I corrected myself with, "May I please go?"

"I don't know, Dolly. He lives all the way over on Spruce Avenue."

"It's okay, Mom, I can walk. I used to walk further than that every day for church."

"Yes, but his is a night time party. It will be dark."

My heart sank. I looked at her pleadingly. I was desperate.

Relieved, I saw her face soften, and she said, "You can ask your dad if he will drive you when he gets home. If he will, you may go."

That was a yes. Whenever my mother turned an event over to my dad, it was a yes. He never said no to me.

I was beside myself with happiness. It would be a glorious party with boys and dancing and records. I couldn't believe it.

When my dad got home, he drove me to Jeff's house. "Call me if you need a ride, Dee. I'll come and get you"

"I can walk, Dad. It's not far."

"Well, find someone to walk home with, okay? Is Rosalee going?'

"Yes." A lie.

My dad leaned over me and pushed the passenger door of the Mercury open. "Okay, remember, don't walk home alone."

I jumped out of the car and closed the door. I entered Jeff's brown frame house through a side door that opened to a dark, rug less room. The floor was linoleum and there was a small bar in the corner where some people were drinking cokes. In the corner, there was a small table lamp with a blue bulb, surrounded by several haphazard piles of 45s. This rich intoxicating gloom with loud enticing music set off several couples huddled together on the linoleum floor, pretending to dance. I recognized Bessie and Gilbert who simply held each other close, with little or no movement. Embarrassed, I turned my attention to the record player still amazed that Jeff had all those records to himself and was actually allowed to play them. I wasn't even allowed a radio of my own.

The musical group The Platters was singing "The Great Pretender".

> "Oh, yes, I'm the great pretender,
> Pretending that I'm doing well,
> My need is such I pretend too much,
> I'm lonesome and no one can tell."

That song was the story of my life, one big pretense. Pretending to be happy when there was hardly a moment when I wasn't afraid of something. I was scared to death and yet I had to pretend to be having a good time. How could I have a good time while I was in a state of panic?

Two of the smaller boys sifted through the records, looking for something.

"Let's find a Lindy or something fast. This is too slow," said one of the boys to the other. I recognized Jeff's younger twin brothers, Grover and Benjamin, who looked exactly alike. They had dark, brown hair, thick and curly, small but well-shaped bodies, athletes-to-be, like their brother, Jeff. They both had happy, grey eyes that seemed ready for any devilment that might come their way.

My mood changed a little now because all the class was pouncing on me, saying congratulations for making the cheerleading squad, acting like I was important.

Avery asked me to dance. Oh my, I was again in terror. The captain of the football team. Why would he dance with me? I was in a panic as I tried to remember what I had been taught at ballroom dance class. I thought he might be doing a box step but there was no box formed. Then maybe it was a fox trot. I didn't know. I remembered to let him lead and tried really hard to follow him. Avery pulled me closer. Oh dear. This was much closer dancing than in dance class. Mr. Appleton would not approve.

It became impossible to guess what kind of a dance it was. I felt a lump on my leg. Did Avery have something in his pocket? His hands were sweaty and so were mine. I had never been so nervous. The thing in his pocket was hot. It almost burned my leg. I moved back. He moved forward. Every time I move away from the heat, Avery moved forward. He seemed to want his leg right there.

The dance ended, thanks to God, and I walked away. I didn't know what to say because he didn't say thank you. In dance class, it was the boy's place to say thank you. I couldn't figure out what the girl was supposed to say when the boy didn't say thank you so we just awkwardly parted company with no sound at all.

I didn't dance too much, but many people talked with me. Then Jeff called out the last dance. Again it was "The Great Pretender."

> "My need is such,
> I pretend too much,
> I'm lonesome and no one
> Can tell."

Avery asked me to dance again, and it was the same, the heat of his pocket and me trying unsuccessfully to politely move away.

> "Too real is this feeling of make-believe
> Too real when I feel what my heart can't conceal."

The dance ended, but Avery's clammy hand didn't move away. Instead, he pulled me closer to him and whispered, "May I walk you home?"

I said yes, thrilled that he would want to. My heart was pounding again. It seems my life was meant to be spent in stark terror. My father told me not to walk home alone, but I'm sure he meant I should walk with my girlfriends. I don't think either Dad or I had thought of what to do if a boy wanted to walk me home.

I had heard in school that if a boy walked you home, he would probably try and kiss you goodnight. I had already decided to let Avery try it. As we walked up my walk, he leaned towards me to kiss me. I moved toward him just as the all too bright porch lights turned their glare on us. *Oh no, not my dad.* My father greeted Avery with a knowing grin as I tried to crawl under the stone beneath me. I was mortified and furious with my father. How could he take my first chance for a kiss away from me? He had no right.

"Hello, Mr. Morgan," Avery said politely.

"Hi Avery, why don't you come in?"

Come in? What in the world for? More terror engulfed me as I desperately tried to figure out what Dad, Avery, and I were going to talk about in the living room together.

Avery said, "No, thank you." He looked embarrassed, too.

"Goodbye, Dee. I'll see you tomorrow. Goodbye Mr. Morgan." He turned and walked down our path. I had lost my chance and would not get another.

I didn't say anything to my dad as I entered the house. I was just too angry.

He said nonchalantly, "How was the party?" and went back to watching the fights on television. He didn't seem really interested.

"It was nice."

The next day at school was great. For once, I knew about the party that was the subject of the conversations, and I was glad to feel a part of a group.

"I heard Avery Steerforth walked you home," Colleen smirked.

I answered, "Yes."

"Did he kiss you?"

"No, my dad came to the door."

"Oh yeah, my dad does that too. It's horrible."

The bell rang for Art class. As I went down to the basement stairs to get to the laboratory, Avery stopped me on the landing. I peeked at his pocket to see if I could figure out what caused the bump last night.

He caught me on my upper arm and squeezed tight. It hurt. He handed me a note with the other hand and walked on up the steps.

I read. "If you want pt, you can have pt, It is 7 and 1/2 inches long."

I had no idea what "pt" meant.

In Art class, I showed the note to Colleen.

She was shocked as she read it. She whispered, "You better show this to your brother right away. Do you know what it means?"

I answered, "No." I had no idea.

"Show it to your brother." Colleen really liked my brother. I, for one, would have never showed him anything, but she insisted.

"Promise me you'll show your brother."

"Okay." I was trying to be nice to Colleen after she got angry with me for making the squad without her.

When I arrived home, George was upstairs in his room.

"Avery Steerforth gave me a note. I don't understand it. Colleen said I should show it to you."

George glanced at the note, and then looked again. He turned white, said nothing, ran downstairs, and called to my mother. "Where's Dad?"

"He's down in the garage."

I heard George go down the cellar steps two at a time towards the garage.

Then I heard the loudest bellow I've ever heard from my dad. "I'll KILL HIM!"

Oh dear, what had I done. My father bounded up the cellar steps two at a time. He climbed those steps as fast as he did when the fire bell sounded and that was fast.

"Spence, what *is* the matter?" It was my mother calling from the kitchen.

"I'm going to beat that kid within an inch of his life."

"Who, Spence, who?" I went to the top of the stairs and looked down. My mother was blocking the front door. "No, Spence, no. Don't go."

"Move out of the way, Anne. I'm going to kill him."

I saw the back of my father. His shoulder muscles were big anyway and now they were huge and tense inside of his shirt, bursting with rage. My mother looked terrified. I didn't blame her. My dad was an amateur boxer. I wouldn't want to be beaten up by him.

The moment seemed like forever as my mother unsuccessfully tried to block my father from going out the door.

"Move OUT of the way, Anne."

After what seemed like forever, my mother relented and let Dad past. He flung open the door and disappeared outside. I looked out the window. In the twilight, my dad's white shirt shone. He ran up the street towards Avery's house, the fury in him almost smoking, out of control.

My mother said, "George, go with him. Don't let him hurt that boy." She held the door open and George bounded after my father, his white fruit boots reflecting in the twilight as he ran. They were as fast as the wind.

My mother went immediately to the phone.

"Exel 8-5515, operator, please hurry."

It was the school telephone number.

"Hello, Mabel. Where is John Emerson?" My mother asked the secretary for the guidance counselor.

"Yes, I need him right now."

She wrote something down, said thank you and phoned again.

"Yes, operator, Exel 8-1222 and hurry please."

"Mr. Emerson, this is Anne Morgan. I need your help. Spence is on his way to Avery Steerforth's house. He's furious at something to do with Dolly. Spence says he is going to kill one of the boys." My mother's voice was as frightened as I had ever heard it. "He'll do it, John. He'll do it. I know him. You've got to stop him."

"Yes, he's headed to his house right now. I'm going to call Charlie Malone next."

Charlie was a fireman, a friend of my dad's and a favorite of mine.

"Thank you, John." There was silence. She made another call.

"Charlie, it's Anne. Spence is on his way to Avery Steerforth's house. He's furious. He says he's going to kill him."

There was no more conversation. Before she had even hung up, I saw Charlie's car coming from the firehouse speeding down our street. Charlie, at the wheel, his face in a deep concentrated grimace, drove fast. Andy Black, also a fireman and one of my dad's friends, sat next to him, pointing up the street as if to give directions.

My mother looked, relaxed a little, and sat down in the living room

"Dolly, what in the world did you tell George?"

"Nothing, it was about a note I got from a boy in school," I answered.

"What did the note say?"

"It said, 'If you want pt, you can have pt. Pt is seven inches long.'"

My mother looked puzzled. "Where is the note now?"

"I don't know. I gave it to George."

"Go upstairs and look on the top of George's dresser, see if you can find it and bring it here."

I looked on George's dresser and there it was. I picked it up, read it again, and stopped dead in my tracks.

Then I knew, that I had made a terrible mistake. The note didn't say, "If you want pt, you can have pt." When Avery wrote it, he dotted the I's with little round circles. I mistook them for the letter P. The note really read: "If you want it, you can have it. It is 7 and 1/2 inches long."

This time I knew exactly what it meant, and I understood why Colleen had become upset.

This was the end of my life. I would be the laughing stock of school for telling on Avery.

I handed the note to my mother. "Oh, dear God." She was angry in a different way than I knew before. Her back stiffened. "When and where did he give you this note?"

I explained.

"Well, I hope for his sake, your father does not catch up with him." She seemed to have changed her mind. If Dad caught up with him—fine.

She looked straight at me. "Do you understand what the note says?"

"Sort of."

"I'm going upstairs to call Grace. I need her advice."

My mother asked advice of Aunt Grace a lot, which was usually good for me. Aunt Grace talked her into letting me go places and buy things when she normally said no.

"We'll see what to do when your dad gets home."

My mother talked with Aunt Grace as I waited in silence wondering why I was always in trouble.

"I don't know Grace. All I can tell you is Spence is absolutely furious. Grace, I've got to go. Spence is home. Call me later." Aunt Grace always called my mother. If my mother wanted her she rang her phone and hung up after two rings, so as not use too many message units.

I heard my dad call to Charlie and Andy as the fire truck drove away. "Thanks, Charlie. Thanks, Andy, I owe you one."

I was sent upstairs to my room, as my mother and father talked in lowered voices in the dining room. I moved to the top of the stairs, my usual eavesdropping position. I couldn't hear too much except that my father didn't hit Avery.

"That kid had the luck of the Irish with him tonight because I would have killed him had Charlie and Andy not shown up. That kid is a spoiled, conceited brat."

"Spence let John Emerson take it from here. That's his job." My mother spoke quietly, trying to soften my father.

My father snapped back, "If I ever catch him around her again, I'll finish what I started. He'll be unrecognizable."

"Let Mr. Emerson handle it, Spence." She was back to calling Mr. Emerson by his last name. This meant she was more in control of herself. I was glad.

My father ignored her. "Just don't let me catch him around her, period."

My party-girl life came and ended that day. And, it was my entire fault. I was so stupid that I misread the note and Avery got into all kind of trouble because of me. His parents were told; he was suspended from school and was kicked off the football team for the rest of his senior year.

When no one was looking, I hit myself on the side of my head, over and over again, "You are just dumb, just dumb."

§§§§§§

No one asked me out. I was considered "jail bait." And, Avery treated me like he wanted to poison my whole lunch tray. My father took over my social life. He and the other fathers took turns driving us to functions.

In some ways, I actually liked my dad's attention because as he became more active in my life, the beatings from my mother lessened. He chatted with my friends as he drove us to and from functions, and he joked with the other fathers about the parties. The girls liked my dad. I was proud of him. When he could not drive, he arranged for Barbara's father to take me in his cab. I never walked to or from a party. When Dad wasn't around, the firemen seemed to be. At the Fourth of July carnival, at the annual parades, at church, after school, I sensed the comforting presence of them, mostly in the background, the volunteer firemen, cheerful, shouting hello, companionable and ever watchful of Spence's daughter.

My Dad found me a job as a switchboard operator after school and during the summer. "Number please. Thank you. Number please. Thank you," I spoke all day long into the headset at the switchboard. The job and homework pretty much canceled any social life anyway.

After Avery graduated, other boys asked me out sometimes, and I went. But there was little chance to be someone's girlfriend, not under the watchful eye of my father and his friends.

Hope and hate and I stuck together, and we somehow made it through. Hate was the bossy one, but every time hate tried to take over my life, I yelled it out on the football field. And always, behind hate, beautiful, ever optimistic, dear hope would surface to remind me that some day I would be free. Some day I would be my own person, and mistakes would be allowed.

I did change some. I loved cheering, and I got some invitations. Mostly I waited. I waited for the day I would be free of the Morgan family jailhouse. Each night I went to sleep, looked up at the sky, at my lucky star, Monk Webber. Next to him, was the new bright star of hope, shining in the darkness to light my way.

In the next few years, I returned to my early habit of going to daily mass. I didn't know that God would again visit me and send me another great gift, a gift for which I would be grateful for the rest of my life.

16

"If we cannot now end our differences, at least we can help make the world safe for diversity." John Fitzgerald Kennedy

The undergraduate college years went by like a rushing circus train. I'll never forget college. I'll never forget Leah Day Hall. I'll never forget Carolyn, my first best friend. I'll never forget the first time I got drunk and my first grade of D. Most of all, I'll never forget the exhilaration of finally being on my own. Autonomy is truly God's greatest gift. The Morgan Family Jailhouse was far behind as I began to see my dreams becoming reality. I studied hard, joined almost every organization, became sorority Treasurer, became Class Treasurer, but most of all I just became.

As my senior year approached, I just didn't want to go home. I was, after all, good at something. I was good at going to college. Scared, yes, but also determined, I won a post-graduate grant to Pennsylvania State University.

It was hard to believe, but I made it to graduate school. Here I was, amidst the hustle and bustle of students all loaded down with books in their arms rushing to and fro because registration day was at hand. I too, was frantic, looking for the address where I was to live.

I wasn't completely on my own in the undergraduate years because I lived on campus. Here at Penn State, only my classes had been set. For everything else, I would be completely on my own. The university provided only a suggested list for housing in town.

The independence excited me—I feared nothing. I was free to make my own decisions as to my life, and I dreamed about this for so long that it seemed completely natural as I walked up and down South Allen Street, my suitcase getting heavier and heavier. The graduate school gave me an address on South Allen, 123 & ½ and yet there was no 123 & ½. There was a 123 and a 125, but no 123 & ½. I looked at the index card again. It did indeed say 123 & ½. I began to think the university had made a mistake. I was going to have to walk all the way back to the campus and try to find what the address should be. If only there was a place to put my suitcase. It was getting really heavy. My feet hurt, too. I had walked all day all over the huge campus dragging this suitcase everywhere.

I was pretty unsure of myself as I entered a jewelry store that had the address 123. "Excuse me, Sir." I spoke to the kindly looking gentleman behind the counter with a jewelry glass in his right eye. There was a soft paunch like Mr. Wilson's pushing gently against the small glass counter.

"Yes?" He smiled as he looked up and his gentle face encouraged me.

I continued. "Excuse me, Sir, I'm sorry to trouble you, but can you tell me where 123 & ½ South Allen Street is?"

He let out a huge laugh, a guffaw, which reminded me of Father McAvoy. "How come no one can ever find that place? I really must change the sign to make it easier." He smiled again as if to reassure me that my walk with the heavy suitcase was nearing an end. "The apartment is over this store, right above us." He pointed up. I looked. He chuckled, enjoying this little joke on me. "I guess you're wondering how to get to it." Tired as I was, I didn't quite see the humor, but I tried to be polite. I was puzzled and out of patience. There was no sign of a staircase.

"Don't worry, little lady, there is no ladder required," he smiled again. He seemed like a thinking man, quiet and smart. "Just go out the front door to my store, turn right, and go down the next alley. At the end of the corridor you'll see a door. Go into that door and up the stairs. The door to the apartment is right in the center upstairs. It's a little dark in the hallway, so be careful."

"Thank you, Sir." At last, I thought, my long walk with the heavy suitcase might be over.

I picked up the suitcase, hoping my new roommate would like me and that this was the end of my long journey. I never had an apartment before. I was pretty scared, but at the same time, exhilarated to be free in a world that seemed a lot more welcoming than my home.

The alley was dark. To some it might be dreary, but to me, it was my first apartment, another chance at happiness. I didn't see the darkness—I saw only the bright light of hope leading my way.

As I clamored up the steps, I tried not to make too much noise, but the suitcase insisted—clunk, clunk.

As I reached the top, a door opened. "Excuse me, Miss, I'm sorry to have made so much noise. My suitcase is heavy."

"Hi," a blond woman with smiling blue eyes responded. "Have you come to see the apartment to share?"

"Yes," I answered, taken aback by her beauty, the long flowing yellow hair, and the blue eyes. "Are you Loni Randall?"

She nodded and smiled again.

Encouraged, I went on. "I got your name from the campus graduate school registrar."

"Well, come in and see how you like the apartment. You might not want to stay. It's small."

I studied her as she explained the apartment. She was indeed beautiful, with full rosy lips accenting the clear blue eyes and long dark lashes. Complementing her beauty was her voice, which had a lilt to it and a touch of an Irish accent. She was about my height and held her head high as the curly tresses fell over her shoulders. She wasn't fat, neither was she thin. Her body was sensuous and appealing. I could tell by looking at her that she had a boyfriend. Certain kinds of girls always do. I could always tell the girls that boys like. That place in the hearts of men could never be mine. I was too scrawny, too smart. I knew that already. Sometimes a girl could overcome smarts with extra good looks, but I didn't have the beauty.

Loni took my coat as she turned into a small, narrow living room behind her. Snuggled between the living room and the kitchen was a table and benches forming a booth. Through the kitchen was a small hallway. She turned right toward the booth, and I followed. She paused.

"I'm a secretary on campus, and this is my apartment. They accepted me for graduate housing because I work at the campus, although, I'm not a student there." She looked at me and hesitated a little. "Perhaps you'd rather have another graduate student like yourself for a roommate. You're not required to take this place if you don't want to. They will give you other choices."

I didn't answer. I kept thinking how nice she seemed.

She turned back and looked me squarely in the eyes. "I see you're hesitating. You don't have to take it. But come in and look around just in case. She passed the little booth with the benches and the small table. "Here's the living room." There was a couch, an easy chair, and a small television forming a circle around a large bay window that looked out on to South Allen St. I could see the pedestrians walking quickly by, having so much to do to get ready for school. I was one of them.

Loni, still talking about the place, squeezed back past the table and me and turned into the other side of the kitchen. A row of cupboards, a stove, a sink, and refrigerator on one wall seemed to me to be the coziest little kitchen in the world. Past the kitchen on the right of the hallway was a bathroom with a shower. The little hallway gave way to a yellow bedroom, which reminded me of the artists, Paul Gauguin and Vincent Van Gogh in *Lust for Life* when they lived in their yellow house in France. On the wall near the door were two twin beds that were only a few inches apart. The bed near the window was rumpled. The one near the door was made.

Loni touched the bed that was made with well-manicured nails as I thought how nice it would be to have time for things like doing my nails. I was usually studying and everything else seemed like time stolen from my books. "This would be your bed if you come." She shrugged her shoulders and glanced awkwardly around the room. "That's it. That's all there is. I know it's small. Perhaps you would prefer something bigger? You look surprised. Is it too small or is it because I'm not a graduate student?"

I wanted to say that it looked like Heaven to me, that it was wonderful, that it was beyond happiness to think of it as mine—that she was beautiful and kind—that I never saw anything as lovely as this apartment and her—that I was the happiest person in the world to find it.

I didn't say any of it.

"I like it. Would you consider letting me stay? I'm in the graduate school here for two years."

She smiled. I'm glad you like it. The rent is forty-two dollars and fifty cents per month. Can you afford that much? It includes water, electric, and heat. We would have to split the telephone bill."

"Yes. I can afford it." My grant didn't cover housing. My mother had offered to pay my rent for one year if I promised to live at home after I graduated and pay her room and board. I had promised instantly because I was desperate to go to graduate school and decided to worry about tomorrow when it came. Today is now, and I found an apartment with a beautiful blond woman named Loni.

§§§§§§

Oh, how happy we were, Loni Randall and I—she, the street-smart life of the party with the lilting laugh and funny German boyfriend named Gunner, and I, the naïve bookish dreamer. We shopped for groceries together, planned meals, and took turns cooking. No one was the boss—we made our decisions together.

Early one morning, as I studied in bed, Loni leapt off her bed. "Dee, guess what." She went quickly to our shared closet.

I was groggy from studying well into the night and then getting up early. I didn't respond.

She went on. "Today's the day I was telling you about. Senator John F. Kennedy is coming to the campus to campaign. He'll be at the Main Hall at ten o'clock this morning. Are you coming with me?" She searched the closet for something to wear.

"I can't Loni. I've got to study." This was my mantra when Loni persistently tried to get me out and about as much as she could.

"Come on, Dolly-Grad; take a break for one morning, that's all. What are you studying for? Can't it wait until tomorrow?"

Loni call me Dolly-Grad whenever she wanted to tease me about being an egghead. I hated the name Dolly, and she knew it, although, when she said it, it didn't sound as bad as my mother's constant nagging. Loni spoke with love and understanding, and the word came out differently from her lips.

I answered with my head still in the book, "Political Science 501—we have a test on Monday. Who is John F. Kennedy?" From my protected cocoon of college campuses I knew little of the outside world.

"Oh, Dee, he's a handsome United States Senator from Massachusetts. He was in the Navy and he commanded a PT boat. Monday is a zillion years away. Come on. Here's a Poly Sci lesson falling right into your lap. You might never have another chance to meet a U. S. Senator."

I gave in. I was tired of studying and a handsome Navy man intrigued me, as I recalled Mr. Wilson's and my admiration of PT boats. I closed the book and put the notes underneath it on the nightstand between our beds. "Alright, Loni, but no bars after, okay? I'm afraid of this test on Monday."

"Deal—no bars for lunch." Loni threw me my jeans and put on her own.

We hurried to campus where there was already a line weaving up the hill to the meeting. There were tables arranged on the front portico of the Victorian A-Frame that housed some of the history professors. Behind the tables were a few men in business suits seeming busy and always shaking hands with someone.

I couldn't see him well, but as we moved along in the line I got a glimpse of a mighty handsome figure, tan and strong looking although a little thin. He smiled almost all the time, a great big toothy smile. He had a twinkle in his eyes as he looked at each person with interest and shook each hand. Even from my distant perspective it was clear the conversations were lively and full of mirth.

As we approached the top of the hill, someone with a clipboard and pen asked me my name.

"Dee Morgan." I responded to a man in a dark blue suit. He asked me where I was from as he gently nudged me towards Senator Kennedy and announced my name.

"Edgemont, New York," I answered softly. I was overwhelmed and quiet.

Senator Kennedy took my hand. "What town did you say, Dee? I didn't hear you?" His interest was sincere.

"Edgemont, New York, Mr. Kennedy." I spoke up not wanting to be a silent dolt forever. As usual, I goofed. I should have said Senator Kennedy. He was gracious and didn't seem to notice as I blushed a dreadful deep crimson at my faux pas.

Senator Kennedy kept my hand in his as he called to another man, who was strikingly similar in appearance. "Hey, Bobby, we have some support in Edgemont, New York, right here."

The man called Bobby laughed, "Forget it, Jack, that's Westchester County. The whole county is Republican."

We all laughed then, as I answered, bravely, "Everyone minus one."

Senator Kennedy shook both my hands together and smiled a large ingratiating smile. "Please vote for us. We need votes there."

I didn't' tell him that it was my first time ever voting and he had won my heart in thirty seconds.

As I hesitated, Loni, who had just said her name behind, answered, "We will. Senator Kennedy, thank you." She flashed them both a Loni Randall smile as charming as their own. Loni didn't even live in New York. She lived in Pennsylvania. What a liar!

They began questioning Loni about her Irish accent and a lively conversation about Ireland began. As for me, I was silent as a desert. The ground gave way again. He was incredibly handsome. My heart pounded. I blushed; I stammered. I was so mortified I actually hoped he would move on to the next people so my insides would settle down.

"Well girls, I hope to win New York. Will you be voting for me, Dee? You seem too young to vote." He fixed his eyes on me again. This time, the ground didn't just move, it shook. There was an earthquake on its way, and I was about to be swallowed up.

"No, Senator Kennedy, I'm not too young to vote." This time I got his name right. "I've already applied for a proxy ballot, and I shall vote for you." I even remembered my proper English.

"*Shall* being stronger than *will* and implying a promise." Senator Kennedy seemed gleeful as he answered. I smiled right at him this time. I was getting pretty bold.

"You see, Dee, I'm a senator, but I know correct grammar when I see it, I studied English Literature in college. I wanted to be a writer. What do you want to be, Dee?"

"I don't know yet." My usual answer to that question was anything but a teacher, but for some reason I answered simply, "I don't know." That sounded stupid, but I really didn't now. The future seemed far away today.

"Well, maybe you'll be like me, study one thing and be something else. Good luck to you, Dee."

He turned to the next person, but not before he squeezed my hand just a little bit and finished our conversation with, "Thank you, girls." He smiled again at Loni, who smiled back, "Now, go ahead over to the table with my little brother, Bobby, and sign up for the committees you would like to join. We need lots of help." That's why I saw a resemblance. The man he called Bobby was his brother.

I liked the phrase "my little brother, Bobby." The softness in his voice, when, he said "Bobby" made them really pals. My brother and I were not pals. We were strangers. I think that was the thing I was most jealous of that day. Jack Kennedy had a real brother—I had none.

In a blink of an eye, Senator Kennedy seemed to forget all about Loni and me. I was grateful he had turned away, for I was much too long in the sun. Senator Kennedy excited me like nothing I'd ever experienced before.

Loni came up behind me and we headed to the next table to sign for a committee. There was a young woman ahead of me as I waited my turn to sign. She put her name on the list—Judy Wellington—and passed the pen to me to sign.

As I took the pen, someone behind bumped into me. I lost my balance and dropped the pen. The girl in front of me and I both bent over at the same time to pick it up. We bumped heads.

Bobby Kennedy turned. "Ow." He jumped in to help. "Is everybody okay?"

I was still on my knees adjusting my glasses. The other girl spoke first. "I'm sorry, it was my fault." She looked directly at me as she handed me the pen. There was no mistaking those beautiful dark eyes.

We both screamed in unison.

I cried, "Judy!'

Judy screamed "Dolly!" We were in each other's arms. Judy backed away and we looked again at each other. I couldn't believe it. It was Judy. She was right here next to me, her tan skin and dark eyes more beautiful than ever.

I went straight to Heaven. We talked for a long time, right there on the sidewalk. Nobody even asked us to move on. People know when not to interfere. Loni stood alongside listening, herself a little bit awed by Judy and me as we talked about our ill-fated friendship in grammar school. Judy talked about her dad, Hugh Wellington, and how she had moved to England to be with him when her mother died. She explained that she was a year behind me because she had lost a year switching to the schools in England.

That was when I learned another new word from Judy. I once learned the word mulatto because of her, and now she talked earnestly about Jack Kennedy and a new term to me, "civil rights." She called him "Jack" as though he were her best friend and talked about how Jack and Bobby were hope for the black people.

"Judy, are you majoring in Political Science?" It was Loni asking her.

Judy looked right at me with those wonderful eyes and said, "No, English Literature. Dolly used to read to me in the library, and I fell in love with her favorite book, *David Copperfield*."

Judy remembered well. Thomas Wolfe was my favorite author, but *David Copperfield* by Charles Dickens was my favorite book.

"Judy," I cried, "you mean you loved him, enough to study English Literature?"

"Oh Dolly, didn't you know how much I envied you and all your friends in those books. I wanted to know all about them."

I put my head down. "Oh, Judy, you know much more than I do about them now. You're an English Literature Major!" It was my turn to be jealous.

"I'll never know more than you know. I've only studied Charles Dickens—you were transformed by him. You're the real expert. I wish I could have read more of him when I was young, like you. It's a far better knowledge."

"I feel like it's because of me that you chose English Literature, and we've met again. That's the most important thing between us."

As we all agreed with that, Loni, Judy, and I walked away from the campus, all three together, arm-in-arm, blocking the sidewalk and not caring. I began to think of that day when I lost Judy. She was thinking of it, too, I could tell.

I wanted to ask Judy a favor. "Judy, would you mind calling me Dee instead of Dolly? I don't go by that name any more. I changed it to change my personality to a better one and forget all about those days."

Judy thought for a long moment. "Okay, Dolly, I mean Dee, yes, I'll call you Dee if you want. But please don't change your personality. You were and are still the sweetest, kindest child in the sixth grade class. I would never want you to change one iota." She gave me a little hug which reminded me of when her mom hugged us both goodbye, that day long ago on the other side of the tracks.

"No one calls me Negro or colored any more either. We're black people now."

It was then that I started to cry—not just a little cry, but great big wracking sobs. My stomach was on fire, I was gasping for air and yet I cried. I couldn't stop. Judy was holding me on one side and Loni was holding me on the other side, but I couldn't stop. They were holding me so tight that I thought my shoulders would be crushed between them. I felt Loni's breasts against me, warm and comforting, different than my mother's. I felt Judy's thin body next to me, a different body, but just as comforting.

A college student passed by, hesitated, looked and then stopped. "Is everything all right? Do you need some help?" He seemed concerned.

Judy let go of me, looked up, and said, "No, indeed, Sir, believe it or not, these are tears of joy."

The boy laughed and walked on. "Okay, if you say so." Boys don't understand these things.

We three, too, began to laugh. There I was, sitting on a bench crying with my two friends, one new and one old, one black and one white, one with the blackest eyes in the universe, and one with the bluest. I was the happiest person alive. I was not going home to a beating either. Perhaps, I was never going home at all, for it was 1960, the beginning of a new decade, and I had done it. I had gotten away from my mother, even if for just one moment in time.

Judy, Loni, and I joined the campus organization Young Democrats to Elect John F. Kennedy President. We worked our hearts out, made up campaign songs, handed out leaflets, and just plain determined to get JFK elected. I had at least one zillion arguments with my staunch Republican father. I never gave in. I was an adult by government standards—I could vote as I pleased. I picked JFK. He was mine. My proxy vote flew to New York on gilded wings.

My father moaned, "He'll bring back the New Deal," when I telephoned him on Election Night, feeling as though I, and, I alone was responsible for his election.

Funny, but after that, Dad saw me in a new light. He joked with me a lot and was always asking for my fiery opinions about anything and everything political. It became kind of our fun, Dad and me, two political adversaries, at political war, and yet in love with each other.

"Did you read what your friends in Washington did today?" he'd ask whenever he called me at school.

I'd answer, pleased as punch with myself and my "friends in Washington," "Oh no, what have *we* done now? Raised taxes again?" That would be his cue to go into a tirade about something or other stimulating his political fervor. I didn't care a hoot about his opinions. I thought he was "out of it," but I loved him, and he loved me. And I didn't really care what we talked about and neither did he. We just liked to be on the phone together. For years after, we called each other to discuss politics every week no matter where I was until the day he died.

17

"She is free who knows how to keep in her own hands the power to decide." Salvador de Madariaga

The conferring of the Master's Degree was a solemn affair, and Judy, Loni, and I were solemn, too. I said goodbye to Judy as she went back to England and to Loni who married Gunner and moved to Wilkes-Barre, Pennsylvania. I was left to face departure alone. My bags were packed and the apartment cleared. At night I visited the deserted campus, all alone with my memories and my fear of the future with my mother. My stomach ached. I could not face the end of it. I planned to return each fall and maybe every year, forever.

Finally, one cold, rainy morning, when there seemed to be nothing else to do, I just left and returned to Edgemont. I had no idea how difficult life would be for both my mother and me. I missed my autonomy, I missed my friends, and I missed my life. I didn't want to be a teacher. I had a whole new set of skills, and yet the only job available for a girl seemed to be teacher or nurse. I needed financial independence, but how to open that door was my dilemma. If teaching was the only choice, than I would have to grin and bear it.

Every time I brought up a new idea my mother found a way towards teaching. I had reached a point where I hated the word. "Mom, I don't want to be a teacher," I said, "I want to be a writer."

"Well, you can do that and be a teacher, too. You can write children's books."

There was no way out. All I had was a teaching degree. My Master's Degree in Psychology seemed useless because to become a guidance counselor, I needed three years of practical teaching experience. Time was running out and there was no alternative.

My mother arranged two interviews at local schools for me, but I failed to land either teaching job. I just couldn't be enthusiastic in the interviews. It wasn't what I wanted to do. At one interview, I lisped on purpose.

Fall was rapidly approaching while I lived at home with no job and no life.

What's wrong with staying home and taking care of your mother?" My mother continually asked me.

I never answered because there shouldn't be anything wrong with that—but there was.

Every day, I paced up and down Edgemont Avenue, dejected, thinking and thinking. Could I get a summer job first and then see about the teaching problems in September? I could probably find summer employment in a shop or go back to the club and take the switchboard operator's job.

Sometimes, I went to talk with Father McAvoy. We sat in the church garden and drank iced tea with the statue of the Virgin Mary quietly beside us.

"Dee," he would say, "you're like the mustard seed. You must find a place where you can grow. Don't choose too soon, don't get picked too green. With your mind, there is nothing more important than growth." He talked to me about other rich cultures and I longed to find my way to them. I trusted Father and his quiet, wise and reassuring judgment, but my riddle of life seemed too difficult even for him.

Every time, I thought I had found a way out, my mother sabotaged it. How could I hide anything from my nosey mother? I tried a job serving ice cream at Howard Johnson's, but during one of her "search and seizure" forays into my room, she found my Howard Johnson's uniform in the closet and her familiar rage took hold.

She tossed the uniform to the floor. "No daughter of mine is going to work at Howard Johnson's. Don't be ridiculous. You're living at home. You don't need any money. Your dad and I will support you. You can work as a substitute teacher for a while until you find a full-time teaching job. You'll live here until you pay your family back for your education and all that we've given you. After that, we'll see." The trap had closed—disguised as rich benefits from my big-hearted mother. There was no way out. I was never going to get away from her.

§§§§§§

I rode buses to different towns, searching every day, for work. One day, I found myself in the center of a town called White Plains. Straddling the corner of the main street was a shiny, almost all glass building with an inviting glass door.

"Maybe I can get a summer job there. It's a new building," I said to no one in particular, as I descended the bus, paused only a moment, walked into the magical door, and up the gleaming staircase to the second floor. I opened a second glass door into a large room with dark wood desks lined up in rows, a telephone on each desk and a small plaque facing outwards, engraved with the word: **THINK**.

Several men in dark suits, white shirts, and ties were milling around talking or on the telephone. They looked up as I entered. A man in a dark blue suit, white shirt, and a steel gray tie came confidently out of an odorless, glass-paneled corner office in front of the large room. He was older, at least thirty-five, and had a receding hairline where once there was red hair. His face was pale and slightly scarred from teen-age acne.

He looked directly at me. "May I help you?"

I felt like an intruder as I answered, "I'm interested in a summer job. I've just finished college." I didn't tell him what college because I was afraid he'd send me off to get a teaching job. I didn't want him to find out that the only thing in the world I was trained to do was teach.

"We have several openings, but there all for permanent positions. Would that interest you?"

Would that interest me? It might save my life. "Yes, I would be interested," I answered, regretting that I didn't have a nicer dress. I was wearing one of my Aunt Theresa's shirtwaist dresses, faded and worn after years in college as my best dress.

"You would need to take an aptitude test first. Is that okay with you?"

I remembered Mr. Emerson and how well he thought I did on his tests. "Yes, I can take them."

"Well, good." He motioned to a woman who was sitting at an L-shaped desk in the front of the large room, the only desk in the room with a typewriter on it. Maybe I could get a job as a secretary I thought, as I remembered how good I had been in typing class. I envied my high school classmate, Barbara Robbin, at this moment. She took the secretarial courses in high school because taxi drivers didn't make much money and her dad couldn't afford college. She now had a job as a secretary and was working her way through the University of California at Berkeley. I couldn't have chosen that because my mother didn't want secretaries for children.

Mr. Krause started to introduce me to his secretary, "Linda, this is—I'm sorry Miss, what is your name?"

Embarrassed, I realized I hadn't told him. I remembered how easy my dad was with his men friends and tried to imitate the effortless style, but I was tongue-tied. I could barely utter the answer, "Dolores Morgan." I thought about shaking his hand, as my father always did with other men, but thought better of it and stopped in mid air. My mother never shook hands with anyone, but I wanted to be like my Dad. I wanted to shake hands. Do women shake hands in the business world? I didn't know.

"My name is Otto Krause, the Branch Manager here," he said, as he decided for me and offered his hand for me to shake. "It's a pleasure to meet you. This is Linda Harris, my secretary," he turned towards her. "She'll take care of you. Linda, I'll meet with Dolores when you're through." He turned back towards me and said, "Good luck, Dolores," and returned to his glass-paneled office. I wondered if it would be hard to concentrate in there behind the glass doors. I'd be looking out all the time.

"Come with me, Dolores." Miss Harris was speaking to me. She was a brisk, slender, vital person with a tiny waist and small hands who smelled clean and freshly bathed. She looked beautiful in a light blue suit with matching light blue high heel shoes. She didn't shake my hand, so I didn't shake hers. But I wanted to. There was something about her that gave me a good feeling.

I followed her into the testing room where there were several desks and exam booklets already on them. As I filled out an application, I thought about saying I had a mathematics degree or something, but I thought better of it. I was an accomplished liar and every good liar knows that you don't lie about something that can be checked. I shamefully wrote Cortland State Teachers College on the application. I felt a little better as I wrote Pennsylvania State University Master's Degree. I didn't say Master's of Education, which it really was. I thought Master's Degree sounded better. At least Penn State was a real school. Listing my interests was fun, and I wrote about my work for President Kennedy, stopping sadly along the way, to remember Judy, Loni, and me and those great days at school.

After filling in the application, I switched the pen for the pencil in front of me, and laid both down in front of the test booklet, indicating I was ready.

"They'll be ten minutes for each section. You may begin," came the familiar words as Miss Harris started the stopwatch she held in her hand.

I was confident as I picked up the pencil and began. The tests were familiar: arithmetic progressions and spatial relations. True to my pattern, I just couldn't get the last spatial relation.

Miss Harris corrected the exam as I waited.

At the end of the last section, she smiled. "You did well on the tests. Come with me. You'll have a meeting with Mr. Krause next."

Still smelling clean and freshly bathed, she escorted me to Mr. Krause's office and gestured to a small chair.

As I sat down, she handed Mr. Krause the tests. He glanced at the summary sheet on the top, put the test aside, and immediately began talking, "Well, Dolores, you did fine on the aptitude test." He glanced again at the summary sheet. "IBM has a program that I think you may like to become part of."

He explained, "IBM wants to hire people like you to be Systems Engineers and Systems Representatives to support the IBM customers and help us with our IBM business machines. For the first year you'll go to school to learn how to wire our accounting machines. During that year you'll also be working out in the field for us. We call the men—Systems Engineers—and we call the women—Systems Representatives. I think it's a good opportunity for you. If you show us that you can handle the accounting machines, you'll have a chance on several new machines and computers that are coming out soon. They are named with numbers. The one that I think you might enjoy is the 1401. I don't want to bore you with the details, but a 1401 is a new, modern computer that runs using core memory instead of vacuum tubes or drum storage. It has a hexadecimal numbering system. Does that sound interesting to you?"

I hadn't the slightest idea what he was talking about. "Yes, it sounds very interesting." I lied.

I was worried. I had no money and there was no way my mother would pay for this school.

"But, I'm sorry Mr. Krause. I can't do it."

One of the men in the suits put his head into the office. "May I see you later, Otto?"

"Sure, Peter. I'll be finished here shortly," Mr. Krause answered and then turned back to me. "Dee, you say you can't join us. I'm sorry to hear that. Why not?"

"I have no money for school. I need a job. Do you have any summer jobs? I'm a good typist." I was angry with Mr. Krause for describing a heaven where I could never go.

"I'm sorry, Dolores. May I call you Dolores? Is that what most people call you?"

"No, everyone calls me, Dee." I loved my name, Dee, the name I had argued so hard for years ago.

"Please call me Otto and feel free to interrupt me if you have any questions. I was remiss in not explaining clearly. IBM pays you while you go to school. It's part of the job. In fact, if you need to, I can arrange for you to have an advance on your salary as soon as you accept the position—today, even, if you want to. Your salary is $5400 per year, and I can advance you a two-week salary. You may start whenever you want, but don't feel rushed. It's a big decision."

He paused, "Do you have any questions?"

He had to be kidding. I couldn't think straight. I wanted to look intelligent, but I was dumbstruck. I frantically searched my brain for an intelligent question to ask him.

Finally, my brain cooperated. Hoping that it wasn't a stupid question, I asked, "Can you tell me the difference between a Systems Engineer and a Systems Representative?" I was curious as to why the girls were called something different.

"That's a good question, Dee." He said Dee in a way that made me feel proud and grown-up. He talked to me as though I were someone important. "It tells me that you're career-minded, and I like that. Practically speaking, as far as advancement and career paths, there is no difference between the two. IBM feels that Systems Engineer is an un-feminine title and the job title of Systems Engineer would not be attractive to women. We gave the women the title Systems Representative in order to attract bright women like you to the job. The starting salary is the same for men and women, and the chances for advancement are the same. A promotion would move you into the man's track, and all the positions are the same after that." He smiled, stood up, and went to a board that was like a blackboard, but white. "Of course, a lot of our pretty ladies like you leave to have families before they reach manager." He drew two pyramid-like figures on his whiteboard. There were two slots on the first pyramid, which started with Systems Representative and ended with Senior Systems Representative. On the second pyramid there were several different slots, each growing smaller as they got closer to the top. The second pyramid reached all the way up the white board. He pointed out which spot on the pyramid was his, Branch Manager. He drew an arrow showing the Systems Representative moving across into the man's pyramid. I wondered how hard it was to move over, but I really didn't care. I'd be happy to be a Systems Representative forever. I didn't say so because he seemed to want me to be career-minded and career-minded seemed to mean to want to jump over into the second pyramid.

"You may think all this over. Talk with your parents and let me know. It's a big decision, Dee. Don't decide right away. A bright woman like you has many choices. Let me get you a formal letter of employment."

He pushed a buzzer on his desk. Linda got up from her desk outside and entered. Her scent filled the office. I felt shabby again.

"Linda, please write me the standard offer letter for Miss Morgan to take with her and bring it to me immediately. The starting salary is $5400."

"Yes, Otto, I'll be right back with it." She said "Otto" with ease. It seemed disrespectful to me. My mother always addressed the fathers of the students she tutored as Mister.

Miss Harris returned to her typewriter and quickly inserted a piece of paper as Mr. Krause continued describing Heaven to me. I didn't hear a word he said.

Is this happening to me?

Miss Harris arrived, letter in hand.

Is this happening to me?

Mr. Krause looked over the letter and signed it. The blue IBM letterhead at the top smiled at me as he placed it in an envelope and handed it to me.

"I'd be honored to have you join us, Dee. There's a place at the bottom of the letter for you to sign and request a start date. You may start as early as you wish, but the offer expires after thirty days." He reached across with his other hand to give me his business card.

"Please call me if you have any questions."

No one had ever handed me a business card before.

"Thank you, Mr. Krause," I said as I stood to leave. I tried to get up gracefully.

"No, Dee, please call me, Otto. We are informal at IBM." I felt stupid. He had already told me that once.

He stood behind his desk and said, "At IBM we address each other by our first names, and we all have signs like this." He handed me the wooden plaque from his desk. "Keep this even if you don't join us. It's good advice."

I looked at the plaque. It was the same as the ones on all the desks: **THINK**. The idea seemed good to me. It *was* good advice.

Otto offered me his hand to shake again and walked me to the outer door. I blushed bright red as the whole office seemed to stare at us.

The glass doors closed behind me, and I walked down the stairs into the street. I think I walked, but I can't really remember whether my feet touched the ground or not. I doubt it.

As soon as I was out of sight, I sat down on the curb of the sidewalk by the bus stop in the middle of all the traffic. I put my head in my hands and spoke to God for the first time since my aunt's death. "Thank you, God. I know you did this for me. I'm sorry I got so mad that I stopped speaking to you. I should have been more forgiving as You have forgiven me." St. Luke, the Patron Saint of Hopeless Cases was my friend, and St. Anthony, the Patron Saint of Miracles, was surely on my side.

I was free. I had done it. I was not a teacher, and not a writer, either. I was a businesswoman, right out of my earliest childhood dreams.

I lost no time moving on to the next dream. I wanted a car, a Volkswagen Beetle. I'd seen the little Bugs as they were called, and they seemed just right for me. I didn't want a big, ugly Cadillac like Uncle Vincent had or the big Mercury my dad drove. Big cars challenged my queasy stomach and made me carsick. I wanted a small car. As soon as I let enough time go by so as not to look too anxious, I would sign the letter and return it to Mr. Krause. He said I could have a salary advance. To be paid before I even started work? It didn't seem possible. I wondered how much of an advance I would get. I needed a down payment on the car I wanted. I tried to figure out how much two weeks pay would be, but I got confused doing the division in my head and wasn't sure how to subtract the weekends from working days in a year.

I watched the side of the road for the Volkswagen Car Dealer I had passed. As soon as I saw it I got off at the next stop. I entered the showroom. Right in the center of the floor was a light green Volkswagen Beetle. I walked no further. It was for me.

"May I help you, Miss?" said a lean, handsome young man with a Spanish accent and dark black hair as he approached me. He was wearing a white suit, a fuchsia shirt, a light pink tie and tons of cologne. He looked neat but somehow much different than Mr. Krause at IBM.

I explained to him about my new job, about my desire for a car just like this one.

"This car cost $2895 fully equipped. It has a sunroof. You need a $100 down payment and, assuming you qualify for a loan, I can have it ready for you in two weeks."

"I don't know if I could qualify for a loan. I haven't started my job yet."

"Could one of your parents co-sign for you?"

I said maybe, but I knew they wouldn't. I didn't want the salesman to think they wouldn't help me, so I said maybe. But I knew I would never ask. Even if I did ask I wouldn't get any help. George was already rolling in Uncle Joe's money, but there was to be none for me until I started behaving. And I had decided a long time ago; I was not going to "behave." But the car would be mine. I would find a way. I remembered what Otto said about the advance.

"I can get an advance at work, but I haven't started yet".

"How much will you be making?"

"$5400 per year."

"Oh, you'll qualify easily. As soon as you start the job, come on in and this car is yours."

I wasn't going to be able to wait any polite amount of time to sign that offer letter. I was going to sign it right away. I would sign today. I would have to risk looking too anxious.

I went over what the salesman meant by "fully equipped" with him. It had everything I wanted. I almost said no to the sunroof because it was an extra $250, but when he showed me what a small difference in monthly payments it meant, I said yes. The official color of the car I chose was turquoise with cream interior. It was beautiful. The salesman said I should get rust proofing and I did. Everything was ready. All I needed was to start my job.

From there I took three buses to the apartment I had been dreaming about for two weeks. It was a small place in Stamford, Connecticut. It was part of an old house—a remodeled sun porch, with a kitchen and bathroom attached.

I booked it for the beginning of next month and promised the landlady a security deposit as soon as I was paid.

"IBM," she said, "is a good company. I don't doubt you'll pay me. Why don't you start living here right now and pay me when you can."

Everyone was being so nice. I couldn't believe this was happening to me.

As IBM was written into my history, I was so happy that I had to tell someone. I thought of my cousin,

Marie, the businesswoman. She would be happy for me. I found a payphone and dialed her apartment.

"Hello."

"Hi Marie, it's Dolly." Most of the family still called me Dolly because my mother insisted they do.

"Dolly, how are you? Are you through with school?"

"Yes, I've graduated."

"Are you going to teach? Do you have a job for the fall? I hear your mother talking about you becoming a teacher all the time."

"Well, I need some advice." I didn't want to brag but I didn't know how to tell her, so I thought I would pretend I needed advice. I needed no advice. I knew exactly what I was going to do. I was going to be a businesswoman.

"Sure, what is it?"

"Well, IBM has offered me a job with them, and I wanted to know what you thought about my doing that instead of teaching." I was bursting with pride.

"Dolly, that's great. I'm thrilled for you. I'd love to give you advice. How about meeting me for lunch and we can talk about it. Is tomorrow okay?"

Talk about my job. Oh, that would be grand. With her, I didn't have to hide my pride.

"Okay, but please don't tell anyone. I haven't told Mother yet."

"Well, your mom might be disappointed, but it's your decision, Dolly. Let's talk about it tomorrow at lunch. Can you meet me at Schraft's in White Plains? It's right near my office. But, better yet, why don't you come to the office, and we'll go from there. I'll show you around the data processing department so you can see what you're getting into. If you'd like, I'll get you an interview with AT&T. Would you like to try it?"

Oh boy this was too much—another interview. I was getting pretty excited.

"I hear your hesitation. Well, don't' decide now. We can talk about it tomorrow. Take the train and then take the cab to my office. I'll pay for it. I remember what it's like to be a student. Have your mom advance you the money, and I'll pay you when you get here." She chuckled a little. She was making it easy. My mom would like me to meet her and would advance me the money.

"So you're not going to be a teacher. Well, well that *is* a surprise."

I went to lunch and had the interview. The AT&T tests were harder, but the salary was less, $4800 per year.

Right after the interview, I phoned my cousin. "Marie, I think I'd rather try IBM."

I thought she might be angry, but she wasn't.

"It's your decision, Dolly, and I think you've made a good one. I've never regretted being in business. You'll be happy."

"Marie, could I ask you one favor? I'm grown up now and the people at IBM are going to call me Dee instead of Dolly. Would that be okay with you?" I was disobeying my mother again and getting someone else to do it too. It was scary as usual.

"Well, you're an independent business woman now, and I guess you can choose your name. Dee, it is."

I thanked her for her help.

"Think nothing of it, Dee, it was all my pleasure."

"Goodbye, Marie. Thank you again."

"Goodbye, Dee. Keep in touch."

18

"Two roads diverged in a wood, and I—
I took the one less traveled by,
And that has made all the difference." Robert Frost

I signed the IBM offer letter the next day because I simply couldn't wait for any polite period of time to pass. I brought it to Otto and planned to start the next Monday. With my salary advance, I went directly to the Volkswagen dealer, flirted outrageously with the salesman, and spent the next days in my enchanted chariot, a turquoise Beetle. I drove miles and miles with my vinyl sunroof pushed back, going nowhere, feeling the air, the smell of the new leather seats, and the full bloom of freedom.

Only then, when there was no turning back, did I tell my mother and father. My dad was unapologetically proud; my mother relentlessly admonished me.

"How can you do this to your family? This is a job, not a profession. Businesswomen never marry. You'll regret this sooner or later. You're lucky that I saw to it that you'll always have your teaching to fall back on. When you mess this up, they'll be teaching, and you'll finally appreciate your mother and all I've done for you. In the meantime, you'll live at home. White Plains is not far. You can commute from here."

She paraded into the kitchen to call Aunt Grace.

"After all we've done for her; she's going to choose a job instead of a profession. Can you believe it? She'll end up like Marie, an old maid. But, she'll always have a job teaching, thanks to her mother."

My mother's constant pressure was ignored by both IBM and me when IBM assigned me to Newark, New Jersey for a six months series of classes. They paid for everything: our hotel, our meals, our telephone calls—everything—six months of pure relief. I felt free from my mother, no more begging for an extra dollar, no more doing the dishes a hundred times in order to get a dress for the dance. It was over. The relief was all through my body. I felt soft, like the branch of a beautiful shade tree.

My dad enjoyed my job as much as I did. He called IBM "Big Brother," "Big Blue," or sometimes "I'm Being Moved."

I was loaded with money because no sooner did I receive one paycheck, the next one followed. I bought all new underwear, bras in every color, and thanked my body for the size A it stayed. The size A was a welcome sign that maybe I wasn't to be a carbon copy of my mother. I devoted one whole Saturday morning to Bonwit Teller, buying all new shoes, high heel sling backs in every color, pale yellow, pale green, navy blue, red, black patent leather, and pastel blue. I carried them home in my turquoise beetle to my converted sun porch apartment, and stacked them neatly in rows on the top shelf as I had seen my Aunt Grace do so many years before. The family didn't know about the apartment yet. There was no need to tell. My family thought I was staying in Newark with the IBM school. Instead, every weekend I drove to Connecticut and basked in the sunshine that came onto my bright bedroom each morning. I cooked bacon and toast for breakfast and steak for dinner. Each Sunday night my enchanted Beetle and I, sunroof wide open, careened over the Tappan Zee Bridge to Newark and joined the other students for class the next morning.

Every morning I heard the exciting ring of the wake-up call from the hotel, ate breakfast in the dining room, and struggled in class with the IBM accounting boards. Each morning, the other trainees in the class helped me. They were all better at it. Most of them had math degrees from Ivy League schools. There was only one other woman, and she was a physicist. I struggled and struggled with the boards, knowing it was easy for the others but never believing even for a moment that I wouldn't eventually catch on. Perseverance and patience were old friends of mine.

§§§§§§

One night, returning home late, especially tired, I entered the elevator of the hotel carrying the 602 Board that I'd been trying to master with little success.

"Hi," a soft voice from behind thick eyeglasses gently broke my reverie.

"Hi, Jeremy." I remembered Jeremy from class. He could easily pass for a skeleton, tall and lean with his Sherlock Holmes pipe always in his mouth, although not always lit.

"Where have you been all evening?" he asked. "I was looking around for you."

"I was at the lab working on my 602 board."

"Oh, yeah, that was easy. I finished mine in five minutes and had nothing to do all afternoon."

"Well, then what did you do?"

"Rode around in the elevator. I always ride around in Otis elevators. They bring me good luck."

"Oh, because your last name is Otis right?"

"Yeah," he chuckled. "No, my dad works for them."

I looked, and sure enough this was an Otis elevator. I had never noticed what kind of elevator I rode in before. I thought about the horrid elevator in my Uncle's building. That was definitely not an Otis. It was too ugly and smelled terrible.

Jeremy continued, "If it's not an Otis, I don't ride in it. I walk up the stairs. I don't want anyone else to have my business except my dad's company."

I laughed a little. He was funny.

He grinned.

"Well, I'm not having much luck." I showed him the board I had brought home with me. "I couldn't get it to work. I brought it home with me." I started to cry. I was tired and had worked hard, to no avail.

He looked at me, surprised. "Come on to my room, I'll help you finish it. By the way, everybody calls me Jerry."

"Okay, Jerry. Mostly, people call me Dee."

Jerry's room had an orderly feel. It was neat and clean, nothing in sight except a small shaving kit on the dresser and a small hi-fi in the corner. He put on some music, and we finished the 602 board quickly. Mostly Jerry did it for me as I watched. I sensed he wanted to explain it to me, but I knew that I was so tired his words would be lost on me. I think he saw that too.

"Well, there it is." He handed it to me.

"Thank you. I can't let you do this again, though. I need to learn myself. 'Neither a borrower nor a lender be.'" I quoted Judy's mom from long ago.

"Hey, do you like Shakespeare. I love Shakespeare. My degree is in English Literature."

I didn't know it was Shakespeare. I thought it was Judy's mom who said it, but I didn't say anything.

"You know you're going to be successful once you catch on to this because you have all the personality traits that are needed."

"Well, Linda is much better at it than I am. I'm worried I'll fail the class." I was referring to my roommate who had a degree in Physics and found the IBM classes quite easy.

"No. If I were manager, I'd rather have you than almost anyone in the class," Jerry spoke with a certain authority. I guess he knows, I thought. His father is a manager for Otis elevators.

"Why?"

"Because, as I told you, you have traits that attract people to you. That's important in an IBM environment. Don't be discouraged. Once you get the insight into these boards, the rest will come easy." Something about the way he talked made me believe him.

We saw each other every evening after that. He helped me understand the boards and taught me how to play chess. He lectured me on classical music. We talked about Jerry's real interest, music and literature, and how he had come to work for IBM because he couldn't get a better paying job. He explained that it was Mozart and Beethoven that he played on the small hi-fi in his room. I guessed it was his own hi-fi. Boys seemed to have hi-fi sets. George had one at home. I was envious of Jerry's life. He had the education he chose himself. No matter what I dared to dream it always came around to being a teacher.

I slept restlessly each night because someone as nice as Jerry wanted to be friends with me. My boyish figure didn't attract many dates, and I was sure that my inexperience would sooner or later make a fool of me in front of him.

When the accounting machine class finished, all the classmates had a small party in our hotel to say goodbye. I would be going back to New York alone because I was the only representative from White Plains branch. Jerry gave me his address and phone number in New Jersey.

"If you ever feel like visiting New Jersey, just drive over the Tappan Zee Bridge and call me from the first gas station on the Garden State. I live near there, and I can pick you up. Be sure and come any time you feel like it. It's an open invitation."

He handed me an LP record. "This is the "Eine Kleine Nacht Musik" you liked. I thought you might like to borrow it."

"Thank you." He touched my hand as he handed the record to me. My heart pounded like I had never felt before. I hoped he didn't notice how cold my hands were.

"Cold hands—mm. Cold hands, warm heart, they say."

I blushed a fierce red. It was true. He knew. My heart was flipping over with an excitement like none I'd ever known. And he knew because my hands were cold. I was mortified.

As I drove back to Stamford, I thought of Jerry and sighed. All I could do was hope that this whole boy thing would get easier.

"See," the landlady said, as I proudly paid her the first month's rent, "I knew you'd be successful."

I hadn't told her that my mother didn't know about the apartment and that I was too terrified to tell her. The IBM job was bad enough. Now, I was about to move out of our home. My mother was counting on my contribution to the family while I worked. That is how it had worked in her family. The older children paid for the younger ones and I was going against tradition. I would pay her back for school anyway. It was the only way.

My mother seemed so vulnerable, so intent, so disappointed that I had not gone into teaching that I just didn't dare add a new apartment to the pile of problems that always seemed to be hers. I couldn't tell her. I just couldn't.

It was time to talk with George. He would have to tell her. I was tired of lying. I wanted to sleep in my own apartment every night, with my high heel shoes under my own bed and the moonlit night all around my sun porch bedroom.

I telephoned George and we decided on a meeting at Whitey's Bar and Grille, which had been renovated since my childhood days and turned into a restaurant. Instead of a bar and bridge tables there were dark mahogany booths along each wall and the privacy was there by benefit of the high bench-backs. I could talk with George and no one would hear.

I entered the still squeaking door, reminding me of everyone—the firemen, my dad's friends, the ghosts of my childhood.

Whitey was delighted to see me. "Hey, Dolly, how are you doing?"

"I'm fine, Whitey, how are you?"

"I'm getting old, Dolly, like your old man. Hey, he told me you landed a job with Big Blue. You're an amazing girl. What'll you have? Still Coca Cola on the rocks or are you too grown-up for that, now?"

"Thank you, Whitey; I'll have a J&B on ice with a twist of lemon." I drank that because I heard a friend of my father's order it once. Actually, I didn't like it at all. I would have preferred the coke. J&B was too bitter and the smell gave me a headache. I took out a cigarette, a Kent. I smoked Kents because Aunt Grace had switched from Pall Mall to Kent. She said filtered cigarettes were better for your health—less likely to give you cancer.

"Comin' right up, Dolly, J&B with a twist." Somehow I didn't mind Whitey calling me Dolly.

He came from behind the elegant mahogany bar and brought the drink to my table. "It's on the house, Dolly. You sure are a sight for sore eyes."

As I thanked Whitey for the drink, I noticed one of the booths held an upright piano instead of a table. Seated there was a tall, heavy guy, softly playing, who smiled at me, a great warm smile, as his huge hands continued on the keyboard, managing, in between notes, to reach for his cigarette from time to time, his blunt body erect. Next to him was an ashtray full of butts. His feet tapped, his hands glided effortlessly over the keys, and his head bobbed around. He was all rhythm and motion as his pudgy, pockmarked face dreamed like a Buddha. From his piano came the most beautiful sounds. He was like the Hunchback of Notre Dame—outwardly a hunched over, pot-bellied and bald old guy, concealing beauty, youth and music inside. The magnificence of *The Piano Man* could be seen in his eyes and heard through his music. He made me think of Miss Roberts, whose eyes shown at me all day long in sixth grade class and all the others, too—Mr. Wilson,

Mrs. Selbourne, Mr. Appleton, Arturo, and Father McAvoy—all of them, who touched my life and my heart when all was dark and I was lost. They, like my book characters, those great ones to whom I gave the faith of my youth, believed in them as I would kings. Neither my books nor my teachers could help me now, except in the strength they gave me so long ago.

The bright piano man interrupted my daydreams as he flirted even while he kept the music going, "Would you like me to play any of your favorites, Miss?" His eyes danced as though he had a huge secret. The music, magically, kept on.

Whitey turned to admonish him. "Hey, Bruce, hands off. This is Spence Morgan's daughter all grown up. No shenanigans from you. Hear me?" He turned to me, "Don't pay any attention to him, Dolly. He's not good enough for you. And I don't want your old man mad at us."

I did a double take. Bruce—it was Bruce Johnson from that terrible night of the ballroom dance.

He smiled. "Hi, Dolly. I still remember the night you chose me as your dance partner over Avery. You saved me from total embarrassment. You saved my life." He looked at me with a look of adult appreciation for someone who had done him a good turn. "One good turn deserves another. How about choosing a song for me to play for you?"

I glanced at Whitey as he returned to his spot behind the bar, remembering the days of his protection of the little girl that was me. Whitey smiled at me with a nod, giving me the go-ahead I would have never taken without his approval.

I looked at Bruce and chose. "Can you play "A Fine Romance"? It's by Jerome Kern." He looked straight at me, nodded, and began to play. I liked the way he looked at me. His pudgy, pockmarked face was the same as in sixth grade. I guess I had never before noticed the bright light behind those eyes. From my Greek Mythology classes I remembered the Greek god, Selenius, seemingly ugly on the outside, with a huge glow of beauty and divinity from within.

I watched him, enjoying his joyous movements as well as his piano, as I waited for George. Sipping my drink, I mused over some of the old tunes from my childhood days at the movies with Aunt Grace. Bruce played like an angel— "Anything Goes," "As Time Goes By," "Night and Day," "I Love a Piano" and others by Cole Porter, Irving Berlin and Jerome Kern, tunes that were friends of mine still.

The squeaky door warned me, as George sauntered through it, and I was forced to turn to thinking about how to present my departure from home to George in a way that would get him to tell Mother for me.

"Hi, George." It was really dull, this romantic restaurant wasted on George. I felt Bruce's eyes on me even as I looked at George. He cocked his head to the sky talking with his friends above, "Well, will you look at little sis!" Then, to me he said, "Hey, Four-Eyes, how ya' doing? What's this big news you've got? Are you getting married, or pregnant maybe?" Bruce's music intensified.

George swung himself into the opposite bench of the booth, full of the self-confidence that was his right by virtue of being born a boy. The only reminders of his awkward childhood were his slightly pigeon-toed feet, which were now fitted with special shoes, and his constant conversation with his pals in Heaven. It was understandable, in a way, that he was as confident as a prince. He had grown handsome, almost movie star quality, with a brashness that belied the shyness only I knew was in his heart. Today, dressed in a tan camel hair blazer, he looked even better than usual. He only seemed like a scared little boy to me because I knew the life he had led in childhood. My mother had fooled everyone else except me into thinking she had laid the perfect egg in George. George was always performing, programmed, too, to be the hen's best-laid egg, perfect, by God Herself, my mother. Still, to me, behind his eyes was the familiar empty look—he was always somewhere else.

I bristled at the name "Four-Eyes." He'd been calling me Four-Eyes since my years in elementary school. I had contact lenses now, but the name still made me feel ugly and awkward, and I hated it. Well, at least, he didn't call me Dolly. His question about pregnancy turned me scarlet, not because I was pregnant, but because there was no chance that I was. I had no idea of boys. Even Jerry never tried to kiss me.

Actually, boys didn't seem important right now. My life was at stake. Either I got away from my mother or I would die on her jangled vine. IBM had handed me a chance at life. I would *not* fail.

I decided to cut to the quick. "George, I have something to tell you." I looked squarely over at him.

"Well, will you listen to her?" He spoke to that angel high over his shoulder.

He took out a cigarette and looked around for the waiter. He was much more at home in a bar than I was. Still searching for the waiter, he said, "I hope whatever you have to say is not as bad as that business about voting for Jack Kennedy. Boy, was Uncle Joe annoyed about that. Why did you vote for him? He's going to bring back the New Deal."

I saw Bruce out of the corner of my eye, his head and shoulders, bobbing, his face delirious, enjoying his own rendition of "I Love a Piano", another one of Aunt Grace's favorite tunes, from Judy Garland in the movie *Easter Parade*.

"Did you vote?" I questioned George as I tried to change the subject. I lit a cigarette, too.

"I'll have Dewar's on the rocks," he said to the waiter who had taken Whitey's place. The waiter looked at me. "No, thank you," I said. "I'm fine."

As the waiter left, George continued. "Nixon, the whole family voted for Nixon. In fact, the whole town voted for Nixon."

He made me angry, as usual. My answer came from within, well behind the façade I learned to show in family situations. "Yes, vote for Nixon—just like everybody else in this Republican stronghold town and live in a big house on a hill when everyone around you has cholera. It doesn't make sense. I campaigned for Jack because I believe in what he is saying: that 'people who carry tigers on their backs get eaten.'" George and Mother were my tigers. I must get free.

"Well, listen to her, now. You're a flaming liberal, Sis, a cause fighter. And you're only antagonizing Uncle Joe. The guy's got a lot of money. Why not be nice to him?" That was exactly the kind of question only George would ask.

The waiter brought George his drink and placed a dish of pretzels on the table between us.

I tried to get George back on track. "George, I'm not here to talk endlessly about money. I've gotten my own apartment. I want you to tell Mother. I'm leaving.

It's over. I'm finally free of her." I hadn't planned to be angry when I told him, but I just couldn't hold back.

"Why can't you live at home like the rest of us? The folks need the money. You're selfish."

"What does 'selfish' mean? That I'm unwilling to do what you want? Doesn't that make you and Mother the selfish ones? Am I to give away my first opportunity in life for you and the so-called family? I'm living behind a huge stone wall and every time I get a leg up, you knock me back."

He ignored me. "You're going to regret this, Sis— not now, maybe—but later. You'll see." He tapped the table with his fingers, tap, tap, tap. It seemed like a threat.

I flashed him a defiant look. "Well, I don't regret it yet. If later I have to pay the price, fine. I'll see then. I can't live another minute at home. She boxes me in. Last week, I tried to rearrange the furniture in my room and she made me put it back her way. I'm so frustrated that I think I'll jump out of a window if I have to stay there another day. My apartment is ready and waiting. I paid a whole month's rent. I'm leaving."

"You can do a lot of things and still live at home. All you ever do is read—you can do that anywhere."

"Well, let's just say that the bookworm has turned," I watched him for a reaction. There was none as I gave him a wry smile and said, "so to speak".

Bruce hit a chord designed to get my attention, which it did. He looked directly at me as he played "Taking a Chance on Love." He endeared me with a look that seemed to be interested in only his music and me. His shy demeanor of sixth grade was gone. His eyes peered right into my heart, and it became my turn to feel awkward and embarrassed. Bruce's confident gaze seemed to enjoy my discomfit. He certainly wasn't the terrified boy I used to know.

I took another puff of my cigarette and leaned forward towards George. " I can't do anything as long as I live home and neither can you except make money. That's it. That's going to be your whole life—greed and money. Being the rich man your father wasn't—your mother's dream. You're living your mother's dreams, George, not your own. I want to live my own dreams for better or for worse."

"Come on, Sis, you're over-dramatizing as usual. You really ought to be a fiction writer. You're a natural. IBM is one of your most stupid moves. You could have had a profession and you settled for a job."

I was livid that he hadn't one iota of understanding for what I'd been through and the importance of the chance I had found for myself. Nobody helped me. I found it for myself, and I wasn't going to lose it. "She drove me crazy while I was trying to help myself. You were there. You saw her. She manipulated, coerced, and just about drove me to the loony bin with pressure. I love my job, George. I wouldn't give it up for the world."

"And what about marrying, Dolores? Do you really think anyone is going to marry a businesswoman? Look at Cousin Marie. She's an old maid, a spinster. Men don't want businesswomen; they want wives and mothers. Cousin Marie defied her dad and went to work for AT&T, and she never got a husband. She's too old now, she's at least thirty-five, and she'll never have children. No one wants her now."

"Marie didn't defy her father, George. Uncle Charlie encouraged her. He sent her to a college to take mathematics—he *wanted* her to achieve. Mother is the one who disapproves of Marie, not her dad. Uncle Charlie is proud of Marie. She told me herself."

"Yeah, according to Marie. You sure are a sucker for these cousins."

George was born defective. He got a brain, but no heart.

"Are you telling me you expect me to quit a perfectly good job and sit around in my mother's house waiting for someone to marry me?"

"It could be faster than you think. I could fix you up. We could find you someone from Harvard."

"Ugh." Harvard was like a god instead of a college to George. It was magic, wealth, elegance, all the things his noisy, clamored childhood wasn't.

"Those guys are heading for Wall Street, and they'll make more money than you could ever dream of."

"Money, money, money. Is that all you think about? George, I don't even know if I want to get married. The only thing I know about money is that I want to earn my own. I don't want a husband's money. I want my own."

"Okay, have it your way. But don't say I didn't warn you. You'll regret it some day. Maybe not today, but later."

"Are you threatening me?"

"No, I'm just telling, you, Uncle Joe is not happy with this."

"Uncle Joe is never going to be happy with me. I was born a girl. I'm out of the picture. He's not giving me a job in his company like he is you. I'm on my own. That's clear."

"Uncle Joe has money to leave us some day you know."

"Great, George, then you sit around and count assets on Saturday night, I want to live. All I'm asking is you tell Mother. I'm afraid to. Tell Mother I've got a place to live, that I moved out. She'll accept it if you act like you approve."

"How are you going to pay her back for your education? You owe her."

"I'll pay her anyway. Tell her I'll pay her the $100 per month until I've paid her back. I just won't be living at home while I do it. If you won't tell her, she'll never know. I don't care. I want out. It's like a fire inside of me. I want to be free."

I put out my cigarette sensing Bruce's gaze again on me. I was awkward with cigarettes and sensed that I wasn't anywhere near sophisticated enough to be casually putting out a cigarette and getting up to leave. I wondered if George could tell just how big and grand and fake this independent facade was.

"Wait a second," he said. "What should I tell her? Where's the apartment? What is the telephone number? Do you need any money? Here, you probably need money." He put $100 in front of me. "Here, it's a gift." There was that look again. Sometimes George was just a scared little boy who needed approval. Across from me was a brother. Is this what a brother is? I never understand anything. My entire school years were spent listening to adults telling me to learn to think for myself and now that I was doing it, nobody seemed to want me to, even my brother. Does my own brother, who witnessed almost every minute of what I'd been through, want me to stay trapped forever?

I softened a little, and I almost took the money, just so that look of his would go away, but I couldn't. "I have no telephone, and I'm earning my own money." I handed him back the $100. He didn't take it. It fell to the table. "I know you don't understand, but I don't want your money, George. I have what I want—my soul. It's okay if you don't want to tell her. I was unfair to ask you to do something I don't have the guts to do myself."

George's shoulders slumped a little, and he looked down. "I'll tell her. She won't like it, but I'll tell her." He put the money back in his pocket and got up to go.

So long, Brother, it was nice being related to you.

I wanted my independence, and I was going to have it. In some ways, the victory was empty. If independence was so great, then why was my heart as heavy as stone.

I hesitated only a moment. I had made a mistake. I spoke right at George. "George, I'm sorry to bring you into this. I was wrong. This is between my mother and me. I'll tell her myself. I have to earn my independence. Did Britain give the colonies permission to be free? No. I'll tell her myself. I know you are trying to help me, but I'm alone in this—alone is the same as independent."

I picked up my brown suede purse and stood as tall as I could.

Bruce saw us get up to leave. He smiled at me, bobbed his head in my direction and began to play "There Goes My Heart." He was quite a tease. I liked him. I had a feeling about him—that I would see him again. I wondered about him. What would he be like on a date—without his piano to protect him and his music to speak for him? I sneaked a look back only once more to see him smiling at me, as I continued my journey to the old, familiar squeaky door.

In that same instant, I saw George, too, staring at me with the most astonished look I'd ever seen. I learned then what the books meant when I read "his mouth dropped open." George's chin could have touched the floor. And mirrored back to me in his gape was my own astonishment. No one was more surprised than I of what I was about to try and accomplish. I was about to confront my most feared enemy, my mother.

I wasted no more time. The door squeaked closed behind me, as if to say goodbye and good luck.

In the dimming dusk light, I sat on the restaurant steps, took out my checkbook, and wrote a check for $100 to give to my mother, the first of the payments for college. I wouldn't live at home, but I would pay her back for the Master's Degree as I had promised.

My turquoise royal carriage responded to my touch, and we were off. I opened the sunroof and looked up at the starry sky, now turning black. The North Star blinked just like it had the day I lost Judy and had only my friend Monk. And there he was again—watching over me. The stars told me what I already knew, "Dee Morgan, you will *not* fail."

§§§§§§

I headed for the house. My mother would be there. She was always there. That home was her life, and she was determined to make that same jailhouse mine forever. My life was just beginning. I must not waste another minute.

The house was dimly lit when I arrived. My mother, father, and Brenda were quietly at the dinner table, no music, no fiery political discussion, no nothing, just emptiness, just a thick, thick loneliness that penetrated the air and the walls.

The front door was open.

"Hey, Princess," my father stood up from his seat at the head of the table. "Come on in and sit down. Would you like a drink?"

"No, thank you, Dad, I'm not staying." Brenda cowered as if she expected trouble. My mother stiffened in her seat next to Dad. I faced her square on.

"Mother, I've gotten an apartment. I just came home to pick up a few things of mine. I'll be moving to Connecticut."

My father stiffened, too. I didn't sit down. I didn't know if I could go through with it in front of him. Brenda's face was set in panic. I felt just terrible leaving her. She was completely dominated by my mother without the personality to fight back. I vowed to stay in touch with her.

"Your father told you to sit down." My mother, as usual had turned a polite man's welcoming gesture into an order. She crossed her arms in front of her and looked up at me, sure of herself.

I didn't sit down. I had to go through with my plan. If I lost this round, I may never have another chance.

She seemed to ignore that I didn't sit down, tapping her fingers on each folded elbow, a sign of her power that she could draw upon at will. "Now, what, pray tell, is this nonsense about an apartment?" She said apartment in a way that meant it was clearly a lower class type of place, not after all, a house like she owned. She breathed; her breasts pushed her elbows forward and her fingers kept tapping, a sign that she wasn't going to wait very long for me to obey her. She breathed again. Her back stiffened. "Doesn't this just perfectly demonstrate your selfishness? You are unappreciative of all we've done for you. I paid for your

Master's degree. I expect to be paid back. You will live at home and pay me back in rent."

Rent. With our family, it was always about money.

I reached in my purse and retrieved the check I had written. "I will pay you as we agreed—$100 per month. Here is the first installment."

My father looked at me. He knew. We exchanged long looks. We were saying goodbye. My heart broke.

My mother continued, "So—Miss Hoity Toity, you are all set to walk out on your father and me?" My father and my mother—the team.

I sat down next to her and tried to reason with her. I said softly, "I'm not walking out on anyone. I only want to live my life. You've lived yours, and I want to live mine."

My mother stood up and looked down at me. When she spoke my whole past with her caved in on me. She stood still, her arms still crossed. "And—what if I say no?"

I gave up then. There would never be any reasoning with her. It was her way or no way.

I hesitated only a moment, stood up, looked her squarely in the eye and answered, "Well, why don't you try it, Mother, and see what happens." I turned and walked out the door. I would come back to get my things another day. The deed was done.

I hurried down the path where I had walked so many times before in the days when I had no choice but to return. Down the slate steps I scampered to my enchanted Beetle, my walk only slightly slower than a run. My heels hit the pavement too quickly as though they were trying to match the tempo of a song. They slapped against the slates, slap, slap, slap, not like Bruce's piano beat, but angry, like violence—slap, slap,

slap—like someone hitting someone else. I shuddered away from that unwelcome image, as the door to my enchanted chariot opened, none too soon. I was to be protected again, in the silence of my Beetle cocoon. I made it. I held on to the car door. It steadied me.

As I turned to get in, I looked up. My dad was on the front porch, waving goodbye. I looked again and my heart broke again as I slid into the driver's seat. This was my promise to myself. I would not return. Is this how Thomas Jefferson felt when he wrote the Declaration of Independence? Independence, the right to rely on one's self, is taken, not given, and, it does exact a price.

I drove to no place in particular and found myself on the Tappan Zee Bridge. I crossed over and saw the gas station Jerry told me about. I dialed the number I had memorized.

"Hello," a woman's voice answered.

I got up all my nerve. "Is Jerry there?" I asked politely hoping she wouldn't ask who it was.

She didn't. Instead, she answered softly, "Yes, he is. Just a minute, please. I'll go and call him."

I heard a loving voice, "Jerry, there's a call for you. Pick up the phone in the library, and I'll hang up."

A mother that didn't listen in on the telephone. A mother who didn't ask who it was and decide if you were allowed to answer. I was envious again.

"Hello." I heard classical music playing softly in the background. There was music in Jerry's house and an emptiness of chaos. No yelling or orders being given. An astonishing peace was on the other end of the phone. This quiet house in the background probably had a library room with books on the wall. Some day I would have that for myself. Thousands and thousands of books on every wall reaching to the ceiling with a wooden stepladder to access any book I wanted, any time I wanted..

"Jerry, this is Dee Morgan, from class." I said my last name in case he may have forgotten. "I'm at the gas station you told me about."

I was afraid he'd say he was busy doing something else, but he answered quickly in a way that made me know he was glad to hear from me.

"Great. I'll be right there. Are you in the Howard Johnson's? Don't move. I'll pick you up, and you can follow me back here."

A few minutes later a small Renault pulled up and out came Jerry, gracefully, with his large pipe in his mouth. His intelligent eyes were behind wire-rimmed eyeglasses, and he was looking at me in the bright lights of the roadside stand with obvious pleasure. He was wearing a pale yellow sweater, which seemed a little big on his tall, slender frame.

"Hi." He removed his pipe to say hello and then put it right back.

"Hi." I didn't have anything to say. I only knew I had accomplished the impossible. I had gotten away from my mother, and I could do anything. In some ways I was fearless, but in other ways, I was overwhelmed by fear. Delighted by the way my heart leapt each time he unexpectedly came into view, the way the ground shifted under my feet when he tugged on his pipe and smiled at me. I was also afraid, afraid of the absolute newness of my emotions. I would surely make a fool of myself and soon.

Jerry removed his pipe and held it lightly in his left hand. I was used to that pipe from school. It was almost a part of him. The large Sherlock Holmes bowl seemed incongruous next to his slight frame and, yet, it was a part of him.

"I told my mother and dad about you. Mom is fixing some cake. She wants me to bring you back home with me for a spot of tea." A wry smile crossed his face.

Jerry talked as though evening tea with his mother was something he took for granted. He said the word "Mom" as though he were sure of her love. Again, I felt envy. Tea? With Jerry's mother? It sounded so, well— classy.

As I drove behind Jerry to his house, I was scared, and I was glad. I bet I could change the rule that businesswomen never marry. After all, I had gotten away from my mother—everything else was going to be easy.

Jerry parked the car in a long semi-circular driveway. I pulled in behind him and we walked up the walk of a large front yard, through the large white pillars, and onto a gray porch that wrapped all around both sides of the house. The front door was gray and white with a large, a shiny, brass knocker on the door. On each side of the door were potted red geraniums. It reminded me of Rosalee's house, the night my aunt died. Quiet and clean.

Jerry's mom opened the door as though she had been waiting for us. The house was peaceful inside and smelled of chocolate baking. Classical music played softly in the background; I recognized the piece to be "Eine Kleine Nacht Musik." I loved that record from the day Jerry lent it to me. I played it in my new apartment all the time. I still hadn't returned his copy.

"Hello, Dee," a small, gentle woman with lovely gray hair smiled at me, "Jerry has told us a lot about you."

The man in the moon winked at me as I turned toward Jerry, who reached around me to shut the door. His arm brushed mine, and my body responded as though I'd been struck by lightning. His twinkling eyes told me that he touched me on purpose.

I didn't say that he better not do that. Nor, did I say please don't do that any more as I'm shaking like a leaf and my brain is getting fuzzy. Instead, I tried to look like I hadn't even noticed such a trifle. He smiled at me with the soft eyes that were so like my father's and yet so different. He pushed me gently, signaling me to follow his mother into the parlor.

It was 1962, and John Fitzgerald Kennedy was President of the United States with his dreams for The New Frontier. As for me, it was 1492, I was Christopher Columbus, and this was more than the JFK New Frontier—I had crossed treacherous seas and reached The New World.